CAT SITTER
ON A HOT TIN ROOF

A Dixie Hemingway Mystery

BLAIZE CLEMENT

St. Martin's Paperbacks

This is a work of fiction. All of the characters, organizations and events portrayed in this novel are either products of the author's imagination or are used fictitiously.

CAT SITTER ON A HOT TIN ROOF

Copyright © 2008 by Blaize Clement.
Excerpt from *Raining Cat Sitters and Dogs* copyright © 2009 by Blaize Clement.

All rights reserved.

For information address St. Martin's Press, 175 Fifth Avenue, New York, NY 10010.

Library of Congress Catalog Card Number: 2008030121

EAN: 978-0-312-36957-6

Printed in the United States of America

St. Martin's Press hardcover edition / January 2009
St. Martin's Paperbacks edition / January 2010

St. Martin's Paperbacks are published by St. Martin's Press, 175 Fifth Avenue, New York, NY 10010.

10 9 8 7 6 5 4 3 2 1

ACKNOWLEDGMENTS

Many thanks to:

Kay Adams, Edith and John Rozendaal, Suzanne Beecher, Nancy Thomas, Jane Phelan, Kate Holmes, Greg Jorgensen, and Madeline Mora-Summonte for their support and friendship.

Roland Rio for keeping my computer running smoothly.

Tara Bolesta for taking care of boring stuff like filing so I could concentrate on writing.

Linda and Tom Witter for keeping my house clean when I was too distracted by plot and characters to notice dust.

Doris and Todd Finney for keeping my roots touched up so I didn't get depressed.

Bill Sullivan, true Sarasota crime-scene cleaner, for letting me use his name.

Phyllis Ullrich of Southeastern Guide Dogs for information about service dogs.

Kathy Alexander of Therapy Dogs Sarasota for information and introduction to her therapy puppies.

D. P. Lyle, M.D., of the Writers Medical and Forensics Lab, for information about post-op stages following brain surgery.

Marcia Markland, Diana Szu, Hector DeJean, Jessica Rotondi, and the rest of the super team at St. Martin's.

Annelise Robey and her cohorts at the Jane Rotrosen Agency.

And most of all, Don, Kit, John, David, Amy, Jesse, Kim, Travis, Sarah, and Sierra for being the greatest family in the universe.

If I were who I would be
Then I'd be who I am not
Here am I where I must be
Where I would be I cannot

—Adapted from "Katie Cruel"

CHAPTER 1

It was early April, about nine o'clock in the morning, when I first met Laura Halston. Well, I didn't exactly *meet* her. It was more that I almost ran her down.

I was easing my Bronco around a curve on the single narrow lane in Fish Hawk Lagoon, a heavily wooded area on the north end of Siesta Key. Driving there is like going through a tunnel cut in a mountain. Towering oaks meet overhead to block out the sky, and one side of the meandering street is edged with wildly growing bougainvillea, sea grape, potato vine, and practically every known variety of palm and pine. On the other side, a manicured hibiscus hedge screens a jogging path so nobody can see rich runners sweat.

As I rounded a curve, a woman in running gear leaped into the street from the wooded side and raced toward the hibiscus hedge. If I'd been going a nanosecond faster I would have hit her. I came to a jolting stop as she turned her head, and for a second I saw stark terror in her eyes. At the curb, she swooped in a graceful arc and picked up a dark brown cat with a long lashing tail. Holding the cat firmly in her arms, she pulled iPod wires from her ears and turned toward me in fury.

"Idiot! Bitch! You nearly hit me!"

I don't take kindly to being called an idiot *or* a bitch, especially by a woman who looked like she had an IQ smaller than her size zero waist. She was about my age, which is thirty-three, and I pegged her as either a runway model or a rich man's trifle. Like the cat, she was an exquisite creature, but her beauty seemed accidental, an unplanned coming together of parts that shouldn't have fit but did. Almost albino pale, she was fine-boned and slim, with tousled white-blond hair cut high at the back of her neck and flopping over eyebrows too thick, too dark, too crude. Her eyes were like jade stones set too far apart, her nose was a fraction too long and thin, her chin too pointed. She should not have been beautiful, but she was. She also had the snottiness of a woman accustomed to getting anything she wanted because she was beautiful.

With what I thought was remarkable restraint, I said, "Here's a hot tip. The best way to avoid being hit by a car is to avoid jumping in front of one."

Twin patches of pink outrage gave her pale face some color. "How could I know you were there? I couldn't hear you! You're sneaking around in a . . . in a *stealth* car! What are you doing here anyway? These are private streets!"

I could hear faint music from her dangling iPod earbuds. I was pretty sure it was Pink, so my estimation of her went up a few notches.

I said, "Maybe if you weren't listening to music, you could hear better. That's Pink's latest cut, isn't it?"

She looked surprised. Her mouth got ready to say something mean and then changed its mind.

I said, "Look, I'm sorry I startled you. I'm Dixie Hemingway. I'm a pet sitter. I have a client in the neighborhood."

Her face relaxed a bit, but she didn't seem the type to apologize for being rude.

I said, "That's a gorgeous cat. Havana Brown?"

It was the magic phrase. Pet owners melt like bubble gum on a hot sidewalk when you compliment their babies.

She said, "His name is Leo. An old boyfriend gave him to me, only he called him Cohiba, for the cigars. Dumb, huh? What cat's gonna come when you say *Here, Cohiba*? I changed it right away. He hates being cooped up in the house. Well, so do I, to tell the truth. Anyway, when I opened the door to go running, he ran out with me. I was afraid I wouldn't be able to catch him, so I guess I should thank you for scaring him so he stopped."

The transformation from fury to friendly had happened so fast it was like watching a cartoon. When she wasn't angry, her eyes sparkled with energy and she spoke in a breathless rush, as if she had so much to say that she was afraid she'd never get it all said.

Now that I had complimented her cat and apologized for almost running her down, and she had introduced the cat and sort of exonerated me because I'd made him stop so she could catch him, there wasn't much else to talk about.

I said, "I'm glad you caught him," and edged on past her.

She raised her hand in a hesitant half wave, and in the rearview mirror I could see her watching when I turned into my client's driveway.

Like I said, I'm Dixie Hemingway, no relation to you-know-who. I'm a pet sitter on Siesta Key, which, like Casey Key, Bird Key, Lido Key, and Longboat Key, forms a narrow barrier between the Gulf of Mexico and Sarasota, Florida. Officially, Siesta Key is part of the city of Sarasota, but when you get right down to it, we're not part of anything but ourselves. Our function is to absorb the fury of storms so they weaken a little bit before they hit the mainland. In exchange, we get sea breezes, a direct view of spectacular sunsets, and annual hikes in storm insurance rates that keep our blood circulating nicely.

Before I became a pet sitter, I was a deputy with the Sarasota County Sheriff's Department, but I left with the department's blessing a little over three years ago. I don't like to talk about it, so I'll just say my world exploded in a way that broke my heart and almost destroyed my mind. When I was able to function again, I became a professional pet sitter. It was a good move. The pay is good, the animals I take care of are mostly sweet and lovable, and I don't have to spend a lot of time interacting with destructive people.

I get up every morning at four o'clock, brush my teeth, rubber-band my hair into a ponytail, pull on a pair of khaki cargo shorts and a sleeveless T, lace up my Keds, and begin my rounds. I mostly take care of cats, but I also have a few canine clients and an occasional rabbit or ferret or bird. No snakes. While I firmly believe that every snake has the right to live well and prosper, I get swimmy-headed around creatures whose diet consists of things swallowed still kicking and squealing.

On the key, you either live on the Gulf side or the Sarasota Bay side. Fish Hawk Lagoon is on the bay side at the north end. My clients there were Hal and Gillis Richards, their three-year-old son Jeffrey, and Jeffrey's seizure-assistance dog, Mazie. Jeffrey had a severe seizure disorder, and Hal and Gillis were leaving that morning to take him to All Children's Hospital in St. Petersburg for brain surgery. Mazie would have to stay at home. For the last couple of days, I had come there every morning to walk Mazie so she would be accustomed to me, and Pete Madeira, an octogenarian who sometimes did twenty-four-hour sitting for me, was going to move into the house with Mazie to keep her company. None of the adults looked forward to the moment when child and dog realized they were going to be separated.

Their house was like most houses on Siesta Key— pseudo-Mediterranean/Mexican stucco with barrel-tile roof, lots of curves and arches. In this case the stucco was the color of terra-cotta, and the barrel-tile roof was dark blue. It was surrounded with the same lush green foliage and flowering shrubs that most yards on the key have, the kind of extravagant natural beauty that those of us living here year-round take for granted.

When I rang the doorbell, Hal Richards opened the door. Hal probably wasn't much older than I, but strain and worry had put lines in his face, and thinning hair and a layer of fat softening a former athletic build made him seem older than he was.

He gestured me into the house. "Gillis is giving Jeffrey breakfast, so come on in the kitchen."

I followed him into a large sunny room with a glass wall offering a view of a dock behind the house where a small pleasure boat rocked. Siesta Key has over fifty miles of waterways, so boats are common. From Hal Richards's pallor, though, I doubted that he went out in his very often. Gillis, a softly pretty dark-haired woman in a scoop-neck T-shirt and an ankle-length linen skirt, stood at the sink stirring something in a cereal bowl. Like Hal, Gillis wore the stunned look of people whose world has shrunk to the small arc of here and now.

Jeffrey sat in a child's booster chair at a round table. He had a fading yellow bruise on his cheek, from falling, and a new purple bruise on his upper arm. Dark shadows lay like soot under his drug-dulled eyes. Mazie, a golden retriever, sat close beside the boy's chair. The dog's eyes were bright and healthy, watching the boy with close attention.

Adults with seizure disorders frequently have seizure-*alert* dogs who sense when a seizure is coming and signal the person, then do whatever is necessary to protect them from harming themselves during the attack. Children as young as Jeffrey can't be made responsible for that kind of warning. Instead, they have seizure-*assistance* dogs, who may or may not sense impending seizures, but stay close by the child's side at all times.

Gillis smiled at me and put a bowl of something white and lumpy in front of Jeffrey.

Gillis said, "Jeffrey, say hello to Miss Hemingway."

The kid spooned up a blob of whatever his mother had given him and grinned shyly.

I said, "Is that oatmeal you're eating?"

Gillis said, "It's groats, actually, with some banana mixed in."

I managed to keep my upper lip from lifting, but the word *groats* sounded too much like *gross* to me. Besides, what the heck are groats, anyway?

Gillis smiled. "It's whole oats, healthier than oatmeal. Jeffrey likes it. Don't you, Jeffrey?"

The kid nodded, but he didn't seem excited about it. Actually, he didn't look as if much of anything excited him. I didn't know a lot about seizure disorders, but I knew the erased look that people get when they're on heavy medication, and Jeffrey had it.

Knowing that Mazie was a service dog currently on duty, I didn't speak to her or touch her. But I sat down at the table so she could smell me and feel my energy. She gave me a quick glance, but her job was to be exquisitely alert to Jeffrey and to any change in him, even something as slight as a change in his body odor that would signal an impending seizure. Hal and Gillis went silent, knowing what I was doing and not wanting to interfere.

After a few minutes, I stood up. "Hal, maybe you and I should talk in the living room for a minute."

Hal said, "Good idea."

In the living room, I took an easy chair and Hal sat on the sofa. I got out my client notebook and prepared to take any last-minute instructions or information.

Sometimes people are surprised to learn that pet sitting is a profession like any other. I approach it the same way I approached being a deputy. I was always aware that lives could depend on my being alert, on remembering my training, on handling my job in a professional manner. I feel the same way about pet sitting. Pet owners entrust me with animals they love, and I take that trust very seriously. I'm licensed, bonded and insured, and I never commit to a pet-sitting job without first meeting both the pet and its owners. I go to their house and get the pet's medical history, along with details of its diet and daily habits. I let the pet look me over and get to know my scent. By the time I've finished interviewing new clients, I know everything I need to know about their pet, and the pet feels comfortable with me. I insist on a key to their house, a number where I can reach them, and the name and number of the person they want called in case of an emergency. Just as I was when I was a deputy, I'm always aware that bad things can happen when you least expect them.

Hal said, "I know I explained this before, but the only reason we're doing this is that Jeffrey has temporal lobe seizures—two or three a week—and they're severe. Of all seizure disorders, temporal lobe seizures are most responsive to surgery and least responsive to medication. He's been on several meds, but none of them have done much good, and they cause so much dizziness that he has problems with balance." As if he felt guilty saying it, he added, "They also cause behavior problems. Temper tantrums, that kind of thing. That's why we have Mazie. She calms him down, and she walks close beside him so he can lean on her."

He had already told me about the medication and why they had decided on surgery, but he obviously needed to tell it again.

He closed his eyes and took a deep breath. "As you might imagine, Gillis and I live with the fear of a terrible fall—into fire, water, whatever—or of his cognitive development being . . . well, you know. Do you have children?"

I didn't want to answer him, because a parent numbed by fear over a child's illness doesn't want to hear how another child died. But I also didn't want to disrespect my own child by denying her.

I said, "I had a little girl. She was killed in an accident when she was three. I understand how you feel about Jeffrey."

He looked stricken. "I'm sorry."

For both our sakes, I needed to get the conversation back to why I was there.

I said, "Please don't worry about Mazie while you're gone. Pete Madeira will be here twenty-four/seven, and I'll come twice a day and walk her."

Pete's a former professional clown I'd met through some circus people I know—Sarasota has a long circus history—and he sometimes helped me out when a client needed a full-time pet sitter.

Hal leaned forward and clasped his hands with desperate urgency. "There's a risk to surgery, but there may be a larger risk if we do nothing."

The doorbell interrupted Hal's compulsive explanation. As he opened the door, Gillis and Jeffrey came into the living room, Jeffrey with his arm over Mazie's back and leaning against her as he walked.

Pete Madeira stood at the door, suitcase in hand and a clown nose stuck on his face. He also had a case with him that looked as if it might hold some kind of musical instrument. Pete had visited several times before, so he was as familiar to the family as I was. Hal and Gillis looked relieved to see him, and Mazie wagged her tail as if she were giving Pete her approval. Jeffrey gave him a tired smile, but I doubted that he understood Pete's presence meant he was soon going to be separated from his best friend.

Pete is tall, slim, silver-haired, and handsome in the way men who are bright and curious remain all their lives. He retired a few years ago, but he still does gigs in hospices and children's hospitals. He has woolly caterpillar eyebrows that he waggles for emphasis, and the softest heart in the western hemisphere.

Three suitcases already stood in the foyer, lined up by size like Papa Bear, Mama Bear, and Baby Bear luggage. Pete set his on the opposite side of the foyer.

He said, "I brought my saxophone. I hope that's okay."

Hal said, "I didn't know you played saxophone."

"Sure. That's how I started in the circus. I was in the band, but clowning paid better and was more fun. I just play for my own pleasure now."

"Pete, you're a man of many talents."

Pete grinned and did that thing with his eyebrows.

Gillis knelt beside Jeffrey. "Honey, you remember Pete? He's going to stay here with Mazie and keep her company until we come home."

Pete said, "Hi, pal."

Jeffrey smiled but looked confused.

Pete said, "Want a clown nose like mine?"

Jeffrey shook his head and covered his nose with his hand.

Hal said, "We have to go now."

Gillis knelt beside Jeffrey while Hal picked up their luggage.

Too hesitantly, Gillis said, "It's time for the trip I told you about. Remember I told you?"

Jeffrey stiffened and reached for Mazie, already resisting what was to come.

Gillis said, "Mazie's staying here. Remember?"

Jeffrey burst into hysterical shrieks and flung himself flat against the floor. "I want Mazie to come too!"

Gillis was pale with tension. As Jeffrey's fists churned, Mazie got to her feet and nuzzled his neck. It took me a moment to realize she did it intentionally to forestall a tantrum. Or a seizure. Jeffrey's rigid body relaxed and his cries reduced to a low droning.

Like a man inspired, Pete knelt beside his cases and in seconds held a gleaming saxophone to his lips. Soft sweet music rose above Jeffrey's cries, and in a minute or two Jeffrey stopped crying and looked toward Pete. Even Mazie took her eyes off Jeffrey for a moment to look at him. I remembered Pete telling me once that circus bands had always played to distract audiences when something unpleasant happened, like an aerialist or ropewalker falling.

Gillis gathered Jeffrey into her arms and stood up. Intrigued by the music, Jeffrey put a thumb in his mouth and stared at Pete. Jeffrey's eyes were dull and flat. I doubted he fully realized what was happening, which is probably the only good side effect of children's medication. Mazie began walking in erratic circles around

Gillis, who looked as if she might break down at any moment.

Hal murmured, "Mazie hasn't left Jeffrey's side more than a few minutes in all the time she's been with him."

I got Mazie's leash and snapped it on her collar.

"Come on, Mazie, let's go for a walk!"

Because she was a good dog trained to obey commands, she reluctantly followed me outside and allowed herself to be led to the sidewalk. I took her in the opposite direction that her family would take. She looked over her shoulder several times, obviously confused about the turn of events, but we had rounded a curve when I heard Hal's car drive away, so Mazie didn't see them leave. If I had it to do over again, I might not handle Jeffrey's departure that way, but at the time it seemed the right thing to do.

When I thought it was safe, I led Mazie back home. At the driveway, the woman I'd met that morning trotted by, her tank top dark in spots with jogging perspiration. When she saw me, she stopped and came forward with her hand out.

She said, "I'm Laura Halston. I should have introduced myself this morning. I was a total shrew, wasn't I?"

Her teeth were milk white, with a little inverted V at the bottom of the two upper centrals that was too perfect—one of those subtle signs that tell you a person has given a lot of money to a cosmetic dentist.

I gave her my name again and tried not to stare. I didn't want to be the kind of person who went slack-jawed just because another person had more than an average share of good looks. A lot more.

She said, "Do you run?"

"Run?"

"For exercise."

"Well, I run with a greyhound twice a day. That's plenty exercise."

"I run every morning. It's the only thing I'm disciplined about."

She said it with pride, and stuck out a foot in its expensive running shoe to emphasize that she was serious about running.

Then she put her hands on her knees and leaned toward Mazie. "Hi, Mazie. How're you doing, girl?"

I was once again struck by all her contradictions. She was gorgeous but she didn't seem stuck up about it, she was sensitive to animals, she seemed to say every thought that drifted across her cortex, and she took little-girl pride in the fact that she ran. I liked that.

Mazie tried to be friendly, but she kept looking over her shoulder toward her house. If I hadn't been so taken with Laura Halston, I might have been more sensitive to Mazie's confusion. She knew something was different in her world, and she didn't know why.

As it was, Laura and I said some more innocuous things, nothing of any importance, and she trotted away while I took Mazie back inside the house.

That's all there was to it. There was absolutely no way I could have known that my chance meeting with Laura Halston would one day haunt me, or that knowing her would ultimately make me question myself in a way I'd never done before.

CHAPTER 2

Most people, when they hear about any key in Florida, think Florida Keys, but the Florida Keys are about six hours south of us, damn near to Cuba. They're just a string of barrier islands too, so I don't know why they get to be called the Florida Keys, as if they're the state's licensed keys, but that's how it is. Life's like that. Half the things people take for granted don't make a lick of sense.

To get technical about it, we're roughly fifty-five miles south of Tampa and two hundred fifty-five miles northwest of Miami. We have around seven thousand full-time residents, but during "season" from November to April, our numbers swell to around twenty-four thousand. We lose some of our laid-back panache then, but anybody who manages to be a grouch while living on Siesta Key really has to work at it.

Siesta Key has one main street, Midnight Pass Road, which runs eight miles from the key's southern tip to the northern end. We have two other sort-of-major streets, one arcing around Siesta Beach, one of the most beautiful beaches in the world, and the other running through the Village, which loosely passes as our business district. We're connected to Sarasota by two drawbridges, and a favorite topic of conversation is the amount of time lost waiting for a drawbridge to come down after it rises to let a boat go through. We like to talk about lost time; it makes us feel as if we're as rushed and busy as New Yorkers or Chicagoans. The truth is that most of us don't really need to rush anywhere, we just like the high of pretending to.

Wild rabbits play tag on the cool white sands of our beaches. Gulls, terns, plovers, pelicans, egrets, herons, ibis, spoonbills, storks, and cranes busily search for food along the shore, and dolphins and manatees play in the warm waters of the Intracoastal Waterway, Sarasota Bay, Roberts Bay, and the Gulf of Mexico. Inside the key itself, there are almost fifty miles of canals and waterways lined with palms, mossy oaks, cedars, mangroves, and sea grapes. We also have balmy days, white crystalline sand beaches, brilliant flowers, and every tropical plant and bird and butterfly you can imagine. I've lived here all my life, and I wouldn't dream of living anywhere else.

Some days, if I'm lucky, I don't run into a single human being until at least nine o'clock, when I stop at the Village Diner for breakfast. It isn't that I don't like people or need them. It's just that I sometimes go a little nuts over certain behaviors in certain people, and then I'm not responsible for what I do. I don't have that problem with animals. Animals always have sensible reasons for whatever they do. People, on the other hand, do stupid things that cause other people to die.

Since it was April, a faint scent of cocoa butter hung in the air from late spring break kids splayed out on the beach. Most schools take spring break in March, but no matter when they come, the kids mostly stay on or around the beach, broiling during the day and partying at night. Unless they get too loud at night, the locals take a live-and-let-live attitude toward them.

The day being Sunday, traffic was light on worker trucks and delivery vans but heavy on churchgoing cars. Personally, I feel a lot closer to God when I'm at the beach watching a sunset than I've ever felt inside a church. When I was little, I got the Sunday school God mixed up with the grandfather in *Heidi*, so for a long time I imagined God surrounded by long-eared goats and greeting people in heaven with hunks of goat cheese he'd toasted over an open fire. I liked that about him.

When I got older, my best friends were Hillary Danes and Rebecca Stein, and they made God seem a lot less friendly. Hillary was Catholic, and God made it his personal business to forbid her to see certain movies. My grandmother forbade me to see most of the same movies, but that didn't seem as awesome as God doing it. Then, when we all started our periods, God declared Rebecca a woman responsible for her own actions. That really steamed me. My grandmother sort of did the same thing, but Rebecca got to do a Bat Mitzvah and all I got was lunch at an expensive restaurant on the bay.

While we ate crab salads, my grandmother said, "Is there anything you want to ask me about periods?"

I shook my head. "Not really. They showed the girls a movie at school."

"What about how women get pregnant? You know how that works?"

"The sperm hits the egg and it divides and turns into a baby."

"And you know how the sperm gets to the egg? The man-and-woman business?"

"I think so."

"Well, that's good. I guess if your mother were here

she would explain it in more detail, but my generation didn't talk about those things much. The main thing is that boys would have sex with a snake if it laid still, so don't think it means they love you if they want to have sex with you, not even if they say they do. And don't get any romantic notions about what fun it would be to have a cute little baby, either. It's not like playing with dolls."

I said, "Hillary said the priest told her mom she'd go to hell if she took pills not to have another baby, but she does anyway."

"Huh! If priests were the ones having babies, they'd be guzzling those pills by the handful."

We'd had strawberry sundaes for dessert, and that had been the end of my Presbyterian Bat Mitzvah. Since then, God and I have given each other respectful space.

That morning, I headed for breakfast at the Village Diner where I'm such a regular that the minute she sees me, Tanisha, the cook, automatically starts making two eggs over easy with extra-crisp home fries and a biscuit. Tanisha's a friend I only see at the diner. She and I half solved a crime one time by putting two and two together. Judy, the waitress who knows me almost as well as my brother does, grabs a coffeepot and has a full mug ready for me by the time I sit down.

Before I headed for the ladies' room to wash off dog spit and cat hair, I grabbed a *Herald-Tribune* from a stack by the door and dropped it at my usual booth, sort of marking my territory. Not that I'm particular about where I sit. It's just that I don't like to mess up our routine by sitting at a different booth. It's an efficiency thing.

Sure enough, the coffee was ready and waiting when I came out, and I gulped half of it before I was good and settled. Judy was a couple of booths down taking somebody's order, but she had her coffeepot with her.

When she headed toward the kitchen, she paused long enough to top off my coffee with the calm air of an old friend who knows exactly what you like.

Judy's tall and sharp-boned, with golden-brown hair, caramel-colored eyes, and a scattering of topaz freckles over a thin pointed nose. If she had long flapping ears, she would look a lot like a beagle. She's loyal like a beagle too. If she likes you, it's because she's decided you're worth her trouble even though you're probably going to royally screw up your life. We have never met anyplace except the diner, but I know every detail about all the no-good men who have broken her heart, and she knows about Todd and Christy.

Both our lives had been fairly calm lately. I'd had a bad patch around Christmas, not only because it was Christmas and my third year without Todd and Christy, but because there'd been a murder involving one of my clients and I'd ended up being involved in the investigation. Around the same time, Judy had been about to let a loser move in with her lock, stock, and gun rack, but she'd had an attack of clear judgment and dumped him. We both had a new flinty glint in our eyes, because by God we were survivors. Like loggerhead turtles that drag themselves onto our beaches every year to dig nests and lay eggs that may be destroyed by morning, Judy and I keep going on.

I said, "Tell Tanisha to give me some bacon too."

She waggled her eyebrows because I rarely allow myself bacon even though I love it beyond reason.

She said, "You celebrating something?"

"Nope, just feel like bacon."

"I thought maybe you and that hunky detective had finally done the deed and you were rewarding yourself."

I rolled my eyes to show I thought she was too silly

to even answer. She grinned and sashayed away with her coffeepot, every line of her saying she thought she was clever to say she thought I'd finally decided to lose my self-imposed second virginity.

She wasn't, and I hadn't, and I didn't want to talk about it.

While I waited for her to come back with my breakfast, I scanned the front page of the paper, skimming over the usual boring stuff. Some Washington senator had been caught soliciting sex from a kid on the internet, a lobbyist had been caught paying a huge bribe to another senator in exchange for preferential treatment to his employer, and a local man had caught a pregnant shark and all its babies had died. The fisherman was photographed standing proudly beside the hanging shark. He missed his calling. He should have been in Washington.

Judy plopped down my breakfast plates and splashed more coffee in my mug.

She said, "You hear that?"

I raised my head. "What?"

"The quiet. They've almost all gone."

I nodded. "I've been seeing car transports."

We both got almost misty-eyed at the thought. We year-rounders on the key mark our lives by the arrival and departure of the seasonal residents. In the fall, when we see auto transports hauling snowbirds' cars into town, sandhill cranes returning from Canada, and an occasional magnificent frigatebird soaring high overhead, we know the seasonals are on their way and we brace ourselves. In the spring, when all the migratory signs are reversed, we let out a big sigh of relief. Not that we don't like our seasonals, or that we don't appreciate what they do for our economy. But having them descend on us every year is like having beloved relatives come for long annual visits—we count them as blessings, but we're still glad to see them go.

Judy left, and I turned my full attention to breakfast. If I were on death row facing execution, I would ask for breakfast as my last meal. Of course, I'd want it prepared by Tanisha, with eggs cooked so the whites were firm and the yolk quivery, with a rasher of bacon laid out like little crisp brown slats without a trace of icky white bubbles, and a puffed-up flaky biscuit served so hot that butter melted into it at the touch. And coffee. Lots of hot black coffee.

While I ate, I looked at the Sudoku puzzle in the paper, but it made my brain ache a little bit, so I finally pushed the paper aside. I had been up since four o'clock, and I needed a shower and a nap and some time to myself. When I'd scarfed down every last crumb, I put down money for Judy, waved goodbye to Tanisha, and dragged my weary self out to the Bronco.

Parakeets and songbirds fluttered up like smoke signals as I eased the Bronco between pines, oaks, palms, and sea grape lining my meandering Gulf-side driveway. On the shore, the day's first high tide was rolling in, and a crowd of seabirds was loudly arguing over its catered delicacies.

Rounding the last curve in the drive, I saw Michael and Paco beside the carport washing out paintbrushes. They usually take Michael's boat out on their days off, but they'd decided to paint their house and my apartment before the weather got too hot. Both of them wore brief cutoffs that revealed acres of firm sun-tanned flesh. They were sweat-shimmery topless, with folded bandannas tied around their foreheads as sweatbands. Half the women on Siesta Key would have paid big bucks for front-row tickets to see them like that—the same women who pray every night that a miracle actually can happen to convert a gay man to straight.

A firefighter like our father, Michael is big and blond and broad, with a piercing blue gaze that turns women into blithering idiots. Like me, Michael has our inherited Nordic coloring. Paco, on the other hand, can pass for almost every dark-haired, dark-eyed nationality under the sun, which comes in handy since he's with the Special Investigative Bureau—better known as SIB—of the Sarasota County Sheriff's Department. He's actually fourth-generation Greek-American, with the surname Pakodopoulos—too much of a mouthful for the kids he grew up with in Chicago so they nicknamed him Paco, and it stuck. He's slim and deeply tanned, so handsome it makes your toes curl and so smart it's sometimes unnerving. He mostly does undercover stuff, mostly in disguise, and mostly so dangerous that Michael and I don't even want to think about it. They've been a couple for almost thirteen years now, so Paco is my brother-in-love. He's also my second-best friend in all the world.

When I drove into the four-slot carport, they both looked up and watched me park. It made me itchy to see them looking at me with such studied speculation. I knew that look.

I got out of the Bronco and glared at them. "Don't even think about it!"

Michael said, "Come on, Dixie, it's good exercise."

Paco said, "Yeah, climbing up and down a ladder would firm your butt."

I said, "My butt is firm enough, and I get plenty of exercise walking dogs. Which I've been doing since four o'clock, and I'm beat."

I shaded my eyes and looked at the half-painted house.

If we'd had our druthers, the house would have been built of cypress and left unpainted to weather pale gray, but cypress hadn't been an option when our grandparents ordered the house from the Sears, Roebuck catalog. The new color was the same as it has been since our grandfather put the first coat of paint on it, the cerulean blue of the water in the Gulf on a clear sunshiny day. It takes about six months for salt breezes to scour it pale, so painting is an annual job.

But not mine.

I am firmly of the conviction that house painting is man's work, like assembly-line drilling or sperm donation—things that require rote repetitious movements.

I said, "Looks good!" which made Michael and Paco beam like little kids getting a gold star on their paper. Men are like puppies, they're easily distracted by compliments.

CHAPTER 3

My apartment rides above a four-slot carport next to the frame house where my brother and I went to live with our grandparents when Michael was eleven and I was nine. Our firefighter father had been killed a couple of years before while saving somebody else's children, and our mother had just up and left one day.

We didn't see her again until we were grown and she came to our grandfather's funeral. Oddly, she had her suitcase with her. She left it in the chapel vestibule before she came down the aisle and took a seat on the front row. Michael and I were across the aisle, and until the minister looked pointedly at her, we didn't notice her. I turned my head to see what he was so taken with and met my mother's gaze. Her face was awash with tears, but otherwise she looked exactly as I remembered her when she'd left seventeen years before.

I squeezed Michael's hand and he leaned around me to see her. We all smiled automatically and uncertainly, as if it were the socially acceptable thing to do but we weren't sure it was the honest thing to do. My mother pursed her lips in a mimed kiss across the aisle, the way she had always done as she left our bedroom after tucking us in, and I was suddenly shaken with sobs for all the kisses lost, all the love withdrawn, all the pain that could never be forgotten.

After the funeral service, we were all awkward with one another. Our grandmother had died the year before, and it didn't take long to figure out that our mother had returned not out of grief at her father's passing but out of a greedy hope that she had inherited the beachfront property he'd bought when he was a young man and land on the key was cheap. As soon as Michael set her straight about who now owned the place, she took her suitcase and left again.

Her brief visit hadn't changed anything. When she left, we didn't know where she went and she didn't make any effort to stay in touch, not even when the next loss threatened to pull me under to dark oblivion. I don't think of her much anymore. Or at least I try not to.

Pushing the remote to raise metal hurricane shutters, I climbed the stairs to the covered porch that runs the length of my apartment. The porch has a small glass-topped table, two ice-cream chairs, ceiling fans to stir the air, and a hammock in one corner for napping and daydreaming. French doors open to a minuscule living room furnished with my grandmother's green flower-printed love seat and easy chair. A one-person bar separates the living room from a narrow galley kitchen, where a window lets in light over the sink and allows a view of treetops. The bedroom is barely big enough for a single bed pushed against one wall, a nightstand, and a dresser holding a photograph of my husband and child. In the photograph, Todd is thirty and Christy is three. If they had lived, Todd would be thirty-three now, same as I am, and Christy would be six.

One day I will be forty, fifty, sixty, perhaps ninety or a hundred, but Todd will remain thirty and Christy will always be three. I imagine them in a different universe, eternally the same age they were when they were killed.

The air was humid and stale, and I flipped the switch to turn on the air-conditioning unit set high on the bedroom wall. On the way to the shower, I tossed my clothes and white Keds in the stacked washer/dryer in an alcove in the hall outside my tiny bathroom. With the morning's fatigue and cat hair washed off, I fell naked into bed and slept a couple of hours, then padded barefoot to my closet. The closet is the most spacious room in the apartment, big enough to serve as an office as well. A desk sits against one wall, and shelves for my shorts and T-shirts and Keds fill the opposite side. Between them, on the back wall, there's a floor-to-ceiling mirror and a short rack of listless dresses and skirts reaching toward the floor like banyan rootlets hoping to acquire greater purpose.

I pulled on clean shorts and a knit top and went to the kitchen to get a bottle of water from the fridge. I wanted cookies, but I didn't have any. I switched on the CD player to fill the apartment with Patsy Cline's voice—there's something about Patsy's steady tumtee-*tum*-tee, tumtee-*tum*-tee rhythm that helps organize my brain—and went back to the closet-office to take care of the business side of pet sitting.

I'm very meticulous about keeping records and sharing them with pet owners. I list times I arrived and left, what I did while I was there, and anything out of the ordinary that I noticed. It can be important to know exactly what date I felt a tiny lump under a cat's skin, or when I noted that a dog's eyes were pained or dull. I keep a record of everything, maybe more than I need to, but it makes me feel better to know I'm doing the very best job I possibly can.

When I finished, I still wanted cookies and I still didn't have any. A furtive peek over the porch railing revealed that Michael and Paco had put away the painting supplies, and Michael's car was gone. Which meant they had gone off on some errand. Which meant they wouldn't know if I snuck down to their kitchen and stole cookies. Not that they'd care, but it was sort of exciting to think I could get away with something they didn't know about.

Michael always has cookies, cookies that he personally makes in his big commercial oven, cookies that are so good you have to be strict with yourself or you'll whimper when you eat them. I was out like a flash, thumping down the stairs to go filch some of his cookies.

Michael is the cook of the family. He's also the cook at the firehouse. If he could, he would travel the world cooking for anybody who was hungry or lonely or downtrodden. He would cook for happy people too, but it gives him a great sense of satisfaction to feed needy people, and if he thinks their lives are improved because of it, that absolutely makes his day.

Except for Ella Fitzgerald, Michael and Paco's kitchen was empty. Ella is a true Persian-mix calico—meaning she has some Persian in her ancestry and her coat has distinct blocks of black, white, and red—and she makes funny scatting sounds like Ella Fitzgerald. Left on my porch by a woman departing the country, Ella had liked me well enough, but the first time she sniffed the air in Michael's kitchen, she knew she'd found her true love. Lots of human females feel that way about Michael too. Fat lot of good it does them.

When I came in, Ella jumped down from her perch

on a bar stool at the butcher-block island and came to twine her body around my ankles. I knelt to stroke her hair and kiss her nose.

She said, *"Thrrripp!"*

I said, "I totally agree."

She trotted beside my feet when I went to inspect the cookie jar. Just as I'd expected, it was full of freshly baked cookies. Coconut and chocolate chip and oatmeal raisin. I made a small stack on a paper napkin while Ella flipped the tip of her tail and watched me. Cats have too much dignity to beg for table goodies like dogs do. They just give you unblinking stares until you break down and give them something.

I got a couple of kitty treats from her special canister with the design of a cat on the front and added them to my stack. Then I scooped Ella up in one arm and pushed through the kitchen door to the wooden deck and the beckoning redwood chaise. With Ella happily sitting on my stomach, we both munched our treats while the surf made gurgling noises at the shore and seabirds swooped and called to one another above us.

Ella finished her treats, licked her paws, and stretched out to purr, her warmth comforting against my body. All my cookies were gone too, and for a little while I closed my eyes and enjoyed the aftertaste of cookies, the warmth of a kitty on my tummy, the fresh clean scent of the sea, and the familiar sound of seabirds circling overhead. There was a time when I was numb to moments of pleasure like that, so I was not only floating on a tide of bliss, but aware that I was. I suppose we have to experience the loss of pleasure to truly appreciate it when it comes back.

It was almost time to make my afternoon rounds, so I finally roused Ella and stood up to go inside. I stopped when a dark blue Blazer crunched down the lane and stopped next to the carport.

Oh, noodles, it was Lieutenant Guidry.

If Michael and Paco came home and found him here, Michael would have a cow. Just the sight of Guidry reminded Michael of all the times I'd been in mortal danger because of some murder investigation I'd got myself involved in.

As Lieutenant Guidry of the Sarasota County's Homicide Investigative Unit got out and started toward me, I tried to convince myself that Michael's distaste for Guidry was the only reason my heart had started jiggling.

Guidry is fortyish, with skin eternally bronzed, dark short-cropped hair showing a little silver at the sides, gray eyes bracketed by fine lines, a beaky nose, and lips that are never indecisive. As always, he looked as if he had come from a fashion shoot rather than a crime scene. Woven leather sandals, pleated linen trousers the color of wet clay, a dark gray shirt, and an unstructured linen jacket in an expensive shade of wine red. No tie, but something told me he'd recently worn one and removed it. Oh, man, he'd probably gone to church that morning. Probably had rosary beads in his pocket.

Feeling very heathenish, I noted how his jacket hung from his square shoulders without any pretension, but somehow it managed to look like something an Italian count would slip on before he went out to inspect his estate. From the elegance of his wardrobe and the casual ease with which he wore it, I knew he had grown up with money. A lot of money. But Guidry's past was none of my business, and I had no intention of ever asking him about it.

Still, I wondered for the millionth time what his background was. What was it that made him walk with such aristocratic confidence? What was it that made him wear the kind of clothes you see in films where Italian playboys are hanging out in sidewalk bistros on the Riviera? All I knew about the man had been dropped in bits and pieces that I'd collected like a starry-eyed groupie. I knew he was from New Orleans and that he'd been a cop there, but New Orleans cops are probably no more elegant than cops in any other city.

I knew he'd been married once, but if being married turned men into model look-alikes the world wouldn't be so full of fat slobs.

He had spoken French to me once. Actually, I had thought he was speaking Italian, but he had laughed and said, "Italian is one of the few things I'm not." That's all I knew about him.

Except that he was a terrific kisser. Oh, yes he was.

For reasons that neither of us ever intended or wanted, Guidry and I had been drawn together by some grisly murders. We had also been drawn together by chemistry. Neither of us had ever intended that either.

Our chemistry had resulted in one kiss that had left me feeling like a volcano that had spewed out a few hot rocks but was still gathering steam to blow sky high. That had happened around three months ago, right before Christmas. Thirteen and a half weeks ago, to be exact. Not that I'd been counting, or that I'd been disappointed that I hadn't seen him since Christmas Eve, because I wasn't.

I didn't any longer feel that being attracted to another man made me disloyal to my dead husband. I'd got over that. But I had a lot of reservations about falling in love with another cop. Too many people had died and left me, and it seemed to me that I might be better off with a man who had a nice safe desk job. Somebody like

Ethan Crane, for example, an attorney who had also kissed me and set off some hot tremors.

But both Guidry and Ethan must have had as many doubts as I had, because after a few weeks of eluded opportunity—sometimes mine and sometimes theirs—they had all but disappeared from my horizon.

Guidry stopped in front of me, and for a second we scanned each other's faces as if we were using visual Braille.

He said, "Enjoying the fresh air?"

My head bobbed up and down like one of those fool dogs that people put in their back car windows. For some reason, I always become incoherent around Guidry.

He said, "Ah, I just wanted to ask you . . . uh, the thing is, somebody donated tickets to the sheriff's office for a shindig Saturday night. A black-tie thing . . . there'll be dinner . . . some kind of entertainment too, I think . . . it's a fund-raiser for the Humane Society—you know, the animal people. I should go, you know, as a member of the department, and I know you like that kind of thing. The animals, I mean, so I wondered if you'd like to go with me."

Ella must have been as astonished as I was to hear Guidry lose his usual cool smoothness because she sat up in my arms and studied him. Guidry narrowed his eyes as if he wasn't accustomed to a cat's scrutiny.

As if I had a lot of pressing engagements, I said, "This *coming* Saturday?"

"Yeah, sorry. I just got word about it, or I would have asked you sooner."

I said, "I love the work the Humane Society does."

Guidry passed the back of his hand across his forehead as if he'd suddenly suffered a pain. He tends to look like that when I talk about animals.

He said, "That's why I thought you might like to go to the dinner."

"Okay."

He looked relieved. "Pick you up about seven?"

"Great."

"Well, okay, then."

We smiled at each other for a moment, both of us blinking a little bit because it was probably the first time in our acquaintance that we'd had an entire conversation—if you could call it that—that hadn't revolved around a murder.

He gave me a half wave and turned back to his car.

I watched him walk away and then felt something with claws clutch my chest.

I said, "Guidry, did you say black-tie?"

He turned back. "Yeah."

"Okay."

I was proud that my voice didn't squeak. He got in his car, waved again, and backed out. I looked at Ella, and she looked at me. Maybe it was my imagination, but it seemed to me that her eyes looked as alarmed as I felt. I had just accepted an invitation to a black-tie event that was to be held in six days. Which meant I had six days to go find something fancy to wear, because I sure as heck didn't have anything in my closet.

I took Ella back inside Michael's kitchen and kissed her goodbye.

I said, "I have to go see to my pets. And I have to buy some new clothes. You're lucky, you can just wear the same fur all the time, but women have to wear special clothes for special occasions. Oh, God, shoes too. Okay, I'll just do it. It's really no problem. No, really, it's not."

She didn't look convinced.

I said, "Don't tell Michael and Paco I stole cookies, okay?"

She tilted her head back, looked solemnly into my eyes, and blinked twice, slowly. In cat language, that means *I love you*.

Even so, she was probably planning to rat me out.

CHAPTER 4

My afternoons are pretty much a repeat of my mornings, except I don't groom any of the pets. Instead, I spend more time playing with them or exercising them. My pet-sitting day ends around sunset, and it's very satisfying to know that I've made several living beings happy that day. That I left their food bowls sparkling clean and fresh water in their water bowls. That I brushed them so their coats shined, and played with them until all our hearts were beating faster. That I kissed them goodbye and left them with their tails wagging or flipping or at least raised in a happy kind of way. That's a heck of a lot more than any president, pope, prime minister, or potentate can say, and I wouldn't switch places with any of them.

Morning or afternoon, my first stop is always at Tom Hale's condo. He lives in the Sea Breeze on the Gulf side of the key. Tom and I swap services. He handles my taxes and anything having to do with money, and I run twice a day with his greyhound, Billy Elliot.

Tom has curly black hair that hugs his head like a poodle's trim, and he wears round eyeglasses that give him a cute Harry Potter look. Until you look into his eyes. His eyes betray a time of intense suffering, a look that says he can endure whatever pain life sends, but hopes, oh God, that it won't happen again.

His transition came during a casual saunter down a lumber-and-door aisle in a home improvement store— one of those huge places that sells everything from flashlights to entire kitchens. To this day he doesn't know what caused it, but there was an avalanche and his spine was crushed under tons of lumber. And that was just the beginning of the cataclysmic change. Within a couple of years, Tom had lost his CPA firm, his wife and children, and most of the money he'd got in a law-suit against the store. About all he had left was Billy Elliot, a dog he had saved from the fate that befalls rac-ing dogs who have quit winning. Billy Elliot returned the favor by saving Tom from utter loneliness and de-spair. Dogs are like that. Dogs don't stop loving you when your luck turns sour.

Tom had been pretty much of a hermit until last Christmas, when he had fallen in love with a woman named Frannie. Since then, he'd been looking more relaxed and a little heavier. Happiness seems to make men gain weight, while it makes women skinnier. Fran-nie was nice enough, but I suspected she wasn't a dog person. I would never have told Tom, but the truth was I didn't think she was good enough for him and Billy Elliot.

I knocked on Tom's door, then used my key to go in. Billy Elliot bounded to meet me in the foyer, and we kissed hello as if we hadn't just left each other a few hours before. Tom was working on taxes or something at his kitchen table, so I hollered hello to him and took Billy Elliot out to the elevator and downstairs.

Billy Elliot needs to run hard laps around the park-ing lot for at least fifteen minutes, and then it takes him another ten minutes to find the right bushes to pee on, the right patch of grass to make a deposit. By the time I've collected it in one of my poop bags, and he's made one final streak around the parking lot, we've spent a good thirty minutes outside. When we got back upstairs, Tom was still working and didn't come out to chat like he usually does. I stuck my head in the kitchen to say hello and saw a strained face and bloodshot eyes.

I said, "You okay?"

He waved his hand dismissively. "I'm fine. Stayed up too late."

I could tell he didn't want to talk, so I told him good-bye, gave Billy Elliot another smooch, and left them. But I was suspicious about Tom's explanation. I would have bet good money that Frannie was the problem, not late hours. I hoped they worked it out, because he had been happier since Frannie came into his life. As much as I didn't think she was good enough for him, I didn't want him to lose her.

By the time I worked my way to Mazie's house, it was nearing five o'clock. I parked in the driveway behind Pete's car and rang the doorbell. Mazie was close beside Pete when he answered the door, and they both looked anxious.

Pete said, "Mazie has been searching all the rooms for Jeffrey. She's whimpering too, like she thinks she's lost him."

That's exactly what Mazie probably thought, that somehow she had lost her boy. That would be bad enough for any companion dog, but for a service dog it would be even worse. Her job was to stay close to Jeffrey, so she would think she had failed in her duty.

I said, "Pete, have you ever brushed a golden retriever?"

His brow furrowed like Mazie's. "Excuse me?"

"Let's take Mazie to the lanai and I'll demonstrate."

Nothing in the world is as calming as brushing a dog, and dogs like it too. Even though I don't usually groom pets during an afternoon visit, this day wasn't an ordinary day for Mazie.

I led her to the lanai, and Pete followed with two mugs of hot coffee. He put one on the table for me, and said, "Jeffrey's awfully young to have to fight for his life."

I didn't answer him. I didn't want to talk about what was happening to Jeffrey. It hit too close to home, made me remember too vividly how small and fragile Christy had looked in death.

Pete fell silent and watched me pull an undercoat rake through Mazie's hair.

Nature gave golden retrievers double coats to keep them warm in winter. That's an asset up north, but in Florida it's like wearing thermal underwear in August, so they shed it. You have to keep it raked out or it'll be all over the house.

Mazie looked over her shoulder at me and smiled, not because she was glad she wouldn't be carpeting the house with dog hair, but because getting rid of it made her feel cooler and lighter.

Pete watched closely and didn't speak until I'd finished with the undercoat rake and got out my boar-bristle brush.

I said, "You finish off with the brush to fluff her topcoat and make it shine."

He said, "I'll call you the minute I hear something about Jeffrey."

Over Mazie's head, I met his knowing eyes. I guess I hadn't fooled anybody. Certainly not Pete, and probably not Mazie. They both knew I was afraid for Jeffrey. I wished I weren't, but I knew only too well that there are times when the worst happens, and there's not a damn thing anybody can do to stop it.

Mazie was calmer once she was brushed, but when I snapped the leash onto her collar and led her outside she didn't happily swish her tail. I wondered if she had lost trust in me since I had taken her away while Jeffrey and his parents left. More than likely, she was simply confused and unhappy because her people had left her and strangers had taken their place and she didn't know why.

We took a long walk, following a meandering sidewalk past houses almost invisible behind palms, oaks, and thick shrubbery, all the way to the far side of the lagoon. Occasionally through the hibiscus hedge screening the jogging path on the other side of the street, I saw a dark shape running on the track. Mazie and I didn't run until we made a U-turn and retraced our walk. Then, as if by tacit agreement, we both broke into an easy trot that gradually turned into a hard run. By the time we got to Mazie's driveway, we were flying.

A car rolled up behind us in the street, and a voice yelled, "Hey!"

It was Laura Halston, waving to us from a red Jaguar convertible. In big dark sunglasses that hid her eyebrows, and a blue Dallas Cowboys cap pulled low over her hair. I wouldn't have recognized her if I'd seen her on the street.

She nodded to grocery bags piled in the backseat. "Had to go stock up on essentials. Coffee, wine, Pepperidge Farm cookies."

"No ice cream?"

"Well, hell, sure. Ice cream's a given."

Then she turned her attention to Mazie, who was looking up at her with anxious eyes. "Oh, sweet Mazie, don't worry about Jeffrey. He'll come home all better."

To me, she said, "I know about Jeffrey's surgery. Poor little guy."

Relieved that I didn't have to keep it a secret, I said, "Pete Madeira will be staying in the house with Mazie. He's a clown, so if you see him wearing a red nose, don't be alarmed. He also plays saxophone, so if you hear music, that'll be Pete playing for Mazie."

She said, "I dated a saxophone player once. Sweet guy. Great kisser."

We chatted for a few minutes more about nothing, the way women do when they like each other and don't much care what they're talking about. I didn't divulge any more information about Mazie's family, and she seemed to understand that I wouldn't, that I was a professional, and that it would be unprofessional to talk about my employers.

I hadn't had a close woman friend since high school, when Maureen Rhinegold and I used to go to Turtle Beach and sit behind a sand dune and try to get high smoking marijuana. We were abject failures at it—we mostly just coughed and gagged—but we kept at it until my brother caught us and told me he would kick my butt clear to Cuba if I ever smoked weed again. We had drifted apart after Maureen married a rich man and I became a deputy married to a deputy. Talking to Laura stirred up a nostalgic wish for the kind of closeness I'd had with Maureen. There had been an easy trust in that closeness that I missed.

Laura must have wanted to prolong the chat too, because she said, "Say, do you have time for a glass of wine?"

I felt a bubble of excitement, as if one of the girls at the popular table in the high school cafeteria had invited me to sit with her. Trying not to sound like a lonely soul grateful for an invitation, I said a glass of wine sounded fine, and that I would take Mazie home and be at her house in a flash.

She said, "I'll be in the kitchen, so just come in through the garage door."

Every time I met the woman, I liked her even more. Except for being gorgeous, she seemed refreshingly uncomplicated. Straightforward, friendly, generous, and a pet lover. How could I *not* like her?

Back in Mazie's house, Pete was puttering around in the kitchen.

"Hal called while you were gone. He said the surgery is scheduled for tomorrow morning at seven. Gillis will spend the night in the hospital with Jeffrey, and then she and Hal will take turns sleeping in a recliner by his bed. He left his cell phone number and their hotel number in case we need to get in touch. He said he would call after it's over."

He gave me the numbers and I wrote them down, even though Hal had already left his cell number and hotel number and the hospital's number several times. We were all repeating ourselves, doing an overkill of efficiency to make ourselves feel organized enough to keep Jeffrey safe.

Pete said, "Is it okay if I give Mazie a treat? So she'll associate me with good things?"

I shook my head. "Sorry. The rules for service dogs are that only their trainer can give them treats. But she's a smart dog, she knows you're a good person."

"I guess all we can do now is pray for the boy. For all of them, really."

I went over and kissed his cheek. Mazie wasn't the only one who knew Pete Madeira was a good man.

I said, "I'm going to leave my Bronco in the driveway here, but I'm going to have a glass of wine with Laura Halston. She lives next door. Have you met her?"

Pete's face took on a guarded look. "I met her this

morning. Mazie and I went out to get some air and she came over. Said she was doing some gardening."

"I don't know her well, but she seems like a very nice person."

"Can't always tell about people by the way they look, Dixie. She's pretty, but pretty is as pretty does. We had a woman in the circus with the ugliest face you ever saw, but she had a beautiful soul. That woman next door has a beautiful face, but don't let that fool you."

That was the first time I'd ever heard Pete say something mean or cynical, and I was disappointed in him. On the other hand, Laura was so outstandingly beautiful that she might have made him uncomfortably aware that he was no longer a man who might attract her.

I said, "Don't worry, I'm just having a glass of wine."

I didn't stay to debate the wisdom of spending time with Laura, just blew kisses at Pete and Mazie. As I hotfooted it over to Laura's house, I could feel Pete and Mazie watching from the doorway, both of them with worried faces.

CHAPTER 5

Once I got past the greenery that hid Laura's house, I was surprised at how modest it was. An L-shaped frame bungalow, it had a covered carport on the long side and a multi-glass-paned front door on the protruding side. The former deputy in me made me think how those square panes of glass in her front door made the house easy to break into, but I certainly didn't intend to mention it.

I skirted the red Jag, rapped twice on the door to the kitchen, and turned the knob. But before I pushed the door all the way open, I stuck my head in to announce myself.

I heard Laura say, "Don't come here, Martin. And don't call me again. Not ever." Her voice was hard and angry, full of bitter animosity.

I froze with my head inside the kitchen and the rest of me outside. Laura stood at a bar on the far side of the kitchen, cell phone at her ear, her face drawn tight. She had taken off the dark shades but still wore the Cowboys cap.

Motioning me in, she said, "Goodbye, Martin."

Hesitantly, I pushed the door open and got my whole self inside. But the instant I was completely in, a banshee scream sounded at my feet and caused me to leap like a kangaroo. Leo streaked to Laura's side and glared at me.

I said, "Oh, I'm so sorry! Did I step on him?"

In a heartbeat, Laura's face went from savage fury to wry humor. As if stepping on a cat were a trifling thing, she said, "It's his own fault. He has this awful habit of sitting beside a door and stretching his tail across the opening. Gets his tail stepped on all the time, but he keeps doing it. I don't know if he's too dumb or too stubborn to give it up."

Waving her cell phone for emphasis, she said, "He's a lot like my soon-to-be ex. Either too dumb or too stubborn to know when it's time to let something go. That was him on the phone, being a complete ass, as usual."

I said, "If this is a bad time—"

"Oh, no! This is a perfect time. I have much more need of a friend than I do to talk to my ex!"

I liked being called a friend.

Putting the cell phone on the bar where a bulky black land phone squatted, she took off her cap and shook her hair. She wore a long skirt with a brief ribbed cotton sweater and high-heeled espadrilles. Even with her Cowboys cap and dark glasses, she would have been the glamorous one at the supermarket.

She said, "I have to get out of these clothes. There's a bottle of Chablis in the fridge. If you'd rather have red, there's some in the rack. Wineglasses in the far right cabinet."

She scooted down a hallway, and Leo trotted after her. In a minute or two, I heard two screeches, one from her and one from Leo.

She hollered, "Leo! You've got to stop doing that!"

In a softer voice, she said something else I couldn't make out. Whatever it was that Leo had done seemed to be forgiven.

Left alone, I considered the wine options. I actually prefer red, but I didn't want to risk staining my teeth before the evening with Guidry, so I got out two wineglasses and poured Chablis in both of them. Men wouldn't do that. Men eat garlic and onions without worrying about their breath and they drink whatever they damn well please no matter what kind of stains it may leave on their teeth. Women are dopes. But I was a woman, so I would drink white wine.

Searching for napkins, I opened several drawers that held flatware and cooking stuff, then pulled out a drawer that turned out to be a deep pull-out storage cabinet. It held all kinds of cat supplies—cat vitamins, packets of kitty treats, bottles of food additives to make coats shiny, and two twenty-pound bags of organic dry cat food. I grinned at the generous oversupply, sort of a sure sign that Leo was Laura's first cat.

Behind me, Laura said, "What are you doing?"

Her voice had gone hard again, and when I turned to her I saw frost in her green eyes. She had changed into baggy drawstring pants and a sleeveless knit top, but that was the only thing about her at the moment that looked relaxed.

I said, "Sorry, I'm looking for napkins. It's an illness I inherited from my grandmother. She got the vapors if anybody used paper towels."

She laughed, easy and friendly again, and padded barefoot to pull out a slim drawer full of cocktail napkins. Flapping a couple at me, she said, "Do they have to be cloth, or will paper do?"

I shoved the drawer of cat stuff closed with my hip.

"My grandmother would have preferred cloth, but paper works for me."

She smiled, handed me a napkin, and picked up one of the glasses of wine. Raising it toward me, she said, "Cheers, new friend."

Again, I was flooded with the warm fuzzy feelings that come with discovering that somebody you like likes you back. The fragrance of some very expensive perfume wafted toward me. I hoped I wasn't sending off wafts of doggie smell.

Leo trotted into the kitchen and stopped beside Laura to give me a calculating once-over. Havana Browns are graceful solid-brown hybrids with emerald eyes and big forward tilting ears. As svelte as they are, they're muscular cats, and it's always a surprise to pick one up and discover how heavy it is. Males like Leo weigh about ten pounds, and every ounce is strong.

I didn't speak to him, just waited for him to deign to speak to me. Cats like for you to acknowledge their superiority right away. Dogs are so happy to have new acquaintances they'll throw away every shred of dignity and approach you first. I'm afraid I'm more like a dog.

Laura said, "I know it's early for dinner, but I'm starving. How about you?"

"Whenever there's food, I'm hungry."

Putting her wineglass down, she opened the refrigerator, dived into the vegetable bin, and began tossing out plastic bags of mystery things, hurling them more or less accurately into the sink.

She said, "I hope you're not on one of those low-carb diets. I was thinking about fettucini Alfredo."

I said, "I love Alfredo and everything he stands for."

She grinned. "I knew you were a smart girl first time I met you."

She got out a wooden salad bowl, and I moved to the sink and began washing romaine while she put water on to boil and chopped garlic. It was nice, very nice, to have that kind of rapport with another person.

By the time we had dinner ready, we had each stepped on Leo's long tail several times and done quick dances of remorse and annoyance, which Leo ignored.

We had also crossed over the divide that separates friendly acquaintances from friends. Laura had told me who her hairdresser was—Maurice at the Lyon's Mane—and I had given her the name of a holistic veterinarian, my gynecologist, and my dentist.

Women need other women as friends. To giggle at dumb things one minute and go deep into our most secret selves the next. Laura and I had that kind of connection, the kind that allows you to explore any idea without worrying that you'll be judged.

We carried our dinner to the living room, a surprisingly impersonal room with oversized white ceramic tile on the floors and louvered shades covering the windows. The furniture was the sell-by-the-roomful type that landlords put in seasonal rentals. No rugs to break the white monotony of the tile. No family heirlooms. No lovingly collected flea-market finds. No photographs, no magazines, no collectibles. The only personal touch was an African violet in a white porcelain pot under a window. I knew that barren look. It was a lot like my own place.

We ate sitting on the floor around the coffee table. Leo lay between us, blissfully resting his head on Laura's bare foot, his long tail stretched out for somebody to trip over.

I confessed that my favorite singer of all time was Patsy Cline, and Laura said hers was Roy Orbison, which we both thought was an amazing coincidence because anybody who's ever given it any thought knows that Patsy and Roy must have come from the same soul. We also agreed that k.d. lang is most likely Patsy Cline reincarnated, and neither of us was embarrassed to say it.

Something thumped outside the window, and Leo jerked upright with his ears pointed toward the sound. Laura went still, with her fork poised in midair.

I said, "It was just a squirrel or something."

She shook her head as if she were mentally lecturing herself.

"I never know whether Leo's heard a serial killer or whether he just gets a kick out of scaring me." Leo lay back down with his tail draped across her lap. She pushed it aside and said, "You know, moving here has brought me the first sense of peace I've ever had."

There was a curious blend of innocence and world-weary wisdom in the way she said it.

I said, "I've never lived anyplace else."

She grinned. "I know. You put on a tough front, but deep down you're just a sweet southern girl who's never seen the ugly side of life."

I bristled. "I am not sweet, and I've seen plenty of ugly."

She laughed. "Sweetie, what you've seen is chicken feed."

The landline phone in the kitchen rang, and an impersonal robotic voice announced, "Call from Number Available."

Laura went still, her jade eyes wary. After a few more announcements, the answering machine switched on. An unctuous male voice spoke loudly enough for us to hear every word.

"Please pick up, Laura. I know you're home. Please don't reject me this way."

Laura scrambled to her feet to race to the phone, but she got there too late to keep me from hearing him. "I'm outside your house. Please open the door to me, Laura. That's all I ask."

Laura snagged the phone from its cradle, her own voice sharp. "You have to stop this! I swear to God, if you don't leave me alone I'll have you arrested for stalking me."

Leo had sat up again with his ears pointed forward. He and I sat frozen in place.

Laura listened a moment and said, "No! I have company now. Please, please, please go away, and don't call me again."

Another pause and then her voice became almost amused. "You misunderstood. I appreciated your help, but that's all. Now leave me alone."

I heard the phone slam into its holder, and she stomped back to the living room with her lips tightened. "So help me, if that man calls again I'm going to report him to the police."

She sat down on the floor again. Beside her, Leo remained at attention.

"Who is he?"

She sighed. "Right after I moved here I twisted my knee running. It swelled pretty bad, so I went to the emergency room to see if it was something serious. This jerk was there, and he must have got my number from the woman at the desk. He calls every day begging to see me. He's a nut."

I'm not exactly an eyesore, but I'll never cause people to go all goggly the minute they see me. I wondered what it was like for Laura to know she had that effect.

Rapping sounded at the front door, and we all swiveled our heads. Through the glass panels we could see the shadowy outline of a large man.

Laura made a fist and shook it toward the door. "Go away!"

The knocking continued, but Laura didn't go to the door.

Outside, the man shouted, "This is quite unacceptable, Laura! Unacceptable and unfair!"

After a while, the figure disappeared. Leo stretched himself beside Laura's feet, and Laura's body relaxed.

Even moderately beautiful women attract men whose fantasies can cause them to go to nutty extremes. A woman as jaw-droppingly gorgeous as Laura probably attracted them by the dozen.

I said, "Has he come here before like that? Demanding to see you?"

"No, he's never gone that far before."

I was tempted to warn her that her front door would be a snap for anybody wanting to break in, but I didn't want to add to her fears. Besides, any door can be opened by somebody really determined.

I said, "If he does it again, you really should call the police."

"I know. It's just that I'd thought I'd left all that behind. Being afraid, threatening to call the police. I hate it."

She leaned to pour the last of the wine in our glasses.

"I was in an abusive relationship," she said. "Very abusive. I'm not over it yet."

"Ah, so that's what it was."

"You knew?"

"I knew you were recovering from something. I recognized the signs."

"Like what?"

I gestured around the impersonal room. "This place, for one thing. I know it's not your home. Are you hiding from your ex?"

She looked alarmed. "You're very perceptive. He's not exactly my ex yet, I've just filed for divorce. He's a very powerful orthopedic surgeon in Dallas. You may have heard of him. He's Dr. Reginald Halston. *The* Dr. Reginald Halston. Before he went to medical school, he was a linebacker for the SMU Mustangs. He's big. Really big."

I could have sworn I'd heard her call him Martin, and I wasn't sure if she meant he was big in size or just big in fame, but I didn't press the point. Plenty of people are known professionally by one name but their families and close friends call them something else. Laura's eyes had widened with awe when she said the name, so he must have been a big deal in Dallas. I said I'd never heard of him, and she looked faintly disappointed.

In a rush, she said, "I was his receptionist for a year before he asked me out. He'd been married twice before, and he has children. He never sees them, but I always knew they were there, waiting in the wings for me to fall on my face. His first wives were college-educated and from rich families. Not like me. I guess I fell in love, but I'm not sure. I have to admit I liked the idea of marrying a rich doctor. And to his credit, I have to say he was never cheap. I could buy anything I wanted, and I did."

She drained her wineglass and ran the tip of her tongue around her lips to get the last drop.

I said, "I'm guessing there was another side to him, right?"

"At night, he would lie in bed and throw scalpels at the ceiling. They never stuck, just fell back down, and he would laugh at me for being afraid one would hit me. He carved my stomach with his scalpels too. He almost killed me several times. One time he choked me until I blacked out and my eyes were red for days from broken blood vessels, but he wouldn't let me go to the hospital. He's so big and strong, I was terrified of him."

She was watching my face closely, and I got the feeling she had never told anybody else about her husband's violence. I was flattered she trusted me enough to confide in me.

"Jesus, Laura, he sounds sick."

"He's insane. If the hospital knew what he's really like, they would kick him out. My folks don't know either. They were so thrilled I had married a rich doctor that I never told them. I told my sister everything, but Celeste is the only one who knows."

I said, "It must have taken a lot of courage to leave."

She laughed shortly. "I left when I found out I was pregnant. I will not let him turn his sick mind on my child. I'm four months now, and nobody knows except my sister."

I looked at her drawstring pants. "You don't show yet."

"I've put on a little weight, but I was too thin before."

"He doesn't know where you are?"

She looked smug. "When I left Dallas, I cleaned out our joint checking account. Then I drove my Mercedes to Arkansas and sold it at a used-car place. I took a bus to Sarasota and bought the Jaguar. I have enough money to live on for a while, and I have some good diamond jewelry. When I need to, I'll pawn it or sell it."

Her face flushed, either with embarrassment at having revealed so much about herself, or because she'd called attention to the jewelry.

"He told me if I ever left him he would kill me."

I said, "He knows how to reach you—"

"He only knows my cell number, and it's still based in Dallas. He doesn't know where I am. But I'm always afraid. . . ."

She didn't need to finish the sentence, I knew what she was afraid of. I also knew that nobody can truly disappear if somebody wants them found. Especially if the somebody has plenty of money to hire good private investigators.

"Is anything in your name here? A lease? The house phone? Utilities?"

She shook her head. "I've thought of all that. The house belongs to my folks. They live in Connecticut and all the bills go to them. They intend to move here when Dad retires, and in the meantime it's a retreat for who-ever needs it. Celeste, that's my sister, lived here for a year when she got a divorce, and one of my cousins stayed here for a while when he was out of work."

"Your sister's in Connecticut too?"

She shot me a look that said I was dangerously close to asking too many personal questions.

"Dallas."

Leo yawned with a big show of boredom, and I leaned to stroke his neck. There were some holes in Laura's story, but people gloss over details in the interest of con-densing an account to its main facts. For now, the fact that she had told me something so painful meant we had crossed an important hurdle in our beginning friendship.

She said, "You said you recognized the signs that I was hiding from somebody. Does that mean you were—"

"No. I was never abused."

A silence stretched, and I opened my mouth and told the thing so hard to say.

"Almost four years ago, my husband and little girl were on their way home, and they stopped to pick up some groceries. My husband was a deputy, and he had picked Christy up at daycare when he got off duty. She was three years old. A man driving across the parking lot turned into a parking place, but instead of hitting the brake he slammed his foot on the gas pedal. He jumped over the wheel stop and hit Todd and Christy and three other people before he crashed into a parked car. They told me Todd and Christy died instantly."

Laura whispered, "I'm so sorry."

That's all. She didn't try to make me feel better about it, didn't tell me to cheer up because they were with Jesus now, didn't tell me she was sure I'd get over it in time. She just absorbed a little bit of my pain. I don't think there's anything more generous one human being can do for another.

I suddenly wanted to tell her more about myself, to be as open as she had been and share the kind of things that women share. I wanted to tell her that I was a lot better now, that I had actually begun to live again. I wanted to tell her that I had kissed two men a few months ago, and that while I had pulled back from both of them, I hadn't closed any doors. I wanted to tell her I was going on a date with Guidry Saturday night. I wanted to tell her all the kinds of things women tell each other when they're close friends. But it was late, and there would be time for those confidences later.

When I told her goodbye that night, I knew I was leaving a new friend.

She said, "I'll see you soon."

But as it turned out, she wouldn't.

CHAPTER 6

Back in the Bronco, I considered my options. I could go straight home, or I could go shopping for something to wear to Guidry's Saturday-night shindig. One good thing about living in a resort town is that a lot of posh shops are open late, even on Sunday. If I got the dreaded dress-buying over with, I could forget it. Or at least not have to think about it anymore. I decided there was no time like the present and headed downtown. For most of my shopping, I think the Gap or Sears, but for the Humane Society party I went to a little boutique on Pineapple Street where the price of a dress would feed a family of five for several weeks.

An hour later, I was on my way home, with a big shiny white bag in the passenger's seat and a dress bag hanging from the do-hickey over the back door. The bag held new underwear, new shoes, and a dumb little purse the saleswoman had described as "just big enough to hold a woman's essentials—door key, lipstick, passport, and a condom." She obviously was accustomed to women who had more interesting lives than mine.

The dress bag held a short black strapless job I had to have the minute I saw it. But when I'd tried it on, it had given me a peculiar feeling—the same feeling I remembered having when I was thirteen and in a store dressing room trying on bathing suits. I had looked at myself in the mirror and realized I had become a woman. It had been exciting and scary. Totally appropriate for a thirteen-year-old, but totally idiotic for a thirty-three-year-old.

At home, the light was on in Michael and Paco's kitchen, so I made a quick stop to say good night and show off my purchases. They were sitting at the island eating key lime pie, and Ella was on her stool adoring them. It was the last night of Michael's vacation. He would leave the next morning for a twenty-four-hour shift at the firehouse, then he would be home forty-eight hours—a rhythm that has been a constant refrain all our lives, beginning with our firefighter father. Paco's schedule wasn't so regular. Undercover cops don't keep normal hours, and Michael and I have adjusted to that.

Michael said, "Where've you been? Want some pie?"

I flourished my shiny bag. "I had to go shopping. Got a new dress. I have a date Saturday night."

Both men gave me looks of astonished pleasure. For the past year, they'd been upping the pressure on me to find a man, have sex, get a life. They had loved Todd like a brother, but they both thought I had dragged widowhood way past its expiration date.

Michael said, "With who?"

"Whom."

Ella Fitzgerald put a paw on the island top, and Paco gave her a stern look. "You know the rules."

She made a meek *thripp* sound, withdrew her paw, and gave a demure twitch to her tail. Paco and Ella have an agreement—if she sits politely and keeps her paws off the table, she's allowed to adore her men from a bar stool. I know some human females who operate under the same rule.

For a moment, I thought Ella might have made Michael forget his question, but he was still waiting. I said, "Guidry asked me to a big party next weekend."

Paco said, "Hot damn."

Michael's mouth drew up like he'd just bit into a green mango. "Guidry."

Paco said, "Michael," in a warning kind of way, like *Shut the heck up, your sister has a date, for God's sake, so don't quibble about who the guy is.*

Michael nodded, shrugged, and stuck a fork in his pie with a little more force than was absolutely necessary. Paco and I exchanged rolled eyes. Paco is protective too, but he's not as extreme as Michael. I guess that's because he hasn't been protecting me since he was four and I was two, the way Michael has.

I pulled the dress out of the bag and held it in front of me. Ella sat up straighter and squinted her eyes, while Michael and Paco made the noises men make when a woman says, "What do you think?"

Fathers probably teach those noises to their sons when they're young—"Stand up when you're introduced to a lady, use your napkin instead of your sleeve, and make admiring noises when a woman shows you anything, no matter what it is, and asks you what you think about it. Never, never, never say you have no opinion."

Paco said, "High damn time you bought something sexy."

"I got shoes and underwear too. The works."

Paco grinned. "I do believe you're about to take old Guidry to bed. You remember how the girl thing goes?"

Unlike Michael, Paco thought Guidry was a fine candidate for ending my self-imposed celibacy.

"I'm just going to a party with him." My face got hot when I said it, because to tell the truth I wasn't at all sure I remembered how the girl thing went.

Michael got to his feet and noisily rinsed his plate. "There's leftovers if you're hungry."

"No, thanks, I had dinner with a new friend."

His eyebrows raised hopefully. "A guy?"

"No, a woman." Next thing I knew, I was telling them all about it, like a little kid reporting her cool new friend.

"She lives next door to the little boy I told you about last week, the one who's having surgery for seizures. He's three years old. Surgery is tomorrow morning. The woman is Laura Halston. She has a Havana Brown cat named Leo. Longest tail you ever saw, and he's always leaving it across doorways so it gets stepped on."

Michael said, "What'd you say the cat is?"

"Havana Brown. They're sort of rare. Brown all over, even their whiskers. I think they're called Havana Brown because they're the color of the cigars. She said the boyfriend who gave him to her had called him Cohiba, but she changed his name to Leo."

"She should have named him Castro."

I rolled my eyes, partly to disparage Michael's humor, and partly because he'd missed the point. The point wasn't Laura's cat, it was that I had a new woman friend.

I said, "She's here hiding from her husband until their divorce is final. He was abusive, and she's left him because she's pregnant. She said she didn't want him inflicting his cruelty on their child. He's a well-known surgeon in Dallas."

Paco's eyes narrowed. "Hiding how?"

"Oh, just that she's living in a house her parents own so nothing is in her name."

"No car?"

"Yeah, a car, but she bought it with cash she got from selling her old car. She cleaned out their bank account and drove to Arkansas and sold her car, then took a bus to Sarasota and bought a new one."

"What kind of car did she buy?"

It struck me that Paco was being awfully nosy. He also had a look in his eyes that I recognized. It was his I-don't-believe-a-word-of-this look.

I said, "She drives a Jaguar convertible. Red."

"Uh-huh, perfect car for somebody trying to hide."

"Oh, come on, Paco, if her husband finds her, it won't be because she drives a Jaguar convertible."

He shrugged. "I don't think a Dallas surgeon's wife would come to Sarasota to get a divorce, she'd get it in Texas. That's all I'm saying."

I could feel my face flushing with defensive anger. Being an undercover cop made Paco suspicious of every little thing that wasn't consistent. Usually he was right, but this time he was wrong. I had misjudged Laura at first too, but now I knew she was an honest, good person going through a bad stretch.

Ella chose that moment to hike her hind leg and gnaw on it, as if to let us know that she found it rude of us to discuss anything other than her majestic self. We all laughed, and my irritation evaporated.

I said, "I'm taking my loot and going home to bed."

I kissed two cheeks and one furry head and left them. As I climbed the stairs to my apartment, I looked up at a coconut palm silhouetted in the curve of a waning moon rind. The palm's fronds had fallen away and left a rim of boots around its bulbous head. Caught in the moon's thin arc, the trunk had a priapic look. Or maybe it was just me. When you haven't had sex in almost four years, you tend to see phalluses in unlikely places.

As I fell asleep that night, my thoughts went to All

Children's Hospital in St. Petersburg and to a little boy whose skull would be opened the next morning in hopes of giving him a better life. I knew the anguished fear his parents must be feeling. No matter how skilled the surgeons were, nothing is certain. The operation could fail, or something could go wrong. And because my own child had died, I couldn't keep from thinking the unthinkable—Jeffrey could die. I also knew that if anything went wrong, Hal and Gillis would never forgive themselves for choosing the surgical option. They would question their decision for the rest of their lives, just as I would always wonder if Christy would have died if I had not been working that day.

I muttered, "No!" and punched my pillow. Thoughts like those could only lead to useless pain, and I refused to linger in that hurtful place.

Deliberately, I imagined Jeffrey and his parents coming home. I imagined him running to greet Mazie, with Hal and Gillis standing behind him beaming with joy that he was now free of seizures. With images of Jeffrey playing with Mazie rolling inside my head, I drifted to sleep and dreamed that Christy and I were walking on the beach. She was just a toddler, and her little pink shoes made three-inch footprints on the white sand. I shuffled along behind her, close enough to put out a steadying hand when she needed it, but far enough away to let her feel the thrill of toddler independence.

She looked over her shoulder at me and laughed with sheer joy. The laughter turned into the sound of rain against the window, and I opened my eyes and fought the momentary confusion that dreams bring. It was the first time I'd dreamed of Christy in several weeks. For a long time after she died, she had filled my dreams every night. Now, when weeks sometimes passed without her nocturnal visits, a dream always brought a disquieting sense of having abandoned her.

I went back to sleep until the alarm sounded, and I got up with a foreboding sense of dread.

CHAPTER 7

The sky was still pearly white when I walked out on my balcony next morning, and a gentle sea murmured drowsily to the shore. As I went down the stairs to the carport, I caught a faint vanilla scent, a whiff of fragrance from a night-blooming cereus twined around the oak tree beside Michael's deck. Creamy white and big as dinner plates, cereus blossoms last only one night, but they are magnificent. By June, they are so profuse and fragrant that being outside at night is like bathing in perfume. Since it was only early April, first blooms were there as friendly promises.

In the carport, all our cars and Paco's Harley were damp with morning dew. Michael's shift at the firehouse would begin at eight that morning, and then for the next twenty-four hours his car would be gone. I always instinctively look to see whose car is home and whose is gone, and I always breathe a little easier when both Michael's and Paco's cars are there. I hate to admit that, but it's true.

I took a deep final hit of salt air and cereus, shooed a trio of sleepy pelicans off the hood of my Bronco, and crept down the twisting lane toward Midnight Pass Road. I went slowly so as not to disturb the parakeets roosting in the mossy oaks along the lane. Parakeets are such prima donnas, they make a big to-do if you wake them up.

At the Sea Breeze, where Tom Hale lives, the parking lot was quiet, with the only movement from a few early risers and their dogs. The elevator was coming down when I entered the downstairs lobby, and when the door opened Tom's girlfriend came out, walking fast and frowning like the Wicked Witch of the West. She had a thick square bandage on her chin, and when I spoke to her, she gave me an icy glare. I swear, the more I saw of that woman, the less I liked her. I supposed she must have some invisible stellar qualities or Tom wouldn't be involved with her, but I had never seen them. More than likely, they only came out in bed.

Upstairs, I used my key to open Tom's door and found him sitting in the living room with his arm around Billy Elliot's neck. They weren't watching early morning news, they were just sitting.

I said, "I just met Frannie leaving the building."

Tom nodded and tightened his lips.

I got Billy Elliot's leash and snapped it on his collar. If Tom didn't want to talk, I wouldn't press him.

Tom raised his arms like an orchestra conductor who'd been waiting for his cue. "Okay, here's what happened. She had a small skin cancer removed from her chin. Nothing serious, not a melanoma, she's going to be fine. But she's self-conscious like you wouldn't believe about it. We went out to dinner last night, and when we came home she told me she'd noticed people staring at her. I'd noticed it too. You know how people look at anything unusual, and they were looking at her bandage. I said it wasn't surprising that people stared at her because she's a beautiful woman. She said no, they were staring at her because she was with me. Said she could tell they felt sorry for her."

He spun his chair around to face me. "She brought it up again this morning, and I told her the truth. Nobody was looking at her because she was with a man in a wheelchair, they were looking at her because she had a big honking bandage on her chin. And they weren't pitying her, they were just rude and curious. She got pissed and stormed out."

I wanted to tell him Frannie was all wrong for him and Billy Elliot, but I knew better. Tell a friend who's having a lover's quarrel that you hate his girlfriend's guts, and the next thing you know they'll be back together again and he'll never forget what you said.

As mild as milk, I said, "You might want to consider what kind of woman would think people pitied her for being with you. Not to mention what kind of self-consumed bitch would *tell* you that."

He gave me a half grin. "Come on, Dixie, don't be shy. Tell me what you really think."

"Sorry, gotta go. Billy Elliot and I have an appointment with some bushes downstairs."

I took Billy Elliot out to the hall. Before I closed Tom's door, I saw a full grin on his face.

Billy Elliot and I ran our laps in the parking lot until he was happy and I was wheezing, then we rode the elevator back upstairs to Tom's condo. I could smell coffee brewing and hear the shower running. I kissed Billy Elliot goodbye, hung his leash back in the closet, and let myself out. On the ride downstairs in the elevator, I counted the women I knew who were both single, attractive, heterosexual, smart, the right age, and good enough for Tom and Billy Elliot. It was a short list, but if Tom ever dumped Frannie's self-centered ass, I would be matchmaking before sundown.

By the time I'd walked all the dogs on my list and fed and groomed all the cats, it was almost nine o'clock and I was on my way to Fish Hawk Lagoon to walk Mazie. Just after the light at Stickney Point, I saw a dark form the size of a toddler's fist moving across the pavement ahead of me. Only one thing in the world has that shape and moves with that sprawling bent-leg gait. A baby turtle had decided to see the world.

I veered onto the shoulder and had my door open before I came to a jolting stop. Behind me, a green-and-white sheriff's car stopped in the spot where I'd just been. The driver's door opened, and a deputy in dark green shorts and shirt jumped out and started flagging down traffic. He must have come up behind me while I was pulling onto the shoulder, spotted the turtle, and realized my intention.

I recognized that deputy. He was Deputy Jesse Morgan, an officer I'd met several times before in less pleasant circumstances. I was fairly sure that Morgan thought I was a nutcase. Considering his reasons, I couldn't actually blame him.

Flashing him a grateful grin, I sprinted across the pavement and picked up a three-inch Florida box turtle. As I ran back to my car, Deputy Morgan got back in his car and waited for me to pull back on the road. He didn't smile and his eyes were shielded by dark glasses, but I had the distinct impression that he was pleased. I felt as if he and I had made a new turn in our acquaintanceship.

The turtle's oval shape marked it as female. When I put her down on the passenger floor, she immediately resumed her plan of moving from Point A to Point B, totally ignoring the interval when a force much larger than herself had swooped down and grabbed her.

I've felt that way myself a few times.

Except for the threat of being eaten by birds and killed by humans, nature has been especially kind to female box turtles. If a female meets a male she fancies as a father for her children, she can have a night of mattress-slapping, heel-banging, headboard-butting sex and then store his sperm for six or seven years. She can go to graduate school, start a business, get tenure at a university, make partner at a law firm, all the while secure that she has plenty of desirable sperm ready and waiting. Then, when her maternal urges kick in, she can dig a hole and use the stored sperm to fertilize her eggs. Maybe she has completely forgotten the male who donated his sperm. Or maybe she remembers and a tear rolls down her leathery cheek while she inseminates herself. At any rate, she can repeat the whole sex-and-storage thing as many times as she chooses for the rest of her life. Box turtles may live to be a hundred, so that's a lot of sex with freedom to choose when to be pregnant. How cool is that?

Fish Hawk Lagoon is actually a man-made lake in the shape of an artist's palette. The lake has narrow inlets that allow small pleasure boats access to the bay, and it's a favorite nesting place for ospreys, which are also called fish hawks. The residential area curves around it, and there are picnicking spots interspersed with nature preserves around its perimeter.

I followed the hibiscus hedge beside the jogging trail until it ended at a boggy lakeside area shaded by moss-hung oaks. Thick with ferns, potato vines, lilies, and taro, and bounded on two sides by palmetto and hibiscus, it was as good a sanctuary as a little turtle could hope for. Pulling behind the hedge into a shelled parking area beside the trail, I picked the turtle off the floor and took a minute to study the perfect symmetry of her carapace markings. They conjured a faint echo of drumbeats, a flash of an initiate dipping her finger into pale yellow dye to trace a clue on a dark turtle shell, sounds of female voices raised in triumphant ululation. If creatures that link us to our distant past become extinct, will we lose the unconscious memory of our origins?

With the little turtle's legs valiantly churning the air, I walked toward the bog, then stopped a moment to look at a nesting pair of sandhill cranes on a minuscule sandbar about ten feet offshore. Four or five feet tall, sandhill cranes are magnificent stalk-legged birds with brilliant patches of red on the tops of their heads. Males and females work together to build nests of twigs and weeds, then the male stands guard while the female sits on their eggs, usually just two. He stays close by until the chicks are able to fly by themselves too, not like some human males who leave their mates to raise their babies alone. This couple must have lost one of their eggs, because only one fluffy caramel-colored chick was poking its head from its mom's shoulder feathers.

When I squatted on the loamy ground, the male crane stretched his snaky gray neck, made a high-pitched gurgling cry, and flapped his huge wings a couple of times. With his five-foot wingspan, he looked like Rodan, the old horror-film monster, ready to shock and awe Tokyo. I hoped he had shocked and awed the baby turtle so she would hide from him, because he could easily gulp her down for breakfast.

When I set her down, she zipped out of sight under a clump of taro leaves. She probably thought she had cleverly escaped a giant predator, but it wasn't the sandhill crane she feared, it was me. Like all of us, she would have to learn that some things that seem horrifying are really benign.

From the other side of the hibiscus hedge separating the street from the trail, a man's outraged voice rose above the hum of insects and birdsong.

"How could you do that to me? How? Even for you, it's especially despicable. You've outdone yourself this time. Of all the stupid, selfish, unforgivable things you've ever done, this is the worst!"

Peering through the hibiscus, I saw two people approaching, a woman in jogging shorts, and a barrel-chested bull of a man in a dark suit. Fury surrounded the man in a kind of subliminal red mist. Not that I'm able to see auras. But if I were, I'm positive that's what his would have been—hot, pulsating energy the color of blood. He walked with the heavy-shouldered tread of a man with a thorn in his soul.

He said, "This time you went too far. You won't get away with this one."

They moved forward until I could see their faces. The man had the glossy patina of raw power, the kind that always sits at the head of the table no matter what the meeting is. He looked to be in his mid-fifties, with dark slicked-back hair, deep pouches under heavy-lidded eyes, and a mouth that was accustomed to giving orders. His body was thick and broad-shouldered, but every inch seemed to be muscle. The woman was Laura Halston. She looked bored.

She said, "You can't do a thing to me, Martin. Not now, not ever."

I looked harder at the man, imagining him carving Laura's stomach with one of his scalpels. Now that I knew who he was, I could imagine him as a young linebacker. I could also imagine him stalking like a king through hospital halls while nurses fluttered in his wake.

It was one of those moments when no matter what you do, it'll be wrong. I could have stood up and made my presence known, but then Laura would have been embarrassed to know I had heard an intensely personal conversation. I could have put my hands over my ears or scuttled out of earshot, but it was too late. I'd already heard enough.

I watched Laura step into the street and start walking away from her husband.

In a voice choked with rage, he said, "Don't you dare walk away from me! You owe me, goddammit! You owe me!"

Without turning, she stretched her arm overhead and shot him a finger.

He stared at her back a moment longer and then charged to a car parked down the street. Spraying shell, he roared away.

I waited until Laura had disappeared around a curve in the other direction before I stood up and walked to the Bronco. Then I drove sedately and carefully toward Mazie's house. I might be a voyeur, but I don't speed.

I didn't need a playbill to know that Laura's husband had found her, and he hadn't sounded to me as if he intended to let her go without a nasty fight. Laura had said she was afraid of him. Now that I'd seen him and had a sample of what he was like, I wasn't sure she was frightened enough. With his raw rage, he seemed inherently capable of violence—violence that went far beyond the sick practice of throwing scalpels at the ceiling to frighten his wife.

CHAPTER 8

An ancient story tells about a prince who died and went
to heaven. As he always had, his dog followed him. At
heaven's gate, the gatekeeper said, "You can't bring a
dog in here, he'll have to stay outside."

The man said, "This dog has been the most loyal
friend I've ever had. He's stayed with me through my
every loss and humiliation, and he's celebrated with me
my every success. I cannot enter heaven and leave my
best friend outside. If he can't go in, I won't go in either."

At that, the dog was revealed as a god in disguise,
and they went in together. According to the story, that's
why dogs are called *dogs*, because they're really gods
in disguise.

I thought about that story when I got to Mazie's house.
Pete was in the kitchen crouched beside Mazie, who lay
by Jeffrey's chair with its empty booster seat. Pete's
shaggy eyebrows were so low I could barely see his eyes.

He said, "She didn't eat last night, and she didn't eat
this morning. She's too sad."

I wasn't surprised. Dogs don't have superficial love
or shallow devotion. They don't ever wonder if it would
better serve their own interests to switch their loyalties

to somebody else. Once they give their hearts to one person, that's where their commitment lies, and they grieve the loss of a loved one the same way humans do. For a service dog like Mazie, her sense of loss was even more acute.

I knelt to stroke Mazie's head. "Did Hal call?"

"Not yet. It's too soon."

I went to the cupboard and shook some kibble into my hand, then went back to sit on the floor beside Mazie.

I said, "Jeffrey will be back, Mazie. And you have to keep your strength up so you can take care of him when he comes home."

As I said it, I sent a mental photo of Jeffrey giggling and hugging Mazie, while Mazie's tail beat with wild happiness. Some people think I'm nuts to send pictures to animals, but the animals seem to get them, so I keep doing it.

She lifted her head, sniffed the kibble, and ate one or two nuggets.

Pete said, "She needs to eat more than that."

"If she's drinking water, she can fast for a day or two with no problem. Remember, don't try to tempt her with people food. When she's ready, she'll start eating again."

Pete reddened, as if he might have already offered her a bite of his own breakfast.

Trying to act as if I were as confident as I sounded, I got Mazie's leash and took her for a walk. She came along docilely, but her heart wasn't in it and she kept looking back toward her house. I didn't keep her out long. As soon as she had done her doggie business, we ran home at a fast clip.

I looked toward Laura's house, but all I could see

were trees and the driveway. It was just as well. I was still embarrassed to have eavesdropped, and I needed some time before I saw Laura again.

Back at Mazie's house, I handed her off to Pete, told him I'd be back around three P.M., and scooted to the Bronco with visions of breakfast dancing in my head.

On the way to the diner, I stopped at a traffic light and noticed a hand-lettered cardboard sign taped to a light pole: LOST CHIHUAHUA PUP! REWARD! CALL LYON'S MANE. There was no phone number or address, which I took to mean that whoever printed the sign assumed that everybody knew where and what the Lyon's Mane was. Which they probably did. The Lyon's Mane was the salon Laura had mentioned, a pricey place for people accustomed to big-city stylists and big-city fees. Needless to say, I'd never been there.

A car honked behind me and made me aware the light had changed, so I moved on with the herd. Somebody had been busy putting up that LOST CHIHUAHUA PUP sign, because it was at every intersection. A block away from the Village Diner, I spotted the little guy cowering under an oleander bush. I pulled off the street and got out of the Bronco, moving as slowly as I could so as not to frighten him. Even adult Chihuahuas make me feel like a big ogre, they're so small and dainty. A Chihuahua pup is like a fairy dog, all big eyes and dancy legs.

I knelt down and spoke softly while my hand crept forward, palm up. "Don't be scared, it's okay. I'm going to take you home."

I slipped my hand under the pup's chest and lifted his front paws off the ground, then did a one-hand lift to cuddle him against my own chest.

I said, "How in the world did a little bitty thing like

you get so far away from home? Did a hawk pick you up and carry you? Catch a ride on a turtle?"

He didn't answer, just burrowed into my bosom as if he liked the warmth.

I thought he'd been through too much trauma to add a ride in a stranger's car, so I walked through some parking lots and side streets to the Lyon's Mane. At the salon, I pulled open the glass door and stepped into the odor of shampoo, styling products, and singed hair. A young woman with lizard-green eye shadow and hair in white Statue of Liberty spires stood behind a tall reception desk talking on a phone. Before I got to her, a ponytailed marionette of a man came clattering around the desk on backless clogs. His arms were raised from the elbows and his hands were flapping excitedly.

"Oh, my God, you've found Baby!"

He grabbed toward me, and I hastily put the puppy into his grasping hands. The puppy licked the man's lips while he cooed and kissed its nose.

I said, "He was under an oleander bush. They're poisonous, so I hope he didn't try to eat any of the leaves."

"Baby? Eat a leaf off a bush? Hell, Baby won't even eat dog food! My wife feeds him off her plate."

I smiled and nodded, polite as anything, and edged toward the door. I'd done my good deed for the day, and breakfast was close by.

The man said, "Hold on! There's a reward for bringing Baby home."

I waved him off like Lady Bountiful telling the peasants they didn't owe her anything. "That's okay. Glad to do it."

He stopped patting Baby and stared at my head. "No offense, hon, but who's been cutting your hair? The yard man?"

Actually, I'd cut it myself, and I thought I'd done a

pretty good job. My hair is straight and just hangs there, so cutting it isn't like rocket science. Nevertheless, my hand went anxiously to my head. Suggest to a woman that her hair is bad, and her hand is compelled to feel it.

"You think it's uneven?"

"Doll, if it was any choppier, people would get seasick just from looking at it. Sit down and I'll even it up for you. A reward for rescuing Baby."

I gave a fleeting thought to breakfast, and dropped into his chair. No woman in her right mind would turn down an opportunity to get her hair trimmed by a master stylist.

I said, "Maybe just a teeny bit off."

He flapped a hand from a loose wrist. "Sweetie, you just leave it to me. You're gonna love it. By the way, my name's Maurice."

He pronounced it Maur-*eeese*.

I said, "I've heard of you. My friend Laura Halston is one of your clients."

As soon as I said it, I was afraid I'd mentioned Laura's name to elevate myself from a strange woman in cheap shoes to a person who was in the same league with his clientele.

He said, "Oh, Laura! Isn't she gorgeous? And just as down-to-earth as she can be."

He scooted away to settle the pup in its own monogrammed basket, and I looked at the hair stuff laid out on his workstation. I didn't know what half of it was. A shallow shelf under the work top held a couple of glossy glamour magazines, and I pulled one out and looked at the photograph on the cover. It was the generic photo that every glamour magazine has—airbrushed close-up of a young woman with carefully applied eyeliner and fake eyelashes that somebody spent an hour or two lacquering and separating so they look like heavy fringe, chemically colored hair with extensions teased and gelled and sprayed to mimic the way healthy hair would look if nothing had ever been done to it, and a pouting, seductive mouth plump with collagen shots. We are all supposed to believe that if we only purchase the products advertised in those magazines, we too can look like the cover model, but not even the cover models look like that.

Maurice came back and grabbed a pair of scissors. "Put the magazine down, because I'm going to turn you around so you're facing me instead of the mirror. You just relax."

I immediately tensed up, because my experience is that when somebody says, "You just relax," you're in for a harrowing time.

Maurice spun me around and began to cut and snip like a wild man, sending pieces of hair flying all over the place. I was so disappointed I could have cried. Sarasota women have two hairstyles: Barbie-doll long and high-lighted white blond, or short and chopped off at the nape of the neck. The Barbie-doll do has bangs that hang over the eyebrows, the chopped-off do is frothed up on the crown like meringue. There is no in between.

I stand up for myself against alligators, religious fanatics, and gun-toting madmen, but I am a hopeless coward with hairdressers. I not only thank them for bad haircuts, I pay them and tip them. Then I go home and recut my hair. It's disgusting to be a hairdresser wimp, but I am. And every time, while I'm in the chair being ruined, I rationalize my cowardice by telling myself that my hair will grow out, that a bad haircut won't last forever.

Maurice knelt in front of me to get a better angle with his scissors. He had kind eyes.

He said, "I worry about her."

"Who?"

"Laura. With that awful husband of hers, I think she should hire a bodyguard. But she's so brave, she just acts like there's no danger. And then there's that other man after her. I feel bad that she met him here, but it's out of my hands, you know? She's an adult and she can see anybody she wants to."

Maurice apparently didn't share my disinclination to gossip about his clients, and I felt a bit let down. Laura had apparently told Maurice everything she'd told me, plus he knew about a man she hadn't even mentioned. So I wasn't so special after all. I wondered how many other people knew her story.

He stood up and whirled me around so I could see myself, and I made an involuntary gasp of surprise.

I felt like Julie Christie in the old movie *Shampoo*. My hair wasn't any shorter, and I didn't know exactly what was different, but now it looked as if it needed a man's fingers running through it.

Maurice smiled. "Now that's kick-ass hair!"

The front door flew open and a woman built like a manatee came charging in. She had large dark eyes with lots of dramatic makeup, shiny black hair cut close to her head like a skullcap, and she wore lavender Lycra tights under a bright orange smock. She should have looked ridiculous, but she looked oddly exotic.

In a deep baritone, she bawled, "Baby!" and snatched the Chihuahua pup from its basket.

Misty-eyed, Maurice said, "That's my wife."

I didn't know whether he was on the verge of crying because my hair was so gorgeous or because his wife was so . . . so *much*.

To his wife, Maurice said, "Ruby, sweetie, this is . . . who are you, hon?"

Weakly, I said, "I'm Dixie Hemingway."

As if he'd invented me, Maurice said, "She's the one found Baby and brought him back to us."

With Baby held tight against her jutting bosom, Ruby stuck out a hand twice as big as Maurice's and gave me a firm handshake.

"You're a pet sitter, aren't you? I read about you in the paper. Great haircut."

I allowed as how I was a pet sitter and that I also thought it was a great haircut, but I didn't respond to the comment about reading about me in the paper. There were only a few times my name had been mentioned in the paper, and none of them were because of events I wanted to remember.

Maurice said, "She's a friend of Laura Halston's."

Ruby opened her mouth to say something enthusiastic, but she closed it when the front door opened and a thick man stalked in, glowering like he owned the place and had caught the employees goofing off. He was donkey-butt ugly, with a deeply pockmarked face and thorny black eyebrows. When he raised his hand to his shades to remove them, several diamond rings glittered on fingers thick as cheap cigars. Maurice and Ruby got quiet, and the smile Ruby gave him was so false it could have been lifted off and pinned to the wall.

She said, "Sheila will be right with you, Mr. Gorgon."

He said, "Well, get her up here, I don't have all day."

The young woman with the Statue of Liberty hair whipped around the front counter with a smile as phony as Ruby's. "I'm right here, Mr. Gorgon. You can come on back."

As he strutted away, I watched him with the repulsed fascination I'd give a nest of baby vipers. Maurice and Ruby seemed equally unable to tear their eyes away from him. Even Baby had cocked his ears and was staring at him with big astonished eyes.

Sheila of the white spiked hair bustled around a manicure stand, getting him seated, making sure he was comfortable, offering him something to drink, putting out her bowls and bottles and tools as if she were getting ready to do major surgery. The man all but sneered at her, but he allowed her to touch his broad hands. They seemed to have something of a practiced routine.

As if we all came out of a trance, Maurice and Ruby and I turned away from them at the same moment.

In a barely audible murmur, Maurice said, "Speak of the devil."

Brilliantly, I said, "Huh?"

He leaned close and pretended to arrange a hair behind my ear while he whispered, "That's the man Laura's seeing!"

Since she'd only lived in Sarasota a few weeks, she couldn't have seen much of him. Besides, anybody with two brain cells to rub together would know he wasn't Laura's type. Then I remembered how she'd talked about how rich her husband was, and how much she'd liked being a rich man's wife. This guy sporting diamonds on his hammy hands obviously had money. Maybe his money was enough to make Laura overlook his nasty disposition. I gave the man another look. I knew he wasn't the man who'd called while I was there because his voice was gruff and harsh, not the unctuous smarm of the guy who'd come to Laura's door.

I thanked Maurice profusely, tried to give him a tip which he refused, and left him and Ruby telling Baby how wonderful he was. I didn't say goodbye to Sheila. I was afraid it would interfere with her concentration and enrage her manicure customer.

That's the kind of thing that makes me grateful for my own profession. I don't have to be a different person at work than I am at home. I don't have to suck up to people I despise so that little pieces of my soul get chipped away every day.

As I trudged back to the Bronco, I thought how women tend to envy beauties like Laura, but if we're going to envy anybody, it probably should be women like Ruby. She was a lot happier than Laura, she had a man who loved her whole zaftig self, and she was content with her life. I suspected that Laura's experience with men was that they all wanted to show her off to other men, like a rare jewel in their possession.

Oddly, I felt sorry for Laura. She probably needed a friend as much as I did. Maybe some of her cool self-esteem would rub off on me, and maybe I could help her feel that she was more than just a lovely face.

CHAPTER 9

At the diner, Judy was too busy to talk, but she was quick with the coffee. After she poured the first cup she stepped back to let a young Hispanic man carrying a bright-eyed baby boy in a plastic carrier pass, and for a second he and Judy did one of those sidestepping routines in which each offers right-of-way to the other. While that went on, the baby and I smiled at each other and he waggled his bare feet in innocent ecstasy at being cute and lovable. I tapped one of his plump little brown toes with my finger, and he laughed before his father moved forward and took the baby out of my reach. It's just disgusting what a pushover I am for babies.

Judy hurried away as a middle-aged man and a dewy-eyed young woman—probably office workers taking an early lunch—stopped at the empty booth across the aisle. The girl slid into the booth's bench seat, and the man hesitated a moment as if he might slide in next to her. Flushing, she quickly put her handbag on the seat, and he sat down across from her. A strand of hair had fallen forward over her face. As if it couldn't help itself, his hand floated across the space between them and smoothed the errant hair away from her brow. She looked startled, and he jerked his hand back in a shamed spasm. He wore a wedding band. She wore a look that said she might soon change jobs.

By nature's design, men have the same response to pretty girls that women have to babies. They are compelled to touch them, caress their soft skin, inhale their scent. Lust and tender yearning are two facets of the same diamond.

Judy slid my breakfast in front of me. "Tanisha says hi."

I looked up and waved a thank-you at Tanisha's shiny black face smiling at me through the opening to the kitchen. Tanisha is wide as a bus from eating her own cooking, so she took up most of the opening.

As usual, she had done my breakfast exactly the way I like it—two eggs over easy, extra-crispy home fries, and a biscuit. No bacon, because I have a bacon monitor in my head that knows how much bacon I can eat without ending up big as Tanisha. Some days I tell the monitor to mind its own business, but only when I really, really need fried fat to ease my soul.

Judy scooted away and left me to enjoy my breakfast. The man and the girl across the aisle were busy eating now, neither looking at the other or talking. A little bacon might have made them both feel better.

I ate as fast as I could, dropped money on the table, and waved goodbye to Judy and Tanisha. My mind and body were screaming for sleep.

Except for sloshing surf and squawking seabirds, everything was quiet when I got home. The parakeets were having a siesta, and only a few bored shorebirds ambled along the sand. The day seemed to have lasted a week or two, and my Keds made weary shuffling sounds as I dragged myself up the stairs to my apartment.

Ella was waiting for me inside the French doors,

which meant that Paco had brought her up before he went off to catch a drug dealer or nab a bank robber or do whatever his job of the day was. I picked her up and kissed her nose, feeling better the instant I heard her start to purr. That's the neat thing about cats. You can be feeling like yesterday's cold oatmeal, and the sound of a cat's purring just because you're there makes you feel like you might be worth something after all. She blinked cat code for *I love you* and then twisted out of my arms and leaped to the floor, where she proceeded to hike her back leg in the air and gnaw at the base of her tail.

That's another neat thing about cats. They don't waste time in feel-good sentiment when there's an itch that needs attention.

I stood for a while under warm water and then fell naked into bed and oblivion. I woke up annoyed at myself for going into a funk over things that were, to be honest about it, none of my business. I was a pet sitter, not a surgeon or social worker. That being the case, I needed to keep my mind on my own life and not indulge in the ego trip of taking on other people's problems.

I told myself that Jeffrey had excellent surgeons and caring parents. I told myself that Laura was an intelligent woman with a family she could call for any support she needed. I told myself that no matter how much I sympathized, I actually couldn't make any difference in what either of them was going through.

With that determined, I got up and padded naked to the kitchen to make a cup of tea. Carrying the tea to my closet-office, I flipped on the CD player to let Patsy Cline's no-nonsense, no-equivocation, no-shit voice break the silence. That's what I needed, less of my own morbid thoughts and more of Patsy Cline's soul. While I whipped through the clerical parts of my business,

Ella sat on my desk and tapped her tail in sympathy for Patsy Cline falling to pieces at the sight of an old lover.

After we were done with record-keeping and grooving on the heartbreak of love, I hauled out the vacuum cleaner and sucked up all the dust in my apartment. I scrubbed my bathroom shiny too, until I was high on Clorox fumes. All the time I did it, I heard my grandmother's voice saying, "Cleanliness is next to godliness," which annoyed the heck out of me because it reminded me that I've become as much a cleanliness freak as she was. I swear, all those bromides that mothers and grandmothers repeat must change a person's DNA.

Nevertheless, I felt in control of my little corner of the world when I'd got my environment clean and neat. I almost swaggered when I put away the vacuum. Then I ambled to the closet-office and pulled on a satin thong. I put on a bra too, because I would see Pete later and I didn't want to give him shortness of breath.

I still had some time before I had to leave for my afternoon rounds, so I took Ella out to Michael's deck for a spirited session of chase-the-peacock-feather. Watching a moving peacock feather arouses a cat's innate hunting instincts, so I buy peacock feathers by the dozen. Both of us were a little winded when I got my grooming kit and put Ella on the plank table. Being a Persian mix, she has medium-long coarse hair with an undercoat that can knot up, so she needs to be groomed every day.

As soon as I put her on the table and got out my brush, a squirrel with an exquisitely buoyant tail scampered to the foot of the old oak at the edge of the deck. He picked up an acorn in his paws, turned a backward somersault and came up still holding the acorn. While Ella and I stared at him in round-eyed admiration, he scampered up the tree trunk and disappeared in the branches.

I said, "My gosh, squirrels must be the clowns of the animal kingdom."

Ella said, "*Thrrripp!*" She didn't exactly shrug, but she sounded as if she thought it was time to talk about her and not about a squirrel.

Like all cats, Ella likes her throat brushed more than anything in the world, so I started there. Careful not to tilt my slicker brush and bite her skin, I ran it down her throat while Ella stretched her neck and closed her eyes, swooning at the pleasure of it. It took just a few seconds more to move down her chest and under her arms, back to her throat for a couple of soothing strokes, and to the outside of her front legs. Then a quick pass over the top of her head and neck, a cat's second most favorite grooming spot, a few strokes down both her sides while I ran a protective finger down her spine, and then her bloomers.

For a second, my mind drifted to Jeffrey, but I jerked it away as if it were a dog on a leash going somewhere dangerous and forbidden. Like his parents, I had to believe Jeffrey would come through the surgery with no problems. I had to believe the surgery would completely end his seizures. The alternatives were too terrible to even contemplate.

I finished grooming Ella with a fast flick around her tail and a couple of final strokes down her throat. To distribute natural oils to the tips of her hair and make her coat shiny and smooth, I quickly passed a soft-bristled brush all over her body. All fluffed up, she was a glorious burst of technicolor beauty, and I told her so.

Ella preened contentedly. Deep in her kitty heart, Ella believes she's the most beautiful creature alive. I like that about cats. They don't compare themselves with other cats. They don't talk themselves into feeling dumb or ugly or fat or thin, they just enjoy feeling gorgeous. Too bad humans don't do that.

I put Ella in Michael's kitchen, made sure she had fresh water in her bowl, and gave her a goodbye kiss on the nose. Then I went outside, spritzed the table with my handy-dandy water and Clorox mixture, and headed out in the Bronco for my afternoon rounds.

As I drove, I caught myself humming a tune and beating time to it on the steering wheel. The lyrics had been in my head all morning, as if I had a jukebox in my brain and somebody had fed it a lot of coins. Actually, it was just the first line of a song's lyrics. My grandmother had always maintained that each of us has an invisible Guide who is always with us, and the Guide communicates with us by directing our attention to book titles or billboard signs or song lyrics. I'm not sure I believe the Guide idea, but I have noticed that my mind has a way of knowing things before I'm aware of them, and lots of times I don't catch on until I hear my own voice singing some song I hadn't thought of in years. This time it was "You don't know me."

Silly thing to hear over and over, but I couldn't shake it.

CHAPTER 10

At Tom Hale's condo, Tom was at the kitchen table working on tax returns. He called hello to me and I yelled back, but I didn't stay to chat because Tom and I both had work to do. Besides, I thought Tom might be embarrassed to have told me about his personal problems with Frannie, and I knew I was embarrassed to have been so blatant about how I felt about the woman. We both needed a bit of distance for a few days, the same way I needed distance from Laura for a few days.

I seemed to have become the sort of person who knew so much about my friends' private business that I couldn't be friendly to them anymore.

My afternoon went fast because two clients had returned home that day, one the human of a Siamese couple, and the other the human of an orange Short-hair. All I had to do was pop in to make sure they had indeed returned as planned, collect a check, and be on my way. Two white Persians, Stella and Marie, were almost as easy. The cats were sisters, so content with each other's company that they deemed me important only as the human who combed them and put out food for them. While I ran the vacuum to pick up hair they had flung on the carpet, Stella sat on the windowsill looking longingly at the birds around the feeder, and Marie lay on the sofa watching a kitty video of darting fish. When I told them goodbye, they both turned their heads and gave me languid looks of total disinterest.

Mazie was my last call of the day, and I rang the doorbell with dread nibbling the back of my neck. Both Pete and Mazie answered, and the minute I saw Pete's worried face, I braced myself for whatever bad news he had about Jeffrey. Mazie looked as distressed as Pete, with the corners of her mouth downturned and sad. She looked sharply at me, sighed heavily, then stepped back to let me in.

Pete said, "She was hoping you were somebody else." He said *somebody else* in the tone people use when they're trying to speak in code so a child won't understand.

I said, "Sorry, Mazie, it's just me."

Pete's saxophone was out of the case and lying on a chair. He held a child's picture book in his hand, a finger crooked into it to hold his place.

He said, "I've been reading to her. She seems to like it."

He didn't mention playing the saxophone for her, but I suspected he had been doing that too.

I looked at the book and laughed. It was *The Cat in the Hat*.

I said, "That was Christy's favorite story. She loved Dr. Seuss."

It was amazing how that had just popped out of my mouth, flowing out easily, not choked by sobs or hoarse from a closed throat. I had been doing that a lot lately, mentioning Christy or Todd easily and casually. It was a strange and bittersweet feeling to be able to do that.

Pete said, "Hal called. The boy's still out from the anesthesia."

"Maybe that's normal."

"I don't think so. I think he should be awake by now. Hal said the doctors keep coming in to check on him."

"Well, they would anyway."

Mazie raised her head and looked back and forth at us, like a spectator at a tennis match. Then she heaved another huge sigh. When a dog sighs a lot, it's a sure sign of stress. In this case, it was also a sure sign that Mazie knew that neither Pete nor I knew diddly about what was normal for a three-year-old after brain surgery.

I got her leash and jingled it. "Let's go for a walk, okay?"

Like a dutiful soldier, she hiked with me down the driveway to the sidewalk. We hesitated there, both of us uncertain which way we wanted to go. As if we had held a discussion about it and came to the same decision, we both turned at the same moment and walked toward Laura's house. As we passed it, we turned our heads and peered through the shielding trees, but we didn't see any sign of Laura.

I wondered if Laura's defiance with her husband that morning had been an act. I wondered if she were inside her house needing a friend to talk to. I was her friend, or at least wanted to be, but I couldn't ring her doorbell and say, "This morning I hid behind some bushes and eavesdropped on you and your husband. Want to talk about it?"

No, the best thing to do was to wait a day or two and ask her to have dinner with me. Then, if she wanted to tell me what was going on with her husband, we could talk.

At the end of the block, Mazie and I stopped to look at a couple of great blue herons standing at the base of a power pole. They were watching a fish hawk atop the pole. The fish hawk was downing a flopping mullet, and the herons were waiting to catch the leftovers.

Mazie made a wuffing sound and sat down with her tail wagging, probably a form of doggie applause for such a sensible display. Nature is neither squeamish nor wasteful. In the animal kingdom, every creature aids and is aided by every other creature. Humans, on the other hand, haven't evolved yet enough to do that.

When the show was over, Mazie got up and walked back home with me. It seemed to me that the corners of her mouth were raised a bit, not in a smile exactly, but not in the morose look she'd had before. I felt more positive too. It's good to be reminded of nature's intelligence. Even when we can't see it in our own lives, it's still there.

As Mazie and I went past Laura's house, I didn't even look toward it.

I will never know if it would have changed anything if I had gone to her door right then.

CHAPTER 11

On the way home, Ray Charles was still in my head singing "You don't know me," while I beat time on the steering wheel and grinned at the contradiction of a wide-hipped Silverado pickup with a gun rack in the back and a RAPTURE! sticker on the bumper. Florida is an Old Testament state where God walks with us in the cool of the evening. But he tells us not to get too smart, not to eat of the tree of knowledge, or we will die. And all around us, a sibilant sea whispers the soul's terrifying truth: "If you eat of the tree, you will not die." It's no wonder so many of us are gun-toting fundamentalists.

At home, I pulled into the carport just as the sun plunged into the Gulf in a final burst of Technicolor glory. Paco was on the deck with Ella in his arms watching the show, and I trotted over to join them. Only Paco could manage to look slim and fit in slouchy black sweatpants and a floppy white T-shirt. The pants even accentuated the fact that he has the most gorgeous butt in the universe.

Gorgeous butt or not, he looked lonely.

He slung his free arm over my shoulder and we stood taking in the floating sky banners of turquoise and hot pink and orange. We didn't speak until the colors had finally faded and the sun's glittering path from horizon to shore disappeared.

As the surf wrote frothy messages on the sand, Paco said, "Have you eaten?"

"No, and I'm starving."

"Me too."

We both sighed in unison. Without Michael to feed us, we were like newly hatched chicks without a mother.

Paco said, "There's some turkey and stuff in the fridge."

I said, "We could make sandwiches."

We both perked up. Sandwiches weren't as good as what Michael would have fed us, but we had solved the dinner problem, and we had each other.

I said, "I'll be down in ten minutes," and loped upstairs.

Ten minutes later, I skipped down barefoot and still slightly damp from a speed shower, but decently covered in elastic-waist cotton pants and an oversized T-shirt, a female version of what Paco wore.

In the kitchen, Ella was perched on her stool looking wistfully at the spread on the butcher-block island. Paco had hauled out everything remotely related to sandwich making, and was crouched in front of the refrigerator poking into its innards.

He said, "I can't find the horseradish mustard."

"On the door. What kind of beer do you have?"

He held up a dark glass bottle with a long neck. "Some exotic stuff Michael got at the Sarasota Brewing Company. You can have Golden Wheat, Midnight Pass Porter, or Sunset Red."

"Ooh, cool. I'll have the porter."

I got plates and made room for them by shoving aside cutting boards holding sliced turkey and ham, sliced tomatoes and onions. There was a loaf of pumpernickel bread and one of rye, along with jars of mayonnaise, three kinds of mustard, two kinds of pickles, black and green olives, several varieties of relish, both mild and hot salsa, and some things I didn't recognize. Also chips, both potato and corn. We could have fed half of Siesta Key.

We took seats and fell on the food like happy cannibals, smearing big globs of mayonnaise and mustard on bread and layering on meat and condiments to hoggish heights. Being a lady, I daintily cut my sandwich in half, on the diagonal. Paco just held his carefully so nothing would slip out the bottom. For a few minutes, the only sound was the crunch of crisp pickles and snap of chips.

After a while, I said, "You know the woman I told you about? The one with the sadistic surgeon husband?"

"Yeah?"

"Well, he's found her. This morning I overheard them talking. He was scary."

"All the more reason for you to stay out of it. That woman's situation sounds like a plane crash about to happen."

"She needs a friend, Paco. That's all I'm offering."

"Sounds to me like she needs a good lawyer. Maybe a good shrink."

"Just because she left her husband doesn't make her crazy."

"I'm just saying she needs more help than you can give her."

I couldn't argue with that, so we chewed for a few more minutes without talking.

But I'm the one who, when I was five years old and made to sit in a corner in kindergarten because I talked too much, told my mother that if you went too long without talking all your mouth bones would grow together. I don't have any trouble with silence if I'm alone, but when another person is present, my mouth is still afraid all its bones will fuse if I don't speak.

I said, "You know those songs or commercials that get stuck in your head?"

"They're called ear worms. Comes from some German word that sounds like ear worms and means the same thing. Don't remember what it is."

"Huh. Well, I've got one. I keep hearing Ray Charles singing 'You don't know me.' That's all. Just 'You don't know me' over and over. It's making me nuts."

"Yeah, I hate those things. I hate commercial jingles the most. One time when I was on a stakeout, I kept hearing a voice say, *Raid kills bugs dead.* All the damn night long, I heard that commercial."

I drained the last of my porter and set the bottle on the butcher block.

"The little boy who had surgery hasn't waked up yet. Surgery was at seven this morning. Shouldn't he be awake by now?"

Paco's dark eyes studied me. "You said he's three years old, right?"

My throat worked for a moment in a vain attempt to deny his implicit meaning, but I knew he was right.

I said, "Okay."

In the shorthand communication that develops between people who love and support one another, he was telling me that I was seeing my three-year-old daughter in Jeffrey, seeing her crushed skull every time I thought of Jeffrey's brain surgery, feeling the edges of the same cold anguish I'd felt when Christy was killed. He had warned me not to do that anymore, and I had agreed to stop. Those unspoken codes may be the best thing about families.

I helped Paco put away all the leftovers and tidy up the kitchen, then blew kisses at him and Ella and went upstairs to bed. As I fell asleep, Ray Charles was still softly singing in the shadows of my mind.

"You don't know me," he said, "You don't know me."

CHAPTER 12

By a quarter to five next morning, I was dressed and on my porch, trying to shake the feeling that the day would be a bad one. I was glad that Michael would come home at eight o'clock and would be home for the next forty-eight hours. I've felt safer all my life when Michael was nearby, and I guess I always will.

The sky was clear and milky, moon and stars withdrawn into its haze. Subdued bird twittering and gentle surf made morning music, the sea's breath was cool and smelled of salt and kelp, a new day's forgiveness dispensed with open hand.

There was absolutely no reason for a ton of weight to ride on my chest.

The next few hours flowed with the same smoothness. No unpleasant surprises. Nothing out of the ordinary. At the Sea Breeze, Billy Elliot and I galloped around the oval parking lot until he was satisfied and grinning, and I was gasping for air. After Billy Elliot, I walked a sedate pug and then a pregnant collie mix. When the dogs were all walked and fed and brushed, I saw to the cats on my list. At each house, I fed them, groomed them, and spent about fifteen minutes playing with them. Sometimes we played with a cat's own toys, and sometimes with one of mine.

Dogs don't much care what games you play with them, they're just tickled that you're playing with them at all. You can roll old ratty foam balls around for dogs, or even throw them a cat's toy, and they'll think you're the coolest playmate they've ever had.

Cats, on the other hand, are as fickle about their toys as they are about their food. Wave a peacock feather at a cat one day, and he'll jump for it with ecstatic excitement. Wave the same feather the next day, and the cat will sit with a disdainful sneer on his face and look at you as if you have insulted him, his mother, and all his ancestors back to Egypt.

At Mazie's house, I heard saxophone music as I went up the walk to the front door. Pete answered the doorbell with the sax in his hand, all the lines in his face curving upward.

"The boy's doing fine. Hal called early this morning, said he came out of the anesthetic late last night. He was groggy and confused for a while, but now he's alert. Hal said they'd be moving him to Sub-ICU sometime this morning."

My knees went weak with relief. "Did Hal say what the doctors think about the seizures?"

He shook his head. "I didn't ask. I didn't want to keep him. Poor guy, he sounded exhausted. He just wanted to tell me Jeffrey was out of ICU and to make sure Mazie was okay."

At the sound of her name, Mazie raised her head, then lowered it with a sigh and stretched her chin against her forepaws.

Pete said, "I'm worried about her, but I told Hal she was okay. I didn't want him to worry too."

I knelt beside Mazie and stroked her head. "Jeffrey will be home soon, Mazie, and he's going to be fine."

I hoped with all my heart that I was telling her the

truth—that Jeffrey would come home soon and never have another seizure.

Neither of us enjoyed our walk, and when we came back and turned into her driveway, something at the edge of my vision streaked across the street and into the trees and foliage. I turned my head, but whatever it was had disappeared. I had only caught a quick flash of movement, but I'd got the impression of a small brown animal with a long tail. Somewhat like a lemur, except lemurs live on a different continent. Actually, it had seemed like a small brown cat. To be even more specific, it had seemed like Leo on the lam.

I led a reluctant Mazie down the sidewalk closer to Laura's house. I didn't see any signs of life, but that didn't mean Laura wasn't home. She could be inside reading the morning paper and Leo could have run out when she went outside to get it. She could be in the shower, not realizing that Leo was loose. Or she could be on the jogging trail, completely unaware that Leo had slipped out when she opened the door.

Mazie pulled on the leash, wanting to go home. I hesitated a moment, torn between wanting to let Laura know her cat was outside, and knowing Mazie was right. I was on her time, not Leo's. Besides, I wasn't even sure I had seen Leo. It could have been some other dark cat with a long tail.

Telling myself Leo would eventually come home—if it had *been* Leo—I led Mazie back to her house. Pete was waiting outside the front door like an anxious father.

I handed Mazie's leash off to him and said, "I think I saw Laura Halston's cat while Mazie and I were walking. He runs out every time he sees an open door."

"Why?"

"I guess he's a nature cat. Doesn't like living inside."

"That's how I'd be if I were a cat. I'd join the circus again, be on the move all the time."

"Are there circus cats?"

"Well, sure, lions and tigers. A few people have got domestic cats to do some tricks, jump through hoops, that kind of thing, but cats don't have a strong desire to please people like good circus animals have. Cats are liable to get bored in the middle of an act and just flat quit."

"I think I'll go next door and tell Laura, just in case it was Leo. He might have gone out when Laura opened the door to go running."

"She ran real early this morning. I took Mazie outside to pee, and I saw her run across the street to the jogging trail."

"I'm not even sure it was Leo."

"A bobcat, maybe. People see bobcats in their yards all the time. Bobcats and panthers were here first, poor things."

I didn't think it had been a bobcat I'd seen. I was almost positive it had been Leo.

I left the Bronco in Mazie's driveway and walked to Laura's house, peering all around as I went in case Leo had returned to his own yard. As soon as I started up Laura's walk, I saw that her front door was ajar. When I got closer, I saw Leo in the corner of the small porch. He was gnawing on one of his paws as if something was stuck between his toes. I wasn't surprised that he'd come home. Cats have an unerring sense of direction, and they usually return soon enough when they've run away.

Cats are also skittish, and Leo might streak away if I approached him. I knelt on the walk and talked softly to him.

"Hey, Leo, remember me? Would you let me pick you up?"

He paused in his paw cleaning, tilted his ears toward me, and then went back to cleaning his foot. He seemed to be telling me that he wasn't unfriendly, but to not take him for granted.

I looked toward the door again. If I ignored Leo and rang the doorbell, he might take offense at my nearness and run away. The smart thing would be to call Laura and tell her he was out and let her handle him. Keeping an eye on him, I pulled out my cell phone and dialed information, then remembered that Laura's landline number was in her parents' name and she hadn't given me her cell number. I put the phone back in my pocket and got to my feet.

Leo turned his attention to another paw, going at it with a determined intensity. Whatever his feet had picked up on his dash to freedom was something he didn't want to keep. Watching him from the corner of my eye, I took a few cautious steps toward the door and realized my heart was pounding much harder than the situation warranted. I told myself a cat had got out through a door accidentally left ajar, that's all there was to it.

But I knew Leo had been outside now long enough for Laura to have missed him. I knew there was something terribly wrong about that open door. And above all else, I knew what Laura's husband had said to her the day before. He had told her he would see that she paid for what she'd done.

While I debated what to do next, Leo stopped gnawing at his toes and watched me. Old deputy habits made me scrutinize the door facing for signs of forced entry. I didn't see any, but when I looked more closely at the landing, I made out several small dark brown circles.

I don't know why it had taken me so long to see them. Perhaps I had known all along they were there and denied them. Whatever the reason, they told me why Leo was so busily cleaning the pads of his paws.

CHAPTER 13

I took the phone back out and called 911. A deep male voice answered, one of those molasses tones that make you feel like weeping with relief because you've found somebody with broad shoulders you can fling yourself against. It took several tries to get my voice to work, and then it came out sounding like something fired from an old rusty cannon.

I said, "I have reason to believe a woman has been attacked in her home. I'm outside the door now, but I'm afraid I'll disturb evidence if I go in. I'm an ex-deputy."

I felt it was important to say I was an ex-deputy, as if that would make me sound more credible.

The man said, "Why do you think there's been an attack?"

"I overheard the woman's husband threaten her yesterday, and now her front door is open a few inches and her cat's outside. The cat has left a trail of bloody paw prints from the house."

He took the address, Laura's name, and my name.

He said, "Somebody will be there shortly."

I could imagine him calling it in: "Crazy woman thinks another woman has been attacked because her cat's outside and she imagines she sees bloody paw prints. Go check it out."

I sat down on the walk and waited. Leo waited. Leo yawned and stretched, then continued grooming a leg. The house was quiet and calm. The yard was quiet and calm. I was the only thing not calm, but it was very possible that I was a paranoid case. It was very possible that I'd been involved in so many crimes in the last year that I'd come to expect the worst even in innocuous situations.

One of those ear worm things started in my head again, Randy Newman singing "I could be wrong now, but I don't think so."

After what seemed eons, a green-and-white deputy's car pulled into the driveway and Deputy Jesse Morgan got out. The fact that a sworn deputy had come instead of one of the Community Policing officers meant the dispatcher had taken my call seriously, but I did an inward groan. Morgan and I have met over a couple of dead bodies, and I think he sees me as somebody whose presence spells trouble. He may be right.

I stood up to meet him, and it seemed to me that his stride faltered a bit when he recognized me. From the top of his close-cropped hair to the hem of his dark-green deputy pants, Morgan was crisp and all business. The only thing about him that hinted of a life outside law enforcement was the discreet diamond stud in one earlobe.

With his eyes hidden behind mirrored shades, I had to go by his lean cheeks and firm lips to tell what he thought, and he wasn't giving anything away.

He stopped a few feet away and rocked back a bit on his heels. "Miz Hemingway."

I said, "I know how this seems, but I'm concerned

about the woman in this house. I saw her cat run across the street about an hour ago. I think the cat ran out when somebody went in." I pointed toward the dark round circles. "Those are paw prints."

Morgan's head tilted a fraction of an inch toward me, either in acknowledgment of my powers of deduction or because he thought it was a good idea to be polite to a crazy woman.

As he moved past me toward the door, I said, "Don't scare the cat away."

He stopped and turned his head toward Leo. "Tell you what, Miz Hemingway, why don't you go pick the cat up, and then I'll go in the house."

I didn't like the careful way he said it, as if he were humoring somebody who might fly apart at any moment. Still, he had a point. Cautiously, I moved forward and stooped to pick Leo up. As if to show Morgan what an overanxious idiot I was, Leo went limp as a sack of jelly.

Avoiding the paw prints, Morgan zigzagged to the door, rang the doorbell, and rapped on the glass. "Sheriff's Department!"

Silence.

He rang again, rapped on the doorjamb, and called louder. "Sheriff's Department!"

He did that three times, each time louder, then used the back of his knuckles to push the door open. "Miz Halston? Sheriff's Department!"

He walked inside out of my view, but I could hear him calling to Laura and identifying himself. I carried Leo to the end of the driveway and stood by the street waiting. I already knew what Morgan would find.

In a few minutes, he stepped outside with his phone to his ear. His face had gone several shades paler. He paused to talk, and I heard the word *stabbed*. The word confirmed what I'd been expecting. Call it intuition or hunch or simply the fact that I knew Laura's husband was a sadist with scalpels, I knew Laura had been murdered and that the killer had stabbed her to death.

Morgan clicked the phone closed and put it back on his belt. Then he walked to the corner of the house, leaned over with one hand on the wall, and very efficiently threw up.

I had firsthand knowledge of some of the gruesome things Morgan had seen, but I'd never seen him lose his poise. Morgan was an experienced law enforcement officer, and law enforcement officers become inured to scenes that would turn a normal person's stomach. He pulled a handkerchief from his back pocket and wiped his mouth, then slowly turned toward me. I could feel his eyes on me behind his dark shades, and I knew he was debating how much to tell me. His chest rose in a deep breath, and he came down the driveway.

I said, "She's dead, isn't she?"

"The crime-scene guys will want to talk to you."

I said, "I'm going to put Leo in my car."

Woodenly, I walked to my Bronco in the driveway at Mazie's house and put Leo in a cardboard cat carrier. Lowering all the car windows, I left him there and went back to Laura's house. As I got there, a sheriff's car pulled to the curb and Sergeant Woodrow Owens got out. When he saw me, his face registered pleasure, dismay, and sadness all at one time.

Sergeant Owens is a tall laconic African American who had been my immediate superior when I was a deputy. There's not a finer man in the world, or a smarter one. He was smart enough to tell me I was too crazy to carry a gun for the department after Todd and Christy were killed. Actually, what he'd said was, "Dixie, you're way too fucked up to be a deputy."

That's how smart he was.

Now he said, "Damn, girl, I was hoping you'd stopped attracting dead bodies."

"Me too."

He flapped a bony hand at me and went past me to confer in low tones with Morgan. They both went inside the house for a few minutes, and when they came out Sergeant Owens held his mouth clamped in a straight line. Morgan studiously held his head with his chin tilted up, as if he'd decided never to look at the floor again.

While Morgan went to his car and got out yellow crime-scene tape and began stretching it around the perimeter of the yard, Owens whipped out his phone. He spoke in clipped tones for a while, then closed it and walked back to me.

"What's the story?"

"The woman who lives here is Laura Halston. I don't know her well, but I had dinner with her night before last, and she told me she'd left her husband. He's a sadistic surgeon, used to carve her up with scalpels. They lived in Dallas, and she ran away and came here. Then he found her."

"She told you he'd found her?"

My face got warm. "I happened to overhear them talking yesterday. I was putting a turtle out by the lake, and they were on the other side of the hibiscus hedge that runs along the street. He told her he would make her pay for what she'd done. She walked away from him, and he drove off."

"You ever see him again?"

"That's the only time."

"Got a name for him?"

"Dr. Reginald Halston. He's a prominent doctor in Dallas."

He scribbled the name, and I said, "She called him Martin."

"When you were listening to them behind the trail?"

I felt myself blush again. "I wasn't deliberately listening, they just happened to come by while I was there."

"How do you know he was the husband?"

"I heard her talking to him on the phone the night we had dinner. She called him Martin then, too."

"And she said he was her husband?"

"She said he was her soon to be ex-husband."

"In Dallas."

"That's what she said."

"You know a next of kin to notify?"

"Her parents live in Connecticut, but I don't know their name. She mentioned a sister in Dallas named Celeste. She didn't say a last name."

Owens deliberated a moment. "You know anybody else who could identify her body?"

"Besides me?"

"I think it would be better if it was somebody else, Dixie. You don't need to see that."

My heart quivered. Morgan had upchucked at seeing Laura's body, and now Owens wanted to protect me from seeing it.

"It's that bad?"

"It's about as bad as it can get, Dixie."

It's funny how your mind can split at times like that. One side of my brain recoiled from what was happening around me. The other side was cool as grass. The cool side knew investigators would look through Laura's address books looking for names and numbers for her relatives. The cool side knew calls would be made, awful truths said, grim arrangements made.

The cool side said, "I'll take care of Leo until the house is cleaned up."

"Leo?"

"Laura's cat. I've put him in my car."

Owens gave me a slow look, then nodded. "Lieutenant Guidry will be handling the homicide investigation. He'll want to talk to you."

As if on cue, Guidry's dark Blazer pulled to a stop in the street, and Guidry got out and walked to us.

Owens said, "Dixie knows the woman. She spent some time with her night before last."

I said, "I was only with her a few hours. She invited me for a glass of wine, and then we had dinner."

Owens flapped his notebook at Guidry. "The woman has a husband in Dallas. A surgeon. She told Dixie he was a sadist, used to scare her with scalpels. Dixie believes the man came here and found her. She saw the woman with a man she believes is the husband."

Guidry nodded, digesting the scant information without comment.

I said, "She was a runner. Ran every morning. That's how I met her. She'd opened the door to go running and Leo got out. Leo's her cat. I've put him in my car."

Guidry's face took on the pained look he always got when I mentioned pets, but neither man answered me.

I said, "She wore serious running shoes. The expensive kind."

I studied their implacable faces for a moment and knew it was time to shut up.

I said, "If you need me, you know where to find me."

As I turned away, Owens said, "Dixie? We don't need to tell you not to divulge anything about the ex-husband and the scalpels."

Of course he didn't. When word of the murder got out, the usual loonies would come forward to make false confessions. Guilty people would give false alibis. Citizens would call with leads and misguided information. The murder would be public knowledge, but the fact that Laura's ex-husband was a surgeon who liked to play with scalpels was information that only the homicide investigators would know. And me.

Without answering, I turned away and trudged back to the Bronco.

CHAPTER 14

At the Bronco, Leo was peering out the air holes in the cardboard carrier and making piteous noises. I leaned in the window and said, "It's okay, Leo."

My mouth said that, but my feet knew it was a huge lie, and the next thing I knew I was kicking the bejesus out of my front tire, all my rage and horror banging in useless fury.

Behind me, Pete said, "Dixie? What's wrong?"

A surge of adrenaline brought teeth-rattling shakes, and I turned around to lean against the Bronco with my knees stiffened and my elbows braced on the car. Pete had Mazie on her leash, and both man and dog were taking in the fact that Leo was crying in the car, and that Laura's yard was marked by yellow crime-scene tape.

An ambulance and several marked and unmarked sheriff's cars passed by, slowing to a crawl in front of Laura's house and then oozing to parking places by the curb. I knew what the criminalists would do. They would post a Contamination Sheet by the front door to record every person who entered and left the house. Then they would photograph the interior of Laura's house, dust for latent prints, and look for shoe tracks, for fibers, for hair, for anything that might point to the identity of the person or persons who had killed her. Outside, they would walk shoulder to shoulder around the area looking for anything a killer might have dropped.

Pete said, "Something's happened to that woman, hasn't it?"

Still shuddering, I bobbed my head up and down.

Inside the Bronco, Leo made a long wailing noise. Mazie whimpered and trotted toward the sound, moving her tail back and forth in a nervous show of sympathy.

I waited until a final tremor released me, then said the thing that had to be said.

"Laura's been killed."

"I'm so sorry."

I said, "I'm going to take Leo to Kitty Haven until Laura's family comes."

I put my hand on the door handle and then turned to him. "Pete, what time was it that you saw Laura?"

"Oh, it was early. Around five, probably. I get up early, you know, and once I'm up Mazie is up, so we went outside for a few minutes. That lady came down the driveway over there and ran across the street. Just sort of squeezed through the hibiscus there where the running path is."

It was now close to eleven, which meant Laura had been killed within the last five or six hours. The killer could have got inside Laura's house while she was running and killed her when she came back. Then he must have left the door open as he ran away, and Leo got outside.

I pulled the car door open, and Mazie trotted over to look up toward the cat carrier where Leo was still crying. Service dogs are trained from puppyhood to live amicably with other household pets, so Mazie was free of cat prejudice.

With the same sympathetic concern that Mazie had,

Pete said, "Why don't you leave the cat with me and Mazie? We can take care of him, and I'm sure Hal and Gillis would want to help out a neighbor."

I opened the Bronco door and got in. "I'd need their permission, and this is not the time to ask for it."

His shoulders dropped with the reminder of Jeffrey.

While he and Mazie watched me with identical expressions of sadness, I started the engine and backed out of the driveway. As I drove away, I looked toward Guidry's Blazer in front of Laura's house. I reminded myself to tell him what time Pete had seen Laura. On TV, medical examiners can tell exactly what time a person died. In real life, nailing down a time of death usually becomes somewhere between the time a person was seen alive and the time she was found dead.

Leo was quiet on the way to the Kitty Haven. Maybe he was soothed by the car's movement, or maybe he was just relieved to get away from the gruesome scene inside his house.

A yellow frame house with sparkling white shutters and a front porch that begs for a swing, Kitty Haven is owned by Marge Preston, a round white-haired woman who speaks English and Cat with equal fluency. Inside, the décor is a comforting blend of a grandmother's house and a brothel, with lots of burgundy velour, lace curtains, and crocheted tablecloths. Several slack cats were draped on windowsills and plump chair backs in the waiting room. When I carried Leo in, they all looked at me as if I were the most interesting specimen of humanity they'd ever seen.

When I lifted Leo from the carrier, Marge said, "Oh, what a beauty! You don't see many of those."

"His name's Leo. There's been a death in his family, and he needs a place to stay until relatives come."

Marge took him from me and then looked suspiciously at the paw pad he raised.

I said, "He needs a bath too."

"Oh, my."

"Yeah."

I left Marge telling Leo that he was safe and beautiful. Marge knows that even when you've stepped in blood, it makes you feel better to be told you're safe and beautiful.

Heavy with the lethargy that follows a prolonged surge of adrenaline, I drove south like a homing pigeon. At the tree-lined lane leading to my apartment, I turned in with hope tensing my stomach. When I rounded the last bend and saw my brother's car in the carport, I let out a sigh of relief. Michael usually spends his off-hours fishing or cooking, so his car meant he was home cooking. As he had been doing all my life, Michael would see that I held together.

Before I faced him, I slogged upstairs to my apartment's porch and fell into the hammock. I kept remembering Laura's husband saying he would see that she paid for what she'd done. She had said he was abusive and mentally unbalanced, but what he'd done went way over being unbalanced. He had to be a raving psychopath to have killed his wife just because she wanted a divorce.

With a little jolt, I remembered the man who'd called and come to her door while I was there, the one she'd met at the emergency room when she twisted her knee. He'd sounded like a nutcase too, and I'd forgotten about him when I talked to Sergeant Owens. Then another jolt hit. Damn, I'd forgotten about the man who'd come in the Lyon's Mane too, the one Maurice had said was after Laura. If she'd turned him down, his obsessive lust might have turned homicidal. I didn't know if he was as crazy as Laura's husband, but I knew he'd looked capable of brutal murder.

Tears came in a sudden torrent, not only from shock and sadness over the murder of a woman I'd liked a lot but from a deep reservoir of unspeakable fear that lies deep in every woman's heart. No matter how much equality we gain with our brains, our street smarts, and our ability to handle weapons, the fact remains that we are physically weaker than men. Furthermore, we belong to a species that does unspeakable things to one another. Until that changes, we will be vulnerable, and every woman knows it.

Laura Halston had been an intelligent, healthy, able-bodied woman who had taken every precaution to stay safe. And yet somebody a lot bigger, stronger, and more brutal had come into her house and killed her.

Was it somebody she knew? Somebody she had opened the door to? I kept going over what little I knew, gnawing on the details. A hunt might already be on for her Laura's surgeon husband, the well-known Dr. Reginald Halston that she called Martin. I wondered how he would feel when he learned that Laura had been pregnant with his child when he killed her.

Then I reminded myself that I couldn't be sure her husband was the killer. Except I was.

When I finally went searching for Michael, I found him in his kitchen, engulfed in clouds of aromatic steam coming from several big pots on the commercial range. He had an apron the size of a tablecloth wrapped around his broad torso, and a look of beatific joy on his handsome face. When he's on duty, Michael cooks for the firehouse. When he's not on duty, Michael cooks for the firehouse as well as for me and Paco. He has enough soups and stews stored in his freezer to feed all of Sarasota County.

When I came in, Ella Fitzgerald jumped down from her perch on a bar stool at the butcher-block island and came to twine her body around my ankles. After I smooched the top of her head, she hopped back on her stool and licked her paws like a bimbo too involved with her manicure to pay attention to the little people.

Michael said, "What's wrong?"

"You remember the woman I told you about? Laura Halston? She was murdered this morning. They didn't tell me how, but I think she was stabbed to death. I took her cat to Kitty Haven."

Michael laid down his stirring spoon and came close, looking down at me with worried eyes.

"Oh, hell, Dixie. Oh, sugar, I'm sorry."

I leaned into him, and he wrapped me in a bear hug, squeezing me as if he could shut out every hurtful thing. Then he held my shoulders in both hands and looked hard at me.

"You haven't had anything to eat this morning, have you?"

"Michael, I can't eat, I'm too upset."

"You've been up since four, and it's nearly noon. Sit."

Michael is of the firm conviction that ninety-five percent of all wars and social ills would be wiped out if everybody ate a substantial breakfast.

While he whirled into action, I poured myself a mug of coffee from the electric pot on the counter. I drank half of it in one long gulp before I dropped onto a bar stool. Beside me, Ella had decided her nails met her standards and was dreamily staring at Michael with the same love-dazed look that a lot of females get when they see him.

Michael went back and forth between the Sub-Zero refrigerator and the giant range like Godzilla stomping over cities, and before I had finished my coffee he slid a bowl of white stuff in front of me and handed me a spoon.

"Down the hatch, kid."

I took a tentative bite and felt my neck muscles relax. Fragrant white rice stirred into light cream, flavored with cinnamon and nutmeg, with a thin drizzle of maple syrup looped over the top. Soft and creamy. No chunks of anything that required serious chewing, no sharp surprises, no intellectual demands. Just smooth, uncomplicated nourishment that went down easy and warmed my heart.

Ella looked at my rice and made a little pleading sound, but Michael shook his head sternly. "Rice isn't good for you, and you've already had a shrimp."

Ella meekly flipped the tip of her tail. Nobody argues with Michael, not even Ella.

I nodded toward the steaming pots on the stove. "What're you making?"

"Gumbo with shrimp and crab. Rice to serve it over."

"Okra?"

"Don't be afraid of okra, Dixie, it's a respectable vegetable."

"It's slimy."

"Lots of good stuff is slimy."

He turned to waggle his eyebrows at me in a mock-lewd parody, but his eyes remained worried.

"Dixie, I hope you're not going to get involved in another murder investigation. I don't think I can go through that again."

"This one doesn't have anything to do with me."

"You knew the dead woman. You're taking care of her cat. That involves you, doesn't it?"

"I don't know anything other than what I've already told Sergeant Owens."

"Which doesn't answer my question."

I carried my empty bowl and cup to the sink and rinsed them before I put them in the dishwasher.

I said, "Thanks for breakfast."

"Uh-huh."

Michael's forehead was wrinkled with worry, but there wasn't anything I could say that would relieve his mind.

No way was I staying out of this murder investigation. What had happened to Laura could have happened to me or to any other woman. I was going to do everything I could to see that Laura Halston's killer was caught and put away forever.

CHAPTER 15

I stood a long time under a hot shower, but it didn't wash away the memory of the bloody paw prints leading from Laura's front door or my sense of outraged grief. Fatigue made me feel like a balloon that had lost its air, but before I fell into bed for a nap, I called Guidry. Miracle of miracles, he answered his cell phone.

I said, "Guidry, I forgot to tell Sergeant Owens about a man who came to her house while I was there Sunday night. He called, too, and begged her to let him in. She didn't, even after he banged on the door. She said he was stalking her."

"He have a name?"

"She didn't say a name, but she said she'd met him at the emergency room at Sarasota Memorial. She went there with a sprained knee and he was there too."

"Okay."

"There's another man, too. Thuggish guy named Gorgon. I don't know much about him, but Maurice at the Lyon's Mane said he was after Laura too."

"Dixie, I don't know what the hell you just said."

"The Lyon's Mane is a hair salon. It's owned by Maurice and Ruby. Maurice does Laura's hair. Did. Gorgon is one of their clients too. Gets his manicures there. According to Maurice, he was putting a lot of pressure on Laura."

"Okay, I'll talk to Maurice."

"There's something else. A man I've put in charge of the dog next door saw Laura leave her house this morning about five o'clock to go running."

The line was silent for a moment, and I knew Guidry was deciphering what I'd meant about a man I'd put in charge of a dog. I wasn't in a mood to spoon-feed him, so I let him figure it out for himself.

He rallied and said, "He's sure about the time?"

"Not positive, but around that time. He gets up early, and he'd taken Mazie outside for a few minutes when he saw her."

"Okay." His voice was oddly flat.

I said, "Did you contact her family?"

"Her sister will be here as soon as she can. Probably tomorrow."

"When is the autopsy scheduled?"

"Why do you want to know?"

"She was my friend."

"Owens said you barely knew her."

"That's true, but she was still my friend."

"Autopsy will be tomorrow morning."

"Have you found her husband?"

"Dr. Reginald Halston, the surgeon? The one in Dallas?"

I didn't like the way his tone had gone crispy.

"Yeah, that one."

"We have somebody working on it."

After I hung up, I crawled in bed and allowed myself to drift off to sleep. But even as my brain pulled the blinds to darken its rooms, I couldn't ignore an internal blinking red light that said Guidry didn't believe what I'd told him. When I woke up, the red light was still blinking, but I didn't know exactly what Guidry didn't believe or why he didn't believe it.

It was almost time for my afternoon rounds, so I pulled my hair into a ponytail and put on fresh clothes. Then I clattered down the stairs and across the cypress deck to Michael's back door. The gumbo and rice had disappeared, probably into freezer containers, and Michael had disappeared too. Damn. I had hoped he would give me something else to eat. It had been almost four hours since the little bowl of sweetened rice I'd had for breakfast, and it had long since been converted into energy. Now I needed a new source. Preferably one that didn't require any effort on my part, because I was still drained from the morning's shock.

I could have dived into Michael's cavernous refrigerator and found something to eat, but that was almost sure to require heating something or slicing something or spreading mayo or mustard on something, all of which seemed as daunting as climbing Everest.

Ella Fitzgerald trotted into the kitchen and made a few musical firping and trilling sounds, but that didn't fill my empty stomach or tell me where Michael was. I got a handful of cookies from the jar on the counter, gave Ella a pat on the head and promised her I would groom her when I came home that night, and trudged out to the Bronco. Tossing back cookies, I drove to Tom Hale's condo.

From the living room where he was watching TV, Tom said, "Hey, Dixie. Have you heard about this?"

I went to stand beside his wheelchair and looked at the screen, where a young woman pointed at a spot that had been roped off with yellow crime-scene tape. Under the shot on the screen, a hyperventilating banner told us we were watching a special news bulletin. To prove it, the young woman was pertly announcing that a woman had been murdered in the house behind the tape. She sounded so thrilled you would have thought she was reporting a sale on Manolo Blahniks. Not that I've ever worn Manolo Blahniks, but sometimes when I'm waiting on line at Publix, I leaf through a *Vogue*, so I know what they are.

Tom said, "That happened over at Fish Hawk Lagoon."

"I know, I was there when they found her body."

Tom turned his wheelchair to look directly at me. "What is it with you? You have a magnet that attracts dead bodies?"

"I just happened to be next door when her cat ran out, and I went to see why he was out. I saw bloody paw prints from the front door and called nine-one-one."

"They don't say who she is."

"They always wait until they've notified the family."

I didn't look at him when I said that. I'd told Michael her name, and I shouldn't have.

"They didn't say how she got killed either. You say there was blood the cat had stepped in?"

Billy Elliot whuffed from the foyer to let me know he had enjoyed listening to me and Tom as much as he could stand, so I used that as an excuse not to answer. Billy needs his daily runs the way hopeless addicts need their fixes. I got his leash from the foyer closet, snapped it on his collar, and let him pull me toward the front door. But inside, a shrill voice was shouting, *She was stabbed to death! Her ex-husband used to carve his initials on her skin with scalpels, and now he's killed her!*

On the way to the elevator, my cell phone rang. Only a handful of people have my cell number, so when it rings I know it's important. Billy Elliot looked over his shoulder when I answered, the expression on his face exactly the way I feel when I hear people answer their phones in public. Like, *Excuse me, but do you have to do that now?*

Without any preamble, Guidry said, "Dixie, what's the guy's name who says he saw the Halston woman leaving her house this morning?"

"Pete Madeira."

"Got a number for him?"

I gave him Pete's cell number, and did not tell him that Pete was a sweet guy, so to be kind to him. Pete was fully capable of taking care of himself, and Guidry was never rude. Except to me, and then I wouldn't exactly call him *rude*, more like confrontive. Personally, I hate confrontive, especially when it's directed toward me.

This time, he thanked me politely and clicked off. The polite part should have comforted me, but somehow it made me suspicious. Why was he being so carefully polite? It was downright weird.

I said, "Damn!" and slammed the phone into my pocket just as the elevator door opened. A man with a cocker spaniel on a leash stepped out with a disapproving look at me. Billy Elliot looked up with an *I told you so* grin and trotted into the elevator ahead of me.

On the ride downstairs, I started thinking about Laura's murder, and my heart began pounding as if it were happening right then. And to me. That's the problem with imagining things. Your mind sees a picture of something that might have happened halfway across the world, and your body thinks it's happening right that moment, and that it's happening to *you*. I'll bet half the people under gravestones gave themselves fatal heart attacks imagining awful things.

By the time we got to the downstairs lobby and went out the front door to the parking lot, I'd got myself under control. At that hour, we couldn't run as freely as we do at four-thirty in the morning when we have the oval blacktop between parked cars all to ourselves. In the mornings, Billy Elliot zips around like he's a young racer again while I lope along behind him trying not to pass out from exertion. Afternoons, we have to skirt the edge of the track while we watch for careless drivers, but it's still a good hard run for both of us.

When we went back upstairs, Tom was at the kitchen table where he does accounting work. I unsnapped Billy Elliot's leash, kissed him goodbye, and slipped out before Tom could ask me anything else about Laura Halston's murder.

By the time I finished with all the other afternoon calls and went to walk Mazie, shadows were lengthening, the late sun was blotted out by treetops, and I had an empty-stomach headache. Guidry's Blazer and several crime-scene cars were still at Laura's house, but the ambulance was gone. That meant the medical examiner had come, examined Laura's body, and zipped it into a plastic body bag for transfer to the morgue.

Inside Mazie's house, Pete sat at the kitchen table with a cup of coffee and a face alternating between happiness and worry.

Mazie lay beside him, her dark eyes full of sadness.

I said, "Have you heard from Hal again?"

Pete nodded. "Jeffrey's out of ICU, and all the neurological tests are good. Hal says they'll probably move him to a regular room soon."

I pulled out a chair and sat down. "Does that mean he won't have any more seizures?"

He shrugged. "I don't know. I guess it does, but I didn't ask. These things are always one step at a time, nobody can say anything for sure, and even if they do they don't always know."

Pete's voice was full of bitter memories that I didn't probe.

"Has Mazie eaten today?"

"A little bit, not much. She's got so much heart, and it's hurting."

Mazie rolled her eyes up to look at us, but she didn't lift her head.

I stood up and got her leash. "Okay, Mazie, it's time for some exercise."

She sighed, but got to her feet. Outside, we walked in the opposite direction from Laura's house. I moved briskly to get Mazie's blood moving, but I kept the walk short. Mazie was panting hard, a sure sign that she was overstressed. Service dogs need to be of service, that's their entire focus in life. Take away the person to whom they give service, and they've lost their purpose. Every day that passed without Jeffrey to watch over would bring more stress to Mazie.

When we went back inside, I pulled out my cell phone and called Hal. He answered in the hushed tones of someone sitting vigil beside a sleeping child.

I said, "Hal, I know this is an interruption, but would you mind speaking to Mazie for a minute? She needs to hear your voice."

There was a moment of silence, and then Hal's voice, thick with suppressed emotion. "Of course, Dixie. Thank you."

I squatted beside Mazie and held the phone to her ear. Her neck stiffened when she heard Hal's voice, but she stayed very still and listened. I couldn't hear what he was saying, just the faint sound of speech. In a minute or two, her tail moved in an almost wag, and her throat worked as if she wanted to make some kind of reply.

I brought the phone to my own ear and heard Hal say, "We love you, Mazie."

I said, "I think Mazie will be happier now."

"Of course she will. I should have thought of it myself."

"Maybe it would be a good idea to tell Jeffrey you talked to her."

"Yes. Yes, I will."

We said quick goodbyes and I clicked my phone closed.

Pete said, "He should have put the phone to Jeffrey's ear, let Jeffrey listen to Mazie. He needs to know that Mazie wants him to come home."

He had an inspired look in his eyes. I didn't want to spoil it by reminding him that Mazie didn't talk.

I said, "She'll probably eat better now. Next time Hal calls, let Mazie listen to him for a minute. When Jeffrey's up to it, he can talk to her too."

I left him and Mazie looking slightly happier than they'd been when I arrived. Driving away, I did not allow my head to turn toward Laura's house. I could not bear another thought of her murder. There would be time enough for that tomorrow.

CHAPTER 16

When I got home, an orange sun was hanging above the edge of the glittering sea, its heart visibly beating as it gathered courage to drop into that vast unknown. Michael and Paco were standing on their deck raptly watching, and when I joined them they barely acknowledged my presence. We all stood in fixed fascination as the giant orb suddenly let go and slid into those waiting watery arms, turning the sea bronze and sending up piercing golden rays that gilded the wings of celebratory gulls.

Michael put out a hand and squeezed the back of my neck. "Supper's almost ready."

I was so near starving that I felt like my navel had sucked in and stuck to my backbone.

I said, "I'm past ready," and thundered up the stairs to shower and pull on baggy pants and a loose T.

Barefoot, I hustled down the stairs and into the kitchen, where the big butcher-block island was set for three. Michael was at the stove. Paco was beside the island tossing a green salad. Ella Fitzgerald was on her bar stool. They all looked up when I came in and waved something—spatula, salad spoon, tail.

I was sure Michael had told Paco about Laura's murder, but by unspoken agreement nobody mentioned it. While Michael dished up whatever we were eating and Paco put salad into three salad bowls, I poured three glasses of Shiraz from the open bottle sitting on the butcher block. The fact that three wineglasses were out instead of two meant Paco wasn't on duty that night. I didn't comment, I just noted it and felt a bit more relaxed. Those of us who love people whose jobs put them in mortal danger live in a constant state of red alert, even when we aren't aware of it. Having already lost a firefighter father and a deputy husband, I take danger seriously. It isn't just an idea, it's a lurking shadow always ready to destroy your happiness.

Michael set down three plates of yummy-smelling something, opened the oven and mitted a hot loaf of bread onto a dish towel, flopped the sides of the towel over it, and tossed it on the table. We all took seats. Ella Fitzgerald's whiskers twitched, but otherwise she made a good show of not being interested.

I looked at my plate. "Oooh."

Lightly sautéed sea scallops lay over a heap of white beans. The white beans were atop a mound of steamed fresh spinach leaves. The whole thing was topped with a scattering of chopped red tomatoes. It was a red, white, and green dish, sort of an Italian flag of food.

Michael nodded modestly. "New idea. Try it."

I already knew before I took a bite that I'd love it. Anything Michael makes is delicious, and this was downright soul-stirring. The white beans were flavored with garlic and something else that raised them above ordinary white beans, the scallops were delicately sweet and tender, and the spinach and tomatoes made everything else sit up and take notice. I tried not to make a pig of myself, but I had two helpings, plus two hunks of hot bread with butter.

My idea of heaven is a place where people who love one another gather for good food and good conversation, so I was in heaven. It's good to be able to recognize those heavenly moments, good to be inwardly grateful to be so lucky.

We didn't speak about Laura. Instead, we talked about how much better traffic was now that most of the snowbirds had gone home. Paco told us about a procession of bikini-clad young women on spring break following a line of slow-crossing Mottled Ducks that had stopped traffic on Ocean Avenue that morning, and how nobody in the line of cars had objected to the wait—some because they liked the bikinis and some because they liked the ducks. I said lots of bright cheery things too, the way women do to avoid topics they don't want to talk about. And Michael and Paco nodded and smiled, the way men do when they really aren't listening to a word you say, but they love you and don't want you to guess they're thinking about carburetors or football scores or whatever it is that men think about.

After Todd and Christy died, especially in that terrible first year, the only person I told my feelings to was a shrink I went to for a while. I never told Michael and Paco that I wanted to die as well. I never let them hear me rail about the half-blind old man who had run into my husband and child in the parking lot. I never told them how I despised the state for allowing people to renew their driver's license without a visual exam, how furious I was at God for allowing my husband and baby to be taken from me. Michael and Paco had been almost as devastated as I was. Dumping all my emotions on them would have made them feel even worse.

The problem with only telling the good happy stuff is that all the bad, scary, sad stuff that doesn't get told ferments and grows like underground mold, and you never know when it may reach its nasty fingers up and grab you by the throat.

After dinner I helped them clean the kitchen and then told them good night. No matter how shocked I was over Laura's murder, I still had to post my pet visits for the day. I finished entering all the information a little before nine o'clock and was halfway through undressing for bed when the phone rang. I let the machine answer.

A crisp woman's voice said, "Ms. Hemingway, this is Ruth Avery at the Bayfront Village Nursing Unit. Cora Mathers asked me to call and let you know she's a patient here."

I did a one-legged hop for the phone, but she had hung up. In a breathless rush, I pulled on jeans and a less saggy T-shirt and charged downstairs.

Cora Mathers is the grandmother of a former client who got herself murdered while I was taking care of her cat, and she's become very dear to me. She lives in a posh apartment her granddaughter bought her at Bayfront Village, one of Sarasota's best retirement communities. The thought that she was in Bayfront's nursing unit pushed my heart into my throat.

Outside the nursing unit at Bayfront, I careened into the parking lot and practically jumped out of the Bronco before it came to a stop. A smattering of cars in the parking lot said visiting hours weren't over yet, but I knew I didn't have much time. A pleasant-faced woman at the reception desk seemed to brace herself as she watched me barrel into the lobby.

I said, "I'm here to see Cora Mathers. And don't tell me I can't see her, because I'll raise such a stink you can't believe."

The woman turned to peck keys on a computer keyboard and peer at a screen.

Mildly, she said, "She's in Room Two-oh-four."

I gave her a curt nod, probably the way Genghis Khan acknowledged people who stepped out of his way when he was trampling over the countryside, and took the stairs instead of the elevator. I didn't have time to wait for an elevator.

I didn't have to look for Room 204. It was directly across the hall from the stairwell, and the door was open. An old sitcom from the seventies was blaring from a small TV on a movable metal contraption at the foot of the first hospital bed, where a woman with drug-glazed eyes was lying flat on her back looking at the screen.

Hurrying around a curtain separating her bed from the next one, I found Cora sitting in an easy chair. She had one foot propped on a stool and was looking out the window at pale spots of sailboats on the darkened bay. Soaking wet, Cora might weigh eighty pounds, and she's roughly the height of an average sixth-grade child. Except for an exasperated look on her face, she looked normal—which is to say she looked frail and old, but healthy.

When my grandmother was Cora's age—closer to ninety than eighty—she went beach walking every day, read everything published, and seriously considered taking up wind surfing. Cora, on the other hand, is the kind of woman who peaks at fifteen, is matronly at forty, and old at sixty. Age doesn't have anything to do with how many times the earth has revolved around the sun since one's birth, it's about health and being protected. If circumstances had been different, Cora might have ended up as robust as my grandmother, but she started out living hand-to-mouth and scared. Now she's living high on the hog and lonely. In either case, she has faced reality without losing her faith in goodness, which I consider a major life accomplishment.

When she saw me, she threw both arms out wide and grinned. "Well, hallelujah and pass the biscuits! I've been waiting for you all this damn day."

I leaned to hug her slight shoulders. "I didn't know you were here. What happened?"

"Oh, it's the silliest thing. I slipped in the bathroom last night and twisted my ankle a little bit, and nothing would do them but I had to come over here and spend the night. Now they won't let me go home until the swelling goes down. It's plain stupid, is what it is, so I told them to call you."

She was trying for anger, but I could see fear in her eyes. When a resident of a retirement community is no longer able to live alone, they are routinely moved to the facility's nursing wing, and their apartment is sold. Every old person fears they'll be unfairly railroaded into a nursing unit while they're still capable of living alone.

I knelt beside the stool to look at her ankle. It was a little puffy but not bruised. I poked it with a tentative finger, and Cora flinched.

I said, "They feed you okay in here?"

She brightened. "I had bacon and eggs for breakfast."

"No kidding. Real bacon or pulverized turkey skin?"

"Real pork. And real biscuits too. Lunch wasn't bad either, and for dinner I had chicken and dumplings."

Personally, I never have understood the appeal of boiled chicken with pieces of dough dropped on it, but I made enthusiastic noises before I bent over her bedside table to make sure her water carafe was filled.

I said, "I guess they can afford to go all out when they know you'll just be here a day or two."

She looked thoughtful. "That's true. I don't think they feed the really sick people that good." She pointed toward the curtain and lowered her voice. "She's sick as a dog, and all she got for breakfast was Cream of Wheat."

I said, "As long as they're feeding you good, it might not be such a bad idea to let them wait on you until your ankle stops hurting. That racket from the TV bother you?"

She rolled her eyes. "Plays that thing all day long. I think she's a little, you know." She twirled her forefinger at her temple with gossipy pleasure. "Poor thing, nobody comes to see her."

More than likely, nobody had come to see Cora either, but she obviously considered herself more popular than her roommate because I was there. When you get down to it, it's not the fact of things that are important, but how we interpret them. She had more color in her cheeks now that she had perked up, and fear had left her eyes. My own fears were back in the box where they belonged too. Cora was okay, and Bayfront Village had done the right thing to put her in the nursing unit where they could take care of her.

Behind the curtain, the TV noise stopped and an oily male voice said, "And how are we today?"

I stood up straight with my ears tingling. Where had I heard that voice?

A shaky old woman's voice answered. "I'd of stayed in Mississippi if it hadn't of been for the hurricane."

With icy contempt, the man said, "Do you have any idea how weary I am of hearing you say that?"

Cora and I stiffened and gave each other raised eyebrows.

With more force to her voice, the woman said, "I'd of stayed in Mississippi if it hadn't of been for the hurricane."

The man said, "God, what a waste of time and money! All you decompensating old Binswangers should have been smothered at your first cerebral infarcts."

The back of my neck prickled, and I spun to glare at the white curtain. I didn't know what a Binswanger was, but I knew the man had just said something cruel.

A moment of silence followed, and then his oily voice again. "You and the rest of the world will be better off when you're gone."

I couldn't stand it anymore.

I said, "What the hell?" and stepped around the curtain to confront the woman's nasty visitor. All I saw was a man's broad back hurrying out the door. The bastard hadn't even had the grace to say goodbye. I took a moment to make sure the woman was okay, then hurried to the door and looked down the corridor. An elderly man in a wheelchair was pushing himself down the hall, but he didn't look as if he had enough air in him to speak above a whisper.

A nurse came out of the room next door and saw me scanning the hall. "You need something?"

I said, "A man was just in here. Did you see him?"

"A man?"

"He was talking to Cora Mathers's roommate. I don't know her name."

"Grayberg." I noticed she didn't give a first name. Maybe when you stop normally responding to other people, they stop thinking of you as a two-named person.

"He said some cruel things to her."

The nurse studied me. "Are you related to Cora?"

"He told Mrs. Grayberg she should have been smothered when she had her first stroke." That wasn't exactly what he'd said, but it was what he'd meant.

She said, "I didn't see you get off the elevator. The

nurse's station is right by the elevator, and I didn't see you get off."

"I took the stairs. Oh, that's probably where he went. He went down the stairs."

"What did he look like?"

"I just heard his voice and saw his back as he left. He was big."

"Ms. Grayberg watches TV a lot. Maybe it was a man on TV."

"No, it was a real man."

She turned away and started down the hall. Over her shoulder, she said, "I'll watch for strange men."

I could tell she didn't believe me. When I thought about it, I didn't blame her.

I went back to Cora's room and spoke to Mrs. Grayberg. "Was that your son who was just here?"

Her face twisted in a rictus of despair. "I'd of stayed in Mississippi if it hadn't of been for the hurricane."

I couldn't think of any appropriate answer, so I turned up the sound on her TV and went back to Cora's side of the curtain.

I whispered, "Was that Mrs. Grayberg's son?"

"Is that her name? We haven't actually met, what with her being so loony and all. I wouldn't worry about her boy. I don't imagine she even heard him."

From the despair I'd seen on the woman's face, I thought she'd heard plenty, but I didn't say so. It was probably better for Cora to be complacent about him than to be vaguely alarmed like I was.

I promised to come back the next day, kissed the top of Cora's downy head, and retraced my path past her roommate's bed. She had stopped crying and gave me a slight smile.

She said, "I'd of stayed in Mississippi if it hadn't of been for the hurricane."

From the other side of the curtain, Cora laughed. I gave Ms. Grayberg a friendly wave and hoped nobody told her that Florida got hurricanes too.

As I went down the stairs, I probed all the corners of my mind, trying to remember where I'd heard the man's smug, pompous voice before. But it was like trying to dislodge a speck of lettuce stuck in your back teeth. Every time I thought I had it, it stayed locked in place.

I made it all the way to the parking lot before I remembered where I'd been when I first heard the man's voice. It was so unlikely that I sat in the Bronco and argued with myself for a long time before I pulled out my cell phone and called Guidry.

He answered with a curt, "Guidry here."

I said, "I was just at the Bayfront Village Nursing Unit, and a man came in the room to talk to the woman in the other bed. I know it doesn't make any sense, but you need to know who he was."

A beat or two passed, and Guidry said, "Dixie, I'm not even going to try to understand what you just said. Do you have something to tell me?"

I stuck my tongue out at the phone and took a deep breath.

"Cora Mathers is in the nursing unit at Bayfront. She has a roommate named Grayberg. While I was visiting Cora, a man came to visit Mrs. Grayberg. I didn't see him because a curtain was between us, but I recognized his voice, and I'm positive it was the same man who called Laura Halston while I was at her house. She said she met him at Sarasota Memorial in the emergency room. Maybe he's a doctor. Or a nurse."

"You didn't see him. You didn't talk to him. But you're sure it was the same man."

"I know it sounds crazy, but he has a distinctive

voice, and he speaks in a peculiar way. He left before I could get a look at him."

"Peculiar how? Lisp? Stutter?"

"He talks like a college professor too full of himself. Pedantic. Prissy."

"So you want me to go to the hospital unit over at Bayfront and ask this Mrs. Grayberg about him?"

"Well ah, Mrs. Grayberg is a little bit senile. She might not be able to give you much information."

Guidry heaved a deep sigh. "I can't talk any longer, Dixie. I'll catch you later."

He clicked off without saying goodbye, leaving me staring at the phone and wondering what he was avoiding telling me.

CHAPTER 17

I drove home in a fog of fatigue and fury. Even though I'd told Guidry about the other men who'd been irrationally drawn to Laura, I knew it was her husband who had killed her. The man had to be completely insane to think he could follow her to Siesta Key and kill her without anybody knowing. His colleagues would know he was gone, and everybody who knew him and Laura would suspect him the minute her murder became public knowledge. If he'd been a nobody, he might already be cooling his odious heels in a jail cell. Since he was famous and wealthy, he would have an attorney to forestall the moment when homicide detectives talked to him. Guidry was probably collecting irrefutable evidence before he moved.

Just the thought of Guidry investigating Laura's murder sent a chill into my bones, because it was a reminder of Guidry's job. Every day, he dealt with murder—the grisliest, ugliest, most sordid side of humanity.

Being involved with any law enforcement officer means being vicariously close to violence, at least to some degree, but being involved with a homicide detective means being close to the ultimate effects of brutal hatred. I wasn't sure I was strong enough for that. I wasn't sure I *wanted* to be strong enough for that. I wasn't sure I could spend my nights in bed with a man who spent his days investigating murders.

Not that I'd been invited to spend any nights with Guidry. Not that he had ever even hinted that it was on his mind. But it must have been somewhere in *my* mind, and I wished it weren't.

At home, I trudged up the stairs to my apartment and fell into bed. Before I went to sleep, I remembered the noise Laura and I had heard while we ate dinner. Could it have been her husband? Could he have been lurking outside, waiting to make sure Laura lived in that house? I wished I had gone outside and investigated. If I had, he might have been frightened away, and Laura might not have died.

I woke with a start from the remnants of a bad dream. In the dream, my father had hit me. The dream was true. I had been seven years old at the time, and my gentle, patient father had smacked my bottom for the first and only time in my life.

He had been about to leave for his shift at the fire-house, and I had sassed my mother one time too many. "You don't speak to your mother like that," he said. "It's rude and it's unkind, and it's unfair."

I'd been so shocked that I yelled, "I hate you! I wish you were dead!" and ran to my room. Within twenty-four hours, he had died saving a child in a burning house.

With a child's belief in my own magical powers, I believed for a long time that I had killed him. Even now, I sometimes wonder about it. He hadn't been the kind of man to hit little children, and maybe he had been so upset over my hateful words that night that he'd lost his concentration and got careless.

When Todd and Christy were killed, that childish belief in magical powers must have returned because I had the same kind of nagging guilt. I knew the things the religious fanatics said weren't true—that God had not punished me for being a working mother. Even so, I'd grieved that I hadn't remembered to buy Cheerios and orange juice when I went grocery shopping, because if I had, Todd and Christy wouldn't have been in that Publix parking lot when the old man hit the gas instead of his brake.

Now, lying in the darkness before my alarm sounded, I wallowed for a few minutes in slimy remorse. Then I rolled out of bed and stomped to the bathroom, where I stood in front of the medicine cabinet and glared into my own eyes.

I said, "Don't start that crap again! You didn't cause your father to die, you didn't cause Todd and Christy to die, and you sure as hell didn't cause Laura Halston to be murdered!"

My eyes in the mirror gazed back at me with a secret knowing. The old irrational guilt was just a way to cover up what I was truly feeling. I hate it when I come up with insights that push me to be honest with myself, especially when the truth is something I don't know what to do with.

The truth was that primal fear had its talons deep into my shoulders, deeper than I'd realized. No matter what, I had to do everything in my power to make sure Laura's killer was found and convicted. Otherwise, the fear of being a vulnerable victim might be an unwelcome companion for the rest of my life.

CHAPTER 18

Mercifully, the morning calls went smoothly. No accidents to clean up, no signs of separation anxiety in any of the pets, no wistful calls from any of the absent pet owners about *their* separation anxiety. Before I went to Mazie's house, I called Pete to tell him I would be a little late. He said Hal had called to say Jeffrey had been moved to a regular room.

"Hal says he's talking and drinking fluids, but he's not happy. He's asking for Mazie and crying a lot."

Pete and I exchanged silence for a few seconds, both of us imagining a little boy trying to comprehend all the strangeness of a hospital without his best friend.

Pete said, "Mazie's not happy either. Hal talked to her again, but she's still agitated. She's not eating at all, Dixie, and she's not drinking but a little. I brushed her and took her out to do her business, but she's not a happy dog."

"She won't be happy until Jeffrey comes home, Pete. But there's not anything you can do beyond what you're doing."

He said, "The detective called about me seeing that lady next door. He didn't seem to believe me."

"Homicide detectives always sound suspicious."

"They're still over there, all those law people."

I told him I'd see him later, and drove over the north bridge to the mainland and the Bayfront nursing unit. This time I took the elevator so the day-duty nurses could see me get off. A nurse at the desk looked up and smiled as I approached her.

I said, "Hi, I'm here to see Cora Mathers in Two-oh-four."

"Are you the one taking her back to her condo? She said you'd be here."

"Can I ask you something? What's a Binswanger?"

She looked up at me and frowned. "Ms. Mathers doesn't have Binswanger."

"I just wondered what it was because a man called her roommate a Binswanger last night. I'd never heard the word before."

"Who called her that?"

"I didn't see him, I just heard him. He said, 'All you old Binswangers should have been smothered when you had your first infarct.' He had a priggy voice like an announcer on a classical radio station. Do you have any idea who that could have been?"

A mottled red flush rose up her neck and face. "Nobody on staff here would have said that to her."

"I went out in the hall looking for him, but he must have taken the stairs. Could it have been an orderly?"

Her entire body had gone rigid. "I hardly think so. Binswanger disease is a rare form of subcortical dementia."

"So anybody familiar with that word would have medical training."

"As I said, nobody on our staff would have said that to Ms. Grayberg."

"Uh-huh. Well, I'll go get Cora now."

No longer friendly, the woman watched me through

narrowed eyes as I went toward Cora's room. She would probably get together with the night nurse and talk about Cora's crazy friend who was spreading false gossip about a male nurse being mean to the patients.

In 204, Ms. Grayberg was watching an old *I Love Lucy* show. She didn't take her eyes off the TV screen as I walked behind it. On the other side of the dividing curtain, Cora was dressed and sitting in an easy chair reading the morning *Herald-Tribune*. She didn't seem surprised to see me, just smiled and stood up.

She said, "I'm glad you're here. I'm ready to get out of this joint."

She wore a loose muumuu thing that swallowed her. One hand held it up above her little feet, while she reached for her handbag with the other hand.

She said, "I'm having to walk careful, because I'm afraid I'll trip on this dress. I ordered it from a catalog, and it's a little too long."

It was at least a foot too long, and it looked dangerous as hell. I had mental images of her tripping on it and breaking some of her fragile bones.

"Your ankle okay now?"

"It's still a mite tender, but I can nurse it at my own place. They said keep it elevated and put ice on it. That won't be hard."

A volunteer charged in pushing a wheelchair. I wondered if somebody had told her to get Cora out as quickly as possible, or if she always moved that fast. As soon as Cora got settled in the chair with her skirt tucked in so it didn't drag on the ground, I took over the pushing while the volunteer trotted along by our side. The elevator door was already open, and we were gone in no time. I noticed that everybody at the nurse's desk was too preoccupied to tell Cora goodbye. Either they knew who had been so mean to Ms. Grayberg, or they thought I was a lying troublemaker and they didn't want to encourage me.

I pushed the wheelchair across the Bayfront campus to the main building, where everybody from the doorman to the concierge rushed forward to welcome Cora home. The manager came out to assure her that she had only to call the dining room at any time and somebody would bring up anything she wanted. I was pleased to see how well she was treated, and Cora was as gracious as the Queen Mother flaunting her power. For the elderly, money not only buys decent health care, it buys respect.

Upstairs, she got up from the wheelchair lifting her dress with both hands.

I said, "Maybe it would be better if I took that dress to the tailor and got it shortened. Then you won't have to hike it up when you walk."

She looked surprised, as if the idea of shortening a too-long dress was a novel idea.

She said, "I'll go change into something else."

I held my breath while she shuffled into her bedroom. While I waited, I heated a teakettle of water and got out her tea things, because Cora likes to be ready for a cup of tea anytime she wants one.

Cora's apartment has a wide glassed sunroom facing the bay, pink tile floors, a spacious living room, and a small kitchen behind a breakfast bar. It's airy and high-ceilinged and comfortable, thanks to the generosity of her granddaughter. When I'd got her tea things ready and made sure her TV remote was handy, I stood at the glass wall and inhaled the view—robin's-egg-blue sky fluffed with cumulus clouds, white sails dotting a bay whose depths were signaled by violet, purple, jade, and emerald. With vistas like that, people in Sarasota don't need art on their walls.

Cora came out carrying the dress and wearing a velour warm-up suit with baggy pants that she'd pulled on crooked so the crotch seam angled up toward her right hip.

As she handed me the dress, she said, "Ethan Crane called me the other day. He asked about you. I think he's sweet on you."

I made a mumbling sound that I hoped sounded like an answer and made a big to-do of folding the dress into a little square. Ethan Crane is a drop-dead handsome attorney who'd handled Cora's granddaughter's estate. It was true that he was interested in me. It was also true that any unmarried, unattached, undead woman with estrogen in her veins would have been thrilled to have Ethan want her. So what the heck was wrong with me?

Before Christmas, Ethan had invited me to dinner at his house, and I'd gone planning to lose my second virginity—the one I'd assumed after my husband died—but Ethan hadn't given me a chance. Instead, he had walked me to my car after dinner, given me a kiss that seared the soles of my feet, and sent me home hot and astonished.

We probably would have had some follow-up dates if circumstances hadn't intervened. Like a shoot-out when a man got killed, and like Guidry being there when I needed somebody. Ethan had pulled back and seemed to be waiting for a sign from me—either a go-ahead sign or a closed shop sign. The problem was that I didn't know myself well enough to know which sign I wanted to give him. Especially now, when Laura's murder was a stone in my shoe and the ultimate result of Jeffrey's surgery something I couldn't even let myself think about.

Cora's shrewd old eyes were sizing me up. "Something's wrong. What is it?"

I hesitated. I didn't want to stir memories of the way Cora's granddaughter had been killed by mentioning Laura's murder, and I didn't want to make her sad by telling her about Jeffrey's surgery. On the other hand, protecting people from the truth is another way of shutting them out.

I said, "I'm concerned about a dog I'm taking care of. He belongs to a little boy who had brain surgery to stop seizures, but I don't know yet if the surgery was a success. The dog and the little boy are extremely close, and the dog doesn't understand what happened to him. She's under a lot of stress, and there's not much I can do for her. It's impossible to communicate with animals and explain things to them."

Like Paco, Cora went straight to the nub. "It's a terrible thing to lose a child."

I didn't want to go there, didn't want to be reminded that death is always in the wings. Whether you're three or ninety-three, death knows your name.

I said, "Cora, do you think any of your neighbors might know who that man was that visited Ms. Grayberg over in the nursing unit? I don't like the idea of somebody going around talking to sick people the way he talked to her."

"You know, I've been thinking about that man, and I think I know who he was. I don't know his name, but he drives people to the doctor. I was on the elevator one time with him and a man that lives here. Prissy-voiced man. As I remember, he was on the pudgy side, and he had big fat lips."

"He works here at Bayfront?"

"I guess he must. Anyway, he drives people. But don't

worry about him, Dixie. And don't worry about that little boy either. You can only do what you can do, and that's all you can do."

I grinned and took her muumuu. "You sound positively zen."

She looked pleased. "Well, I do try to be positive."

I kissed her goodbye and zipped off with the muumuu. I felt more positive too.

Downstairs, the lobby was buzzing with good-looking white-haired people carrying tennis rackets or shopping bags or just gathered in groups to gossip. All that energy and good humor was almost enough to make me nostalgic for growing old.

Instead of going out the front doors, I detoured to speak to the concierge at the front desk. I said, "You know, Ms. Mathers was in the nursing unit for a couple of days."

"I know, I'm so glad it was something minor."

"She had a roommate over there named Grayberg. I heard a man talking to Mrs. Grayberg while I was there, and I thought I recognized his voice. He left before I could make sure. I think he may work here driving people to the doctor. Do you happen to know who it might have been?"

She blinked at me. "I wouldn't know."

"He talked like a schoolteacher. You know, the boring kind that nobody listens to. He was nasty to her."

Twin lines appeared between her eyebrows, and she went professional.

"I'm sure it wasn't anybody connected with Bayfront. You'd have to ask Ms. Grayberg who he was."

"Thanks, I'll do that."

I gave her a big friendly smile to remind her I was on her good side and went out to the porte cochere, where a valet galloped off to rescue my car. When he eased it under the portico, I handed him a couple of bills. Tipping was prohibited at Bayfront, but he and I both knew that green was a color that got me quicker service.

He said, "You been visiting Ms. Mathers? She's a sweet old lady."

Cora would have despised being called a sweet old lady, but I smiled and agreed.

I said, "When she was over in the nursing unit, a man came in and spoke to her roommate. He had a deep voice and used lots of big words like he was reading the dictionary. I think he may work here as a driver. Do you have any idea who he was?"

He grinned. "That old fart does talk like he's reading a dictionary. That's a good one. That would be Frederick. Used to work here, but he got fired for being weird."

My pulse thrummed, and I had to clench my hand to keep it from throwing more money at him. "What's his last name?"

"Don't know, you'd have to ask the manager. But he's really ticked at old Fred. The dumb boob lost a woman over at Sarasota Memorial. Took her to ER and forgot about her."

I said, "Ms. Grayberg."

He looked surprised. "You know about that?"

"I heard some people talking about it over at the nursing unit, but I don't know the details."

He leaned close, eager to give me the scoop.

"Well, see, Frederick drove people shopping or to doctors' appointments, things like that. Sort of a personal driver, but anybody living here could hire him. So Ms. Grayberg had him take her to Saks to get something to wear to the birthday party they were throwing for her here—you know, they do that for everybody when they make it to one of the big ones, eighty, ninety, a hundred. Anyway, while she was there she had a stroke. So instead of calling nine-one-one like he should've, Frederick put her in the car and took her down the street to Sarasota Memorial. Took her to the emergency room, and then the dumb cluck forgot about her. Didn't call here to report it or anything. The hospital had to look in her purse and get her address to know where to call. So Frederick got fired."

My body wanted to jump out of the car and run inside and ask the manager what Frederick's last name was, but my head told me to be cool. I listened to my head for a change, told the valet goodbye, and drove sedately out of the parking lot. As soon as I saw a driveway into a business lot, I whipped in and took out my cell phone to call Guidry.

I got his voice message, so I was denied the pleasure of saying "I told you so."

Instead, I said, "The man who came to Laura Halston's door when I was there used to be a driver at Bayfront Village. Took people shopping and to doctors' appointments. His name is Frederick. I don't know his last name, but he has fat lips. He was with Ms. Grayberg when she had a stroke. He drove her to the ER at Sarasota Memorial, but he didn't call Bayfront to report her stroke, and they fired him for it. I imagine if you check ER records, you'll find that Ms. Grayberg was there about the same time Laura Halston was there with a pulled knee."

I closed the phone and pulled out of the lot into traffic. I was quite pleased with myself. Smug, even. I'd found out who the man was who'd stalked Laura and come to her door demanding to see her. Since it seemed to me that nobody else was making a lot of effort to get answers, I was glad I was one who was. What the heck was wrong with everybody else?

CHAPTER 19

I was so hungry the palm fronds hanging over the street were beginning to look tasty, but I pulled into Dr. Phyllis Layton's parking lot and hurried inside. I wasn't sure I'd been right when I told Pete there was nothing more he could do to make Mazie happy. If anybody knew better, it would be Dr. Layton.

I charged up to the receptionist's desk so fast that my Keds probably made skid marks when I stopped.

I said, "I don't have an appointment, but if Dr. Layton has a minute, I need to ask her advice about a dog I'm taking care of. She's the dog's vet. The dog is Mazie, belongs to Hal and Gillis Richards."

Behind the receptionist, Dr. Layton's head popped around a corner, with a look in her eyes that said she was a damn busy woman and didn't have time for pop-in visits from pet sitters, but that she knew me well enough to know I must have good reason to be interrupting her schedule. Waggling her fingers at me, she came around to open the door into her inner sanctum.

A comfortably plump African-American woman roughly my age, Dr. Layton has the ability to soothe and command at the same time. I felt more confident the moment we stepped into a treatment room.

She leaned against a metal table and said, "There's a problem with Mazie?"

"She's terribly depressed, has been ever since Jeffrey left to have surgery."

She looked surprised. "I thought that was scheduled for next month."

"It was, but there was a cancellation or something and the hospital got him in a month early, and the surgery was Monday morning. He's out of ICU and in a room, which I hope means the surgery was a success, but Mazie is distraught. She's not eating or drinking much, she's panting and sighing a lot, and she runs around the house all day looking for Jeffrey. I have a full-time sitter with her, a sweet man—he's reading to her and playing the saxophone for her—but she's more agitated every day."

Dr. Layton smiled. "He's playing the saxophone for her? That's nice." More somberly, she said, "A pet's grief can be so intense it can cause them to become ill."

"Jeffrey will be home in a week or so."

"But Mazie doesn't know that. Besides, the future doesn't exist for a pet. All they know is right now, and right now Jeffrey is gone."

Briskly, she went to a wall cabinet and moved some small dark bottles around.

"If this were a permanent separation, I might give her something stronger, like Prozac. But I don't like to medicate an animal unless it's absolutely necessary." She chose a bottle and handed it to me. "This is an herbal supplement that might help calm her. Put ten drops in her water bowl every time you give her fresh water. If that doesn't help, call me and we'll try something stronger."

I thanked her and slipped the bottle in my pocket. Guiltily, I wished I had talked to Dr. Layton sooner. I was letting other things distract me and make me less focused on my work than I should have been, and I didn't like that about myself.

Since it was on my way, I made a fast stop at the Kitty Haven to check on Leo.

Marge Preston took me back to Leo's private suite, a cubicle furnished with a litter box, climbing tower, and a small TV set that played kitty fantasies all day. It was actually a jail cell, and Leo knew it, but it was a posh jail cell with the best food and tenderest jailers any incarcerated cat could ever hope for.

He looked healthy and well fed, but pissed. I didn't blame him. Through no fault of his own, he'd been whisked away from a spacious house and a loving human to this small world with strangers taking care of him. He didn't know me any better than he knew Marge and her assistants, but I spent a few minutes with him anyway. I told him that Laura's sister was coming, and that she would soon take him to a new home. I told him that his world was going to get better in time, and that he would one day be as happy as he had been with Laura.

Marge heard me. As I was leaving, she said, "I hope you were telling Leo the truth."

"I hope so too."

Marge never quizzes me about the cats I bring her, she never pries into their home lives. This time, though, I'd brought her a cat with dried blood on his paws, and she would surely have guessed that the "death in the family" I'd mentioned had been the murder all over the papers and news shows.

She said, "I'm giving Leo vitamin C supplements for stress."

"That's good, Marge. I'll let you know when his family arrives."

The cats in Marge's front room gave me looks of

sweet disdain as I left. They probably considered me underprivileged because I wasn't lucky enough to live full-time at the Kitty Haven.

I was now beyond famished, but my rule for myself is that I don't eat breakfast until I've finished every pet call. I still had to take Mazie for a run, and I particularly wanted to give her the drops from Dr. Layton.

At Fish Hawk Lagoon, the crime-scene people were still at Laura's house, and Guidry's Blazer was among the cars at the curb. I parked in Mazie's driveway and rapped on the door before I opened it and went in.

Pete sat on the sofa with his saxophone in his lap as if he'd just finished playing it. Mazie lay on the floor in front of him.

With an edge to my voice, I said, "Pete, it's not a good idea to leave the door unlocked."

He shot me an annoyed look. "I never lock doors."

"There's a killer loose, maybe you should."

We stared at each other for a beat, each of us defensive and tense. Mazie got up from her spot and made a soft whining noise. Her distress at our snippy voices made me feel like an idiot.

I said, "I'm sorry, Pete. I've let it all get to me."

"I guess I have too. But it can't go on, Dixie. It just can't go on much longer."

He looked close to tears, and I knew he wasn't concerned about a killer. He was distressed because it had been necessary for Jeffrey to undergo major surgery. He was distressed because Mazie was so sad. He was distressed because he was a man accustomed to making people laugh and feel better, and he felt helpless.

I said, "I stopped at Mazie's vet this morning and talked to her about Mazie. She said it's normal for Mazie to be grieving, because she thinks Jeffrey has gone away forever."

I pulled the bottle from my pocket and headed for the kitchen.

"She gave me these drops to put in her water bowl. I'll put some in now, and next time you give her fresh water, put ten drops in. Dr. Layton says that will help calm her. If it doesn't, she'll give her something stronger."

Pete followed me, skepticism and uneasiness making his eyebrows shimmy. "The doctor sent *drugs*?"

"No, it's something herbal. From flowers, I think. She knows Mazie. She wouldn't give her anything that wasn't safe."

I rummaged around in a junk drawer, found a marking pen, and wrote *10 drops* on the bottle.

"I've marked the number of drops. Just put them in every time you give her fresh water."

"She's not drinking much water."

"I know, but let's give it a try."

With Pete suspiciously examining the label on the bottle, I got Mazie's leash and led her outside. We both needed to run off our tension, so as soon as she was willing, I took off at a fast clip. As we ran, I kept glancing right and left, peering into the thick foliage beside the sidewalk and then across the street at the hibiscus hedge that hid the jogging path. Laura's killer could be hidden nearby, watching all the crime-scene activity and feeling proud of himself for causing it.

We ran hard for about five minutes, then stopped to pant awhile before we started back at a more leisurely pace. Mazie seemed less tense, but her forehead was still furrowed in doggy concern.

As we approached her driveway, I saw Guidry and Pete standing next to my Bronco. Pete looked defensive, and Guidry was pulling his notebook from his pocket as if ready to take notes.

As usual, Guidry looked like he was about to give last-minute instructions to the lackeys who ran his mansion. Black linen jacket that I could imagine being cut by an Italian tailor with a thin mustache and an attitude, chocolate trousers with enough wrinkle to let you know they weren't made from the cheap crap that doesn't crease, and a soft charcoal shirt open at the collar. I hated that look. It made me want to go open his jacket and lay my ear to his heart just to listen to it beat. I should have been locked up.

When he heard me and Mazie scuffing up the walk, he looked up and gave me a slight nod. He looked grim, and all the questions I wanted to ask him turned to dust in my throat.

He said, "I'm just verifying some information from Mr. Madeira, and then I need to talk to you."

My heart skipped a beat, but I waited demurely while he and Pete went on with their conversation. It only took a second to know Guidry was asking him about seeing Laura on the day she was killed.

Pete said, "She had a cap pulled down low, one of those baseball caps women wear with their ponytails sticking out."

"You saw a ponytail?"

Testily, Pete said, "I didn't *say* I saw a ponytail, I said that's what women do. Unless they have short hair."

His voice became uncertain as he remembered Laura's short hair. Guidry waited, watching Pete's face.

Pete said, "You know, it may not have been her after all. Come to think of it, I think I did see some hair poking out of that cap. Not a ponytail, but more hair than Laura had. I guess it was some other woman going for a run. They all look alike, with their caps and jogging shorts."

Guidry snapped his notebook closed. "Thanks, Mr. Madeira. That clears up a point we couldn't understand."

Pete looked embarrassed. "Don't think it's because I'm old that I mistook one woman for another. It's the way women dress nowadays."

He and Guidry looked my way, and I drew my knees together under my cargo shorts and T-shirt, and above my Keds—the same kind of running clothes that Laura wore. But I never wore baseball caps.

Guidry said, "It's an understandable mistake."

He gave me a pointed look that meant it was my turn to be questioned.

I handed Mazie's leash off to Pete, told him I'd be back in the afternoon, and waited until he and Mazie had gone inside the house.

Guidry said, "Tell me again when you had dinner with Laura Halston."

"Early Sunday night. I left sometime around seven-thirty, seven-forty-five."

"Pasta?"

"Fetuccini Alfredo and salad."

"Do you mind going in her house and see if you notice anything missing?"

I minded very much. "Guidry, I was only in her house that one time."

"That's one time more than anybody else."

I couldn't argue with that. Numbly, I walked down the sidewalk beside Guidry, waited while he noted the time on the Contamination Sheet by the front door, and then stepped into the house.

Except for black print-lifting dust on every surface, everything in the living room looked pretty much the same as when I'd left Sunday night. In the kitchen, every evidence of our dinner had been cleaned and put away. No wineglasses sitting out, no pasta pot, no salad bowl.

Our lipstick-smeared napkins had disappeared, and I didn't need to open the dishwasher to know that our plates were neatly rinsed and filed inside. Women who live alone don't run their dishwashers every day.

On the counter, a box of dried cat food, with a Post-it note attached. The note had an exclamation point on it, a memo Laura had left herself to buy more. My eyes burned at the memory of how alive Laura had been, how we had both laughed and talked and eaten and drunk as if we had infinity stretched before us.

Guidry looked closely at me. "What is it?"

I cleared my throat. "Nothing. I don't see anything unusual or out of place."

"What's the deal with the cat food?"

"She'd run out, so she put the box there to remind herself to buy more."

He said, "What was she wearing that night?"

I took a minute to think. "Drawstring pants, T-shirt. She was barefoot."

His jaws worked for a second as if he were gnawing on invisible gristle. "That was in the clothes hamper in the bathroom."

I had to ask the question. "Where did he get her?"

"In the shower. Looks like she was taken by surprise."

"He stabbed her?"

"Yep."

I took a deep breath and asked the question I already knew the answer to.

"There was more, wasn't there?"

A shadow crossed Guidry's face, and his lips tightened as if I'd uttered the unsayable. He said, "Her face was disfigured."

I crossed my arms over my chest and looked away from him while I fought to control hot tears that had suddenly filled my eyes. Deputy Morgan had thrown up after he'd seen Laura, and Sergeant Owens had wanted to spare me from seeing her. Laura had been an unusually beautiful woman. Whoever had killed her had wanted to destroy her beauty along with her life.

Carefully, Guidry said, "The mutilation was done postmortem."

I said, "Laura Halston's husband is a sick, sadistic surgeon. He throws scalpels at the ceiling for fun. Mutilating Laura's face is the kind of thing he would do, and have fun doing it."

Guidry didn't respond, just looked at me with level gray eyes.

I said, "She wasn't raped?"

"No rape. And no theft that we know of. She wore some gold and diamond bracelets, and we found a diamond necklace that was pretty valuable."

I understood the implication. Her killer hadn't been a robber or a rapist, he'd been somebody who killed in a furious rage. But the ritualistic cutting was something else. That wasn't rage, it was psychopathic deliberation. And where there is psychopathic ritual, it points to a serial killer. Laura might not be the first person this killer had murdered, nor the last.

I cleared my throat. "What about prints on her body? Deep-tissue X-rays?"

"Negative and negative. Most likely the killer wore gloves."

I closed my eyes against the image of Laura in the shower. She had probably left the bathroom door open, the way women do when they live alone. The killer had probably slipped in while she was showering, pushed the shower curtain aside, and stabbed her while the water continued to run. Laura would have tried to shield herself, would have put up her hands to deflect the blows, but it would have been too late.

It was every woman's nightmare, to be killed at home in her most vulnerable moment.

Guidry said, "Dixie? You all right?"

I said, "Sunday night, there was a noise outside the living room window. A cracking sound, like wood snapping. We thought it was a squirrel knocking a limb against the house, but it could have been somebody outside, somebody waiting for me to leave."

He touched my shoulder lightly. "You couldn't have prevented this, Dixie."

"I want to help find the person who did this. If her husband did it, I want him caught and put away for life."

Guidry's gray eyes were too steady. He was keeping something from me.

I said, "Has anybody talked to the husband yet?"

"We have somebody working on that." His voice was too careful.

"What about her family?"

Guidry started maneuvering me to the front door. "Her sister arrived late yesterday and identified the body. She's at the Ritz."

I would have expected her sister to stay at a less expensive hotel, but for all I knew the sister was loaded.

I said, "I should let her know where Leo is."

"Leo?"

"Laura's cat. I took him to the Kitty Haven. I could pick him up for her when she's ready."

Guidry said, "She'll come to the house after Bill Sullivan has finished up here."

Bill Sullivan is a trauma cleaner who has the gruesome job of sanitizing crime scenes. Blood and body wastes contain bacteria that can cause disease. Carpet and tile often have to be replaced, walls have to be scrubbed and possibly repainted. Since Laura had been killed in her shower, the drain would have to be sterilized.

At the door, I said, "What's her last name? So I can call her about Leo."

"Last name's Autrey, but I wouldn't call her today. It was an ordeal for her to identify her sister's body."

"Of course."

Without making it too obvious that he was getting rid of me, Guidry had skillfully got me outside. It was just as well. I didn't have any other information to give him, and I needed to get out of that house.

He said, "Thanks, Dixie. I know that was hard for you."

"It wasn't hard for me."

"Okay. Thanks anyway."

I didn't answer. Something was going on that he wasn't telling me. As I slogged back to the Bronco and drove away, I reminded myself that I wasn't a part of the investigation and that Guidry had no obligation to tell me anything. But I had the distinct feeling that there was more to his reticence than the mere fact that it was none of my business. For some reason I couldn't pinpoint, I thought Guidry was concealing information because he thought it would hurt me to know it.

CHAPTER 20

I was so famished by the time I got to the diner that I felt bared-teeth feral, as if my growling stomach was giving the world fair warning that I was about to pounce on something and kill it.

Judy took one look at me, poured coffee, and scurried away to make sure Tanisha knew the she-wolf had arrived. She must have filched somebody else's order, because I'd barely finished the first mug of coffee when she brought my food. Nobody talked to me, which was just as well. When I'd thrown enough food down to my monster, I perked up and gave Tanisha a friendly wave. From behind the kitchen's pass-through counter, her wide face dimpled as she winked at me. It's good to have friends like Tanisha. They know your nasty disposition is really hunger, so they feed you.

I left money on the table for Judy, with an extra tip for having to put up with my crankiness, and slumped out to the Bronco. Now that I'd eaten, I needed a nap bad.

Driving slowly behind a motorcycle driven by a shirtless spring break guy with a sunburned young woman plastered to his back, I suppressed a yawn as I drove past the Lyon's Mane. Then a little alarm in my head jerked me awake, and I swerved into a parking space. I wanted to know what Ruby and Maurice knew about Gorgon.

When I went in the salon, Ruby was at the front desk with Baby in tow, and she gave me a dazzling smile.

I said, "I think I may need some conditioner."

She and Baby looked hard at my hair, and she reached to a glass shelf and got a fancy-looking bottle. When I scrabbled for money, she shook her head.

"It's on the house. Next time you come in, we'll charge you out the wazoo, but right now you're still getting rewards for rescuing Baby."

I laughed and tucked the bottle under my arm.

"Ruby, when I was in here before, a man named Gorgon came in. Maurice said he was a friend of Laura Halston's. Do you happen to know anything about him?"

"I know Laura was murdered."

"What about Gorgon?"

"Dixie, when I was a kid in New Jersey, one of our neighbors talked about a man we knew. Next day, the neighbor got shot in the head. Killed dead. You understand what I'm saying?"

Even the conditioner in the bottle understood what she was saying.

I said, "Lieutenant Guidry is the homicide detective investigating Laura's murder. If anybody had any information that might help catch the killer, they could make an anonymous phone call."

"Honey, with caller ID, no phone call is anonymous anymore. And anyway, I don't have any information."

I thanked her for the free conditioner and left. I didn't believe she didn't have any information, but I fully understood why she didn't want to talk to me about Gorgon. I felt jazzed. I was on a roll. Through my own cunning I had verified that Mr. Gorgon was indeed as thuggish as he looked. I hadn't exactly got his mafia ties or anything to connect him to Laura's murder, but at least I had done *something*, which seemed a hell of a lot more than Guidry had done. At the rate things were going, I might have to go out and find Laura's husband myself.

Cora's neatly folded muumuu was in the passenger seat, so since I was near the tailor shop, I decided to drop the dress off before I went home. The shop was in a part of Siesta Key's business district so old the stucco on the buildings could have been applied by one of de Soto's men in the 1540s. It was purely coincidental that it was across the street from Ethan Crane's office. I wasn't even thinking of Ethan when I chose it.

Okay, maybe it crossed my mind a tiny bit. Maybe it zipped across without calling attention to itself, but that's all.

The tailor promised to chop off at least two feet of Cora's muumuu and have it hemmed by midafternoon, and I came out fully intending to get in the Bronco and drive straight home. But my eyes crossed the street and stood at the entry to Ethan's building, and that caused my feet to stop.

My eyes stayed across the street, and after a second my feet said, Shoot, we're going too.

The next thing I knew I was opening the door with its flaking gilt sign that said ETHAN CRANE, ESQ. Then I was standing in the dingy vestibule looking up at stairs that had been trod by so many feet they sagged in the middle.

All that venerable decay and wear would make people expect an old man in the upstairs office, but the sign on the door had been put there by Ethan's grandfather, and most of the feet that had climbed the stairs had been to the elder—now deceased—Ethan Crane. The present and very much alive Ethan Crane was in an office at the top of those stairs.

I told myself I could still go out the door and cross the street and drive home, and Ethan would never know I had been there.

I ignored myself and climbed the stairs, because if I didn't do it then I might never do it at all, which seemed a terrible waste of something. A chance to rekindle a chemistry that had been there from the first time Ethan and I had met, maybe. Or just a chance to remain friends with a great guy.

From the top of the stairs, I could see Ethan moving around in his office. His suit jacket hung on a coat rack, neatly fitted on a coat hanger, but his tie was close at the neck and the sleeves of his blue and white pinstripe shirt were held in place by silver cuff links. I like people who take their work seriously, and Ethan was a professional, head to toe. Ethan was a lot of things, head to toe, things I shouldn't have been thinking about.

Ethan claims to be one-quarter Seminole, and his high cheekbones and straight black hair do indeed look Native American. He'd got a haircut since I'd last seen him. Instead of falling halfway to his shoulders, his hair was neatly trimmed above his ears.

He has damn nice ears.

He saw me and stopped moving, just stood with a law book in his hand and watched me walk toward him. My knee joints felt weird, as if they'd forgotten what their function was and needed conscious direction. I stopped in the doorway and tried to think of something intelligent to say.

Instead, I said, "I'm sorry I never knew your grandfather."

As if it were a perfectly reasonable opening remark, Ethan said, "My grandfather almost single-handedly kept Siesta Key from going the way Longboat and Bird have gone. He wanted Siesta to be for real people."

I said, "I hate to burst your bubble, Ethan, but real estate on Siesta is no steal."

"I didn't say he wanted Siesta for *poor* people, I said *real* people. Big difference. Real people don't barricade themselves in mega-mansions."

I said, "That isn't what I came to talk about."

He quirked one thick black eyebrow, which caused my tongue to have an out-of-body experience in which it leaped across space and licked the eyebrow's arched peak.

I said, "I mean . . . I wanted to, you know . . . just say hello, and tell you . . . ."

My voice trailed off because I hadn't actually had a plan, and because my tongue was still vibrating from its out-of-body moment.

He said, "I think I know what you wanted to tell me. Something like, 'I really dig you, Ethan, but not enough to make any kind of commitment to getting to know you and seeing where it might take us.' Is that about right?"

I opened my mouth to protest, and then snapped it shut. It was exactly right, and I felt like a high school tease.

Ethan pulled his desk chair out, laid the law book on the desk, and sat down. He put both hands behind his head and leaned back. His dark eyes were serious as a coming hurricane.

"Dixie, I've never asked you to make any kind of commitment to me, and I never will. But I'm not the kind of man to play footsie either. You've sent me a different message every time we've met, so now I'm not sure what you want. Hell, I've never been sure about anything with you."

I sat down too, dropping into one of the old butt-sprung leather chairs facing the desk. The chair's arms were darkened by thousands of palms that had gripped them. I rubbed my fingertips on one arm and looked at the mellow sheen of the big mahogany desk where Ethan's grandfather had sat for so many years. Everything in the office, including the law books on the shelves that lined the room, were symbols of continuity, generation to generation. Ethan might look like a man on the prowl with his dark good looks and sure manner, but deep down he was a man of tradition and family values. Not the phony family–values of politicians who use the term as code for white, straight, and Christian, but true family values of honor and integrity and loyalty. A woman would be a fool to turn away from a man like Ethan.

I said, "I don't know what I want either. I just know what I don't want."

He took his hands down and laced his fingers together on his desk. "So what is it that you don't want, Dixie?"

My voice grew suddenly thick. "I don't want to love a man and then lose him. Not again. Not ever again."

Ethan studied my face for a long moment. "I never took you for a coward."

Stung, my face went hot and I stood up so fast my head swam. "It's easy for you to say that, Ethan, you've never lost anybody you loved."

"How can you be so sure of that, Dixie? How do you know what I've lost?"

I couldn't answer that. The truth was that I didn't know much about Ethan's past. I'd been so preoccupied with my own, I'd never asked.

He said, "It may sound trite, but it really is better to have loved and lost than never to have loved at all. And it's cowardly to refuse to love for fear of losing. If everybody in the world operated that way, we would all live like isolated islands, never getting involved with anybody else. Is that how you want to spend your life?"

I looked away, and for a second my throat burned with threatened vomit, bile roiled from some dark ugly place I didn't want to acknowledge.

Ethan's voice softened. "I'm sorry, Dixie. I swore I'd never put pressure on you, and I just did."

Through stiff lips, I said, "It's okay."

"It's not okay, and I won't do it again. And just for the record, that wasn't a proposal or anything. I don't know if we're right for each other; maybe we're not. But when you feel strong enough, I'd like to explore the possibility."

And there it was, the *something* I thought it would be a shame to waste. It wasn't chemistry or friendship that I might be wasting, it was the possibility of love.

I said, "I'm sorry."

"For what?"

"For things too numerous and screwy to go into."

I turned my back and walked out with a determined stride.

As usual, I hoped my butt had looked good as I left. I'm ashamed of that, but it's the truth.

I drove home wishing I hadn't reacted the way I had, wishing I'd kept my big mouth shut. I talked far too much, and it was time to just shut the fuck up.

It was also time to quit stringing Ethan along. He deserved better. A lot better.

When I got home, I went to the closet-office and stared a long time at the black party dress hanging by itself as the closet's featured attraction. The party shoes were parked in their fancy box in a separate spot too, and the dinky little purse hung on a hook like a trophy.

In just three days, I would slither into that new dress,

step into those new shoes, and sling that little purse over my shoulder—with or without a condom inside like the saleswoman had recommended. At the party, I would probably dance with Guidry. In his arms, moving my feet close to his feet, my legs close to his legs, his hand on my back down low.

I groaned.

Guidry was a cop. Ethan was an attorney. Cops get killed a lot more often than attorneys. Ethan was one of the nicest, smartest, sexiest men in the universe, and my hormones stood up and tap-danced every time he was near. And yet I had walked away from Ethan, and I was going to the party with Guidry.

I groaned again, and went and stood a long time under the shower. I was still as stupid when I got out as I'd been when I got in.

CHAPTER 21

After a long nap, I went to my closet-office and listened to messages while I stepped into fresh underwear and cargo shorts. None of the messages were urgent, so after I pulled on a fresh T and laced up clean Keds, I went downstairs to visit with Michael and Ella. At that time of day the air on the key leans heavy on your back, draping its sweaty arms over your shoulders in a dazed torpor. Songbirds were hidden away having a siesta, and only a few seabirds wheeled in the sky. On the shore, some sleep-deprived gulls and terns made stubborn footprints in the sand.

In the kitchen, Michael was bent over a tray of meatballs he'd just taken out of the oven, and Ella was on her preferred perch on a stool at the butcher-block island. They both gave me *I love you* messages when I came in, Ella by blinking her eyes slowly, and Michael by offering me a meatball on a toothpick.

He said, "Wait, there's stuff to dip it in."

He plopped a spoonful of something creamy white into a small bowl and shoved it toward me. "See how you like that."

I rolled the meatball in the dip and took a bite. "Yum. What is it?"

"Mostly ground turkey and sesame seeds, with some spices. The dip is just mayonnaise and Dijon mustard and horseradish."

"Are you taking them all to the firehouse?" I sounded like a four-year-old about to whine.

"Don't worry, I'll leave some here. By the way, Paco and I are going out to dinner tonight."

"Okay."

"How's the kid?"

"He's good, they've moved him to a room."

He gave me a quick sideways look, but he didn't ask anything else about Jeffrey.

Luckily, he didn't even think to ask anything about Laura's murder. If I'd told him that I'd been asking questions about it, his sad look would have changed to one that said *Have you lost your mind?* I protected him by not volunteering any information. He already had enough worry and anxiety from being in a partnership with an undercover cop, he didn't need to worry about his sister too. Also, I didn't want to listen to him yell at me.

I ate another meatball, then washed my hands at the sink and took Ella out on the deck to groom her. I had just put the final stroke on her when Guidry's dark Blazer rolled around the curve.

Damn! Why couldn't he have given me some notice before he came? If I'd known, I could have slicked on a bit of lip gloss and run a brush through my hair. At least I was clean. Half the time when I see Guidry I've just thrown up on myself or I'm covered with dog drool and cat hair.

I hustled Ella inside and said, "I'll be back later."

Ignoring Michael's questioning look, I scooted out without telling him Guidry was outside.

I met Guidry coming toward the deck. He was

carrying a manila envelope. He looked dead serious. He nodded to me, formal as a funeral director. Something about the grim look in his eyes made my fingers fold into my palm.

He said, "I need to talk to you." His voice had an unusual strained sound, as if he wished he weren't saying what he was saying.

I said, "Let's go upstairs," and led the way.

On my porch, he tossed the envelope on the glass-topped table and took one of the chairs. "I want you to look at these."

I searched his face for meaning, but he wouldn't return my look. Suddenly dry-mouthed, I sank into a chair and watched him open the envelope.

He pulled out a couple of photographs and slid them across the table to me. They were mug shots of a man I recognized immediately—the wide jaw, the arrogant tilt of the head, the self-assured look in the eyes. Even in police custody, he had exuded raw power.

I said, "That's the man I saw with Laura. That's her husband."

"You're sure?"

"Positive."

He put the photograph back in the envelope and tapped his fingers on the tabletop as if he were drumming out ideas.

He said, "Since her sister will tell you anyway, I'll give you this much. That man is Martin Freuland. He's the president of a bank in Laredo, Texas, where Laura Halston worked as a teller."

I shook my head like a stunned boxer. "She didn't mention that when she told me about leaving her husband. She must have gone to Laredo for a few weeks and then come here."

"She didn't have a husband, Dixie. Her sister says she

never married, and there is no Dr. Reginald Halston. Not in any state."

"I could have remembered the name wrong. He was a surgeon, played college football. He told her he would kill her if she left him. She didn't want his craziness to infect their child."

"There was no child, Dixie."

"But—"

"She wasn't pregnant. Laura Halston lied to you."

"I don't understand."

"Her sister says she lived in Laredo for several years and worked in Freuland's bank. We've corroborated that. We've even nailed down the exact date she left Laredo. That's the one thing everybody is sure of when they talk about Laura Halston, that she left Laredo, Texas, on February twenty-second."

Stupidly, I felt like a betrayed child. Laura had lied about living in Dallas. She'd lied about being married to a Dallas surgeon. She'd lied about being pregnant. Apparently the only thing she hadn't lied about was having a sister.

I'd been so sure that Laura and I had made a true connection, like soul sisters finding each other in the midst of a jungle. But if what Guidry said was true, I'd been a naïve fool. Laura had simply been acting a role, and I had obligingly played her audience.

Oddly, he said, "I'm sorry, Dixie."

My eyes burned and I looked away. "I hardly knew her."

"But you believed in her. Losing faith in another person is almost worse than losing a friend."

There was a shadow in his eyes that said he spoke from personal experience.

I said, "That man, Martin whoever, said he would make her pay for leaving him."

Guidry tapped the tabletop a few more times. "According to her sister, Freuland and Laura were lovers, and she left him because he wouldn't divorce his wife."

"So he killed her."

"Don't jump to conclusions, Dixie. There's more to this story than a love affair. Freuland is under federal investigation for helping drug traffickers launder money. They believe he handled buffer bank accounts for money that had been delivered in cash to currency exchanges in Mexico. They wired the money to his bank, and he took big payoffs for not reporting it. The feds got an anonymous tip about what he was doing, and the sister claims the tip came from Laura."

I felt as if I were whirling through a wormhole in space. "He killed her because she reported him for laundering drug money?"

Dryly, Guidry said, "It could rile a man up to know he was going to spend the next twenty or thirty years of his life in jail."

I searched Guidry's face. He wasn't telling the whole story. Laura's killer hadn't just stabbed her to death, he had also made ribbons of her face. Stabbing her was a crime of intense passion, an act of rabid vengeance that could have been motivated by fury. But slashing her face had brought a different kind of satisfaction to the killer. Slashing her face seemed more like a psychopath's doing than an outraged banker. Not that a corrupt bank president couldn't also be a psychopath, but it was a stretch.

Dully, I said, "Did you get my message about the man who was stalking her?"

He grunted. "I'm not even going to ask how you got that information. You must send out invisible taser beams that cause people to go into shock and tell you everything they know."

Since I was still in shock myself, I let that pass.

Guidry shook out another photo sheet from his envelope and scooted it across the table. "Ever see this guy?"

It was another mug shot, this one of a puffy man with close-set eyes and marshmallow lips. He looked like the actor who would play an uptight high school principal or a holier-than-thou church youth director, the one who sucked all the fun out of life. In some shots, he wore rimless glasses that added to his professorial look.

I shook my head. "I don't recognize him."

Guidry got out his ever-present notepad and flipped through some pages.

"Name's Frederick Vaught. He's a nurse, or used to be until he lost his nursing license. He was charged with elder abuse after another nurse saw him holding a pillow over a patient's face in a rehab center. The patient didn't die, and there wasn't enough hard evidence to convict him of attempted murder, so he got off by pleading no contest. He got five years' probation, and had to do two hundred hours of community service. That's how he wound up driving people at Bayfront. It was a volunteer position."

"They let somebody like that drive people?"

"His driving record was okay, it was his nursing record that was faulty."

Guidry did that finger-tapping thing again. "Your tip about him was a good one. The ER people remembered him as the driver who brought the Grayberg woman in. And Laura Halston was at the emergency room at the same time. You were right about that."

Damn straight I'd been right about that. Even if I'd been wrong about a lot of other things.

He said, "Several patients under his care died under uncertain circumstances. They were all between eighty and ninety years old."

I thought of how he'd told Ms. Grayberg she should have been smothered at her first infarct, and shuddered. If I hadn't come around the curtain, would he have smothered her right then?

I said, "A nurse would know how to use a scalpel. Maybe he was a surgical nurse at one time."

"Maybe."

He met my gravelly stare and sighed. "As I've already said, don't jump to conclusions."

"But you will pick Vaught up?"

"Of course. If nothing else, he violated about a hundred rules of his probation by going to that nursing facility."

I said, "I asked about that other guy, Gorgon, at the Lyon's Mane. Ruby wouldn't talk about him, but I'm sure he's deep in organized crime."

His gaze measured me for a moment. "Dixie, I would really, really appreciate it if you'd stop asking questions about this murder. That's my job, not yours."

His gray eyes were calm, but his eyelids flickered just enough to tell me he wasn't being completely honest.

"What's the real reason you want me to stop?"

"We're looking for a psychopathic slasher. Killers like that don't need a lot of reason to go after another victim. I don't want you to attract his attention."

I didn't answer him. I didn't want to go into all the reasons why fear wasn't a good deterrent to keep me from looking for Laura's killer. Besides, I wasn't sure I wanted Guidry to know that I was more afraid of fear than I was of a killer.

I took a deep breath and stood up. "I have pets waiting for me."

He nodded and followed me down the steps. Downstairs, we got into our respective vehicles and gave each other sober waves before we started our engines. Guidry went first, easing his car around the meandering lane and causing the parakeets to do their usual paranoid panic. I followed, gripping the steering wheel with both hands like an old woman afraid of losing control.

CHAPTER 22

I weighed about two tons when I slogged into the down-stairs lobby at the Sea Breeze. As I went in, the elevator door opened and Tom Hale's girlfriend came out. She was mincing along on red high heels and carrying a cardboard box so big she had to peer around its side to look ahead. Since she had her hands full, I turned back to open the door for her.

She stopped and gave me a defiant look. "I know what you're going to say, but women have to put them-selves first. If we don't, who will?"

"Excuse me?"

"I need a man who can protect me. Look at what happened to that woman over in Fish Hawk Lagoon! Somebody came in her house and killed her in the shower. That could've been me, and Tom couldn't do a thing to stop it."

I looked from her flaming face to the box in her hands. "Are you saying you're leaving Tom because a woman you've never met got killed?"

"I'm saying a woman needs a man to protect her. Every woman, not just me."

I said, "That's pure bullshit. You're just using that as an excuse to leave Tom."

"You're so crazy about him, why don't you move in with him?"

I considered saying that Tom and I were good friends, but that we had no sexual attraction. Not because Tom was in a wheelchair, but because we just didn't. I considered saying that Tom deserved a woman who wasn't shallow and vapid, and that I was glad she was leaving him. But saying those things would have taken more energy than she was worth. Besides, I had become so sane and well-balanced that I no longer leaped to tell idiots they were idiots. Instead, I only said one teensy thing.

I said, "Lady, I sure hope you've been spayed. It would be a damn shame for you to reproduce."

She snorted and pranced out on her red high heels, leaving me wishing I hadn't regained so much sane self-control. A year ago, I might have gone bananas and pulled out all her flat-ironed hair. As it was, I had let the bitch walk away with all her hairs intact.

Upstairs, I tapped on Tom's condo door and then used my key. He and Billy Elliot were in the living room, and they both gave me doleful looks when I went in.

I said, "Oh, for God's sake! Don't tell me you're actually sad the bitch has gone! Puh-leeze!"

They both looked startled, but Billy Elliot began to grin with his tongue hanging out the side of his mouth.

Tom said, "When your husband was alive, did you feel safer?"

"Of course."

"You thought he could protect you."

"It wasn't that I thought he would protect me, it was just that there were two of us. Even if we were miles apart, there were still two of us, and I always knew if I got in a jam, I could call Todd and he would help me. That made me feel safer."

"Frannie couldn't rely on me like that."

"How come?"

He looked down at his paralyzed legs. "You know."

"Oh, big doo-doo! She could rely on you for lots of things. You solve problems for people every day. You know things, you have information, you know how to get things done. Women don't need a bodyguard, they need somebody with good sense to help them solve problems. Frannie's a poisonous toad. Just get over it."

Peering up at me with narrowed eyes, Tom gnawed on the inside of his cheek for a moment. Then he grinned.

"I just remembered a movie I saw one time where this guy rubbed a lamp and got a genie that fulfilled his every wish. He wanted a pile of money, boom, he had unlimited supplies. He wanted a fancy hotel suite, boom, he was in it. He wanted two or three women, boom, they were there. He wanted drugs and booze and every kind of sex he could think of, boom, he got it all. Anything he wanted, he got. Man, he was beside himself. He'd found nirvana, heaven, the Garden of Eden. Then after a while it started to get old, you know? And he thought he'd leave for a while and spend some time alone. But he couldn't. He was locked in that room with those sluts and the drugs and the booze and the unlimited supply of money. And he realized he was in hell."

"Your point being?"

"At first I thought Frannie was the answer to my dreams. Sexy, good-looking, great in bed, everything a man wants. But for the last few weeks I've been in hell."

"Well, there you go."

"I guess the moral is to be careful what you ask for."

I patted his shoulder. "If I meet a genie, I'll remember that."

I was already reviewing my list of women who were better than Frannie. I figured I'd give Tom a few weeks to get over her, and then play matchmaker.

Billy Elliot and I went downstairs and did our run, and both of us felt happier when we came back upstairs. Tom seemed to have recovered his equilibrium too.

He said, "Speaking of the woman who was murdered, what's going on with that?"

Apparently, he and Frannie had done a lot of speaking about Laura's murder, because I hadn't mentioned it.

I said, "I don't think I told you that I'd had dinner with her. I really liked her. I thought we would become good friends."

"I didn't realize this was a personal loss for you."

"It turns out she lied to me about a lot of things. I thought she was one kind of person, but she turned out to be something else."

"Like Frannie."

"In a way."

"Disillusionment sucks, doesn't it?"

"It looks like Laura hurt some people."

"Including you."

"She didn't hurt me. I barely knew her."

"Uh-huh, and I still have two good legs, and nobody ever broke my heart and left me."

A slight sea breeze moved in to wave palm fronds as I left Tom's place, and my disposition lightened. Funny how the weather seems to have an organic connection to humans and animals. A drop in pressure brings aching joints and pain in old injuries, spring's explosion of new green stirs a surge of adolescent hormones, and winter's snow makes people pack up and move to Florida.

I had to spend extra time on my afternoon rounds on

account of a recent magazine-shredding binge by twin-mitted Ragdolls named Annie and Bess. Ragdolls are large long-haired cats who fall limp in your arms when you pick them up. Then they look up at you with such a sweet expression in their deep blue eyes that you're instantly a goner. Annie and Bess were blue colorpoints with white chins, mittens, and boots. They were loving and gentle, but they knew they were the mistresses of the manor and that I was their servant, so they weren't the least apologetic about flinging paper dandruff all over the house. They watched with bored disinterest while I vacuumed it up, and when I suggested that it might have been a better use of their time to watch the birds outside their window than to tear up a magazine, they merely flipped their tails. In their former lives, they had probably been opera divas.

After they had eaten and I had washed their dishes and put out fresh water, we ran around on the lanai for a few minutes playing jump-for-the-peacock-feather until we were all winded. Then I took them inside, kissed them goodbye, and headed to the Village to get Cora's muumuu. Not that she needed the dress right that minute, but I didn't like to think of her by herself, hobbling around on that sore ankle. I didn't even look across the street toward Ethan's office when I got it. Well, I may have let my eyes slide that direction, but I didn't really *look*.

With the newly shortened dress in a nice shopping bag, I drove over the north bridge and wound my way around to Bayfront Village. I left the Bronco under the portico for a valet to disappear into the bowels of their parking garage, and swished through doors that automatically opened when they felt me coming. As I went toward the elevator, the concierge waved at me, friendly again, and pointed to her phone, meaning she had already notified Cora that I was on the way. I waved back and hustled on to the elevator.

As soon as the elevator door opened on the sixth floor, I could smell chocolate bread from Cora's apartment. Cora had opened her door for me, and when I went in the look of joy on her face was enough to make me forget how rushed I was.

She said, "I figured you'd be here this afternoon, so I made us some chocolate bread."

Cora has an ancient bread-making machine her granddaughter gave her, and she makes decadently delicious chocolate bread in it. She claims her technique is a secret, which is okay by me. The secret results in a round whole-wheat loaf studded with almost-melted spots of oozing dark chocolate. Just smelling it makes my taste buds sit up and smile.

I put the bag with her muumuu on a chair.

"I thought you were supposed to sit with your foot propped up."

"Oh, I do, every chance I get. I'll sit right now, and you can bring me some bread and tea."

She plopped herself in one of the graceful iron chairs at a little round table covered with a pink and turquoise tablecloth.

She said, "Would you mind boiling me an egg? I used up all my zip making that bread."

I said, "I'll boil two. You should have more protein than one."

She watched me over the bar while I clattered around finding everything. I boil eggs the way my grandmother taught me and Michael—cold water almost but not quite covering the eggs, cover the pot, bring them to a rolling boil, then turn off the heat and let them sit exactly three minutes. While that was happening, I made a pot of tea, tore off chunks of chocolate bread from the loaf—because it's best torn, not sliced—and put it all on a tray. When the timer announced the eggs done, I took them out of the water, ruthlessly guillotined them through their shells, and scooped their quivering flesh into a small bowl before the soft yolks had time to run.

When I carried the tray to the table, Cora's eyes lit up in a way that made me suspect she hadn't eaten since she'd been home. For a few minutes, the only sound was the clink of Cora's fork and my soft whimpers of pleasure. Cora's chocolate bread is another thing I expect to be in unlimited supply in heaven, along with bacon.

She said, "Have you heard anything else about that little boy?"

"He's doing well, they've moved him to a room."

As if I'd said the opposite, she said, "I don't worry about dying, you know. To tell the truth, I sort of look forward to it. Not the last-breath part, but the next breath in a new place. I imagine it's sort of like being born, don't you? I mean, coming into this world is no picnic for a baby, all that squeezing and pushing going on around it, but then it pops out in a whole new world."

She leaned forward and lowered her voice, as if somebody else was with us and she didn't want to be overheard saying something controversial. "Between you and me, I never have believed that business about golden streets and angels flying around playing on harps. That would get old real fast. No, I imagine when we die here, the next thing we know we're popping out of our next mother, babies again, starting all over."

"Reincarnation."

She looked blank. "I don't know about that. I just think the good Lord gives us another chance to get it right. I'm gonna do better next time."

I swallowed a lump in my throat. "You've done just

fine this time, Cora. I don't know anybody who's done it better."

To stop all the talk about death, I said, "I'm going to a party Saturday night. A big shindig the Humane Society is throwing. Guidry invited me."

She sat up straight and beamed at me. "That nice detective fellow?"

"That's the one."

"That's why you got your hair cut."

I touched my ends. "You could tell?"

"It was a little uneven before."

"That's not why I got it cut."

She waggled a hunk of chocolate bread at me. "Yes, it is. You wanted to look pretty for that nice detective. Did you get a new dress?"

"New dress, new shoes, new purse, new underwear, the works."

She smiled at me, her papery skin cracking into a zillion fine lines. "Ha! It's about time. That's all I can say. It's about time."

Everybody who loved me seemed to be pushing for me to get involved with a man. Michael hoped it wouldn't be Guidry, Paco hoped it would be, and Cora would have been happy with either Guidry or Ethan Crane. It made me feel a little bit like a filly on the track that people were betting on. Only thing was, I wasn't sure I was ready for the race.

CHAPTER 23

It was close to five when I got to Fish Hawk Lagoon, and shadows were lengthening along the sidewalk. The crime-scene cars were no longer in Laura's driveway, but Bill Sullivan's HAZMAT van was there. I parked in Mazie's driveway and tried the doorknob before I rang the bell. The door was locked, which made me glad and sad at the same time. Glad that Pete had taken my reprimand to heart about leaving it unlocked, and sad that it had been necessary.

Between trying the knob and ringing the bell, I'd heard the sweet strains of Pete's saxophone. I wondered how many hours a day he spent playing for Mazie. The music stopped, and in a few seconds Pete opened the door with Mazie close at his heels. Both man and dog had stressed faces.

I said, "How is Jeffrey?"

"He's talking, but he's weak. Hal held the phone to him so he could talk to Mazie, but Jeffrey didn't understand and just cried. It was a mistake, and we won't do that again. Mazie went nuts for a while, running around like she was looking for Jeffrey."

I said, "She probably thinks he needs her, and that

she's not doing her job. For a service dog, that's about the worst thing that can happen."

Pete looked miserable. "I shouldn't have asked Hal to let Jeffrey talk to her."

"Don't blame yourself, Pete. We all thought it was a good idea. Maybe when Jeffrey is stronger, Hal can try again."

I opened the hall closet door and got Mazie's leash. "Has she eaten?"

"Very little. Just a few bites, and then she wouldn't look at it again. I brushed her this morning, and she seemed to like that."

I said, "Come on, girl, let's go for a run."

Listlessly, she followed me outside and allowed herself to be drawn into a run. We covered about three blocks and then turned and ran all the way back home. Mazie had the joyless look of somebody exercising only because she knew it was good for her. I felt somewhat the same way.

When we got back to her house, a beige Camry was parked behind Bill Sullivan's HAZMAT truck, and a woman with corn-tassel hair stood behind it, looking around the neighborhood. When she saw me and Mazie, she began walking toward us at a fast clip.

A persimmon-mouthed woman, she had the pronounced calf muscles and bony shoulders of someone who took exercise seriously. She looked a few years older than me, early forties probably, and wore a pale blue no-nonsense suit and cream colored pumps. I would have suspected she was a news reporter there to get a juicy murder story, but the handbag hanging from the crook of her elbow matched her pumps, and she wore panty hose. She was too domesticated to be a reporter.

With a wide smile, she said, "Hello, I'm Celeste Autrey, Laura Halston's sister."

She had a brisk, snappy voice with a chirpy undertone, like a kindergarten teacher or the X-ray technician who does your mammogram.

Now that I knew who she was, I searched for a resemblance to Laura. She was fair, but not with Laura's near-albino skin. Her blond hair was neither smooth nor silvery platinum like Laura's, and her eyebrows were plucked to an almost invisible line. Her nose and chin were longer and more pointed, and her eyes closer together. When Mother Nature had dispensed the gifts of beauty, she had been generous to Laura but extremely frugal with Celeste.

Still with that incongruous smile, she said, "There's a man in Laura's house who won't let me in. I don't know who gave him authority to be there, but it certainly wasn't me. He was very rude, said he wasn't finished yet, and that I couldn't come in no matter who I was. I took his license number, and I'll report him to his employer for being so discourteous. He gave me a lecherous look too. I think if he hadn't been afraid I'd call the cops, he would have tried something with me. But that's typical, isn't it? Nobody seems to have any respect for anybody else, they just trample all over you."

All the time she spoke, her lips were stretched in a frozen smile. For a second, I felt as if I were back in junior high listening to the mean girls slicing and dicing reputations with their razor-sharp little tongues.

I said, "That's a crime-scene cleaner. He was sent by the Sheriff's Department. You won't be able to go in the house until he's finished. It's for health reasons."

"You would think I'd have been consulted before they sent somebody. I don't want strangers going through my sister's things. She had some valuable jewelry, just the kind of thing people would take if they're not supervised. I doubt if they even did an inventory before they sent somebody in there. That's inexcusable negligence, but I don't suppose you can ask for anything better in a one-horse town like this."

Careful not to use words like *blood* or *bacteria*, I said, "They won't go through her things, they'll just clean the areas that need cleaning."

"Well, I suppose I can't do anything about it now, anyway. Do you mind if I come in? I don't like standing out here on the sidewalk with the neighbors watching."

There wasn't a neighbor's house in sight, but she apparently thought we were under close observation. With her lips still smiling, her eyes gave me an aggrieved look, as if I were personally responsible for her discomfort. She moved toward the Richards' front door, her high heels making clicking sounds on the walk. No question about it, I had lost control of this situation from the get-go.

I did a fast mental debate and then led Mazie after her. Laura had been a neighbor, and I was sure Hal and Gillis would want me to be hospitable to her sister, even if she had a snotty attitude. I could even halfway tolerate her snarky disposition because I knew she'd suffered a terrible shock. Besides, I wanted to hear what she had to say. I wanted to learn the truth about Laura.

At the door, she stopped and stood aside to let me open it, as hard in her skin as a premature banana.

Before obeying her peremptory direction, I made a feeble attempt at asserting some control. "This isn't my house. I'm here to walk the dog."

"The detective told me about you. Your name is Hemingway."

So much for gaining control. I opened the door and motioned her in ahead of me.

I said, "It's Dixie Hemingway, and I'm very sorry about your sister."

Pete stood up from the sofa, and Mazie strained at the leash to go to him. I didn't blame her. Of the two of us, Pete was the one she could depend on.

I said, "Ms. Autrey, I'd like you to meet Pete Madeira."

Pete extended one hand to take Mazie's leash and the other to shake Celeste Autrey's hand, but she didn't offer it. She didn't even seem aware that Pete was there.

With machine-gun precision, she said, "The detective said you had my sister's cat. I don't know why she kept that cat. That man gave him to her, I suppose that's why. Laura never used any judgment when it came to men. Not when she was a girl and not when she was a woman, just jumped from bed to bed, man to man. Never had any morals, not from the beginning. She was my sister, and I hate to speak ill of the dead, but Laura has always been a slut. Never could turn down any man that wanted her, and believe me, there were plenty of bad ones after her. Martin Freuland was the worst, the very worst. I tried to tell her, but Laura never listened to me. Not ever, not about anything. She wanted his money, and she thought she could get it. Now look what it got her."

Even with that odd smile, her voice held so much acid that Pete's eyebrows climbed toward his hairline, and Mazie edged closer to his side.

Pete said, "If you two will excuse us, Mazie and I will be on the lanai."

Celeste dropped into a chair as if she intended to spend the rest of her life there. I perched on the arm of the sofa. I wasn't sure why she was there, but I knew it wasn't because she was concerned about Leo.

I said, "You think Martin Freuland killed Laura?"

"Of course he did. He found where she'd gone and he came here and killed her. I warned her. As soon as she told me he was here, I told her to leave, but she laughed at me. Laura thought she could twist every man around her finger. I don't suppose anybody could blame her for thinking that. She started with our father and moved on to every man she ever met. It was a sickness she had, a weakness of character. I think she was born with it. But she went too far with Martin Freuland."

I caught an odd note of satisfaction in her voice, as if she were glad Laura had got what was coming to her.

I said, "Laura told me she was married to a surgeon. She said she had gone to work for him as his receptionist and then married him."

Her laughter spewed like ice cubes falling from a refrigerator's icemaker. "She actually said that? Oh, she was good! That's what *I* did, not Laura. *My* husband is a surgeon, and *I'm* the one who was his receptionist. But I'm not surprised she told you that. She was so jealous of me, she stole my life! She tried to steal my husband too, but he saw right through her. Not like most men—she had most men fooled. Men are stupid, you know, they'll believe anything a woman tells them, and Laura knew all the right ego buttons to push. She was oversexed, I think. Maybe it was hormones or some extra chromosome thing. Whatever it was, she never thought of anything except sex."

I thought back to our evening together. Two women sharing secrets have plenty of opportunities to talk about sex, but the topic hadn't come up. Grief does strange things to people, but in Celeste's case it seemed to have turned her into a vile disloyal gossip.

I said, "I didn't know Laura well, but she seemed like a nice person to me. I can't imagine her doing something so bad that it would cause a man to kill her."

Her head snapped toward me, and in the movement a ray of light from a table lamp caught two thin wet trails on her cheeks. Her lips were still pulled back in a parody of a smile, but her eyes were leaking tears. Strangely, she seemed unaware of them.

"Let me set you straight about Laura. From the day she was born, she seduced every man she met, beginning with our father. I was four when she was born, and I don't think Daddy ever looked at me again. Oh, she was cute, no doubt about it. I don't dispute that. Every time we went out in public, strangers would stop us on the street to rave about how pretty she was. Right there in front of me, they'd go on and on about her looks, and she ate it up. I was cute too, plus being smart, but she hogged all the attention. It was a sickness of hers."

She leaned forward and dropped her voice an octave, getting serious. "You know what someone said to me? They said, 'I hate to tell you this, but your sister is a narcissist.' That's what they said, a narcissist. I'd never heard the word before, I had to look it up in the dictionary. It's a mental illness, is what it is. Narcissists are selfish and controlling, just like Laura. They're outrageous liars too, you can't believe a thing they say, and they don't care about anybody but themselves. They use you and use you and use you, and then they throw you away."

Her voice had taken on a corrosive bitterness. "When Laura was eight, she made Daddy take her to a kid's modeling agency. Oh, she knew the effect she had on men, she knew they'd want her. They did too, snapped her right up, and after that, the whole family lived on the money she made. Needless to say, all the photographers were men. Even then, she was using men to get what she wanted. We moved to a big house, my parents got new cars, and neither of them ever worked another day. Laura was their princess, like she's been ever since."

I clamped my teeth tight to keep from reminding her that Laura's mutilated body lay in the county morgue no longer a princess. No longer anything.

She said, "Laura drew in every man she ever knew. Teachers, neighbors, every man around. She was just naturally seductive, even when she was little. She was a bad seed, depraved, no morals whatsoever. She even seduced Daddy. That's how low she was."

With tears glistening on her cheeks like snail trails, she peered at me to see how I was taking what she said. Increasingly willing to give her every opportunity to sink to her lowest self, I gave her my best *I'm listening* look.

"We were still young enough to sleep with our bedroom doors open. Laura's room was directly across the hall, and there was a night-light in the hall in case we needed to go to the bathroom in the middle of the night. One night I woke up and saw Daddy in my door. He was so big he blocked out all the light from the hall. He pulled my door shut, and then I heard Laura's door close too. I knew she had got him to come in there, and I knew what was going on. Can you believe that? She was that depraved. After that he went in her room almost every night. She had him under her thumb but good."

My stomach lurched. Celeste Autrey was not only viciously disloyal to her sister, she had a maggot-ridden mind.

"How old was Laura then?"

"Nine or ten. Our mother knew what she'd done, too. She turned hateful to Laura, really spiteful and mean, but Daddy was so much under her spell that he went out of his way to let us know that Laura could have anything she wanted."

She gave a short bark of a laugh. "It backfired on her, though. It always does, doesn't it? Like they say, what goes around comes around. Daddy managed Laura's career, getting her modeling jobs, making sure she got attention, handled all her money. But he wasn't very good at it, and when he and Mama were killed, Daddy had run up huge debts that he'd expected to pay with Laura's earnings."

"Your parents are dead?"

"Killed in a car wreck when I was in college and Laura was seventeen."

So much for the story Laura had told about parents in Connecticut who owned her house.

With a hint of satisfaction, Celeste said, "By that time, Laura was past the adorable-kid stage, and the catalog ads and magazine cover jobs weren't rolling in anymore."

With a mental image of two young sisters left alone with a mountain of debt that one of them was expected to pay off by being beautiful, I did some figuring.

"You were twenty-one then, right?"

She colored. "The older one, the one who should have helped Laura out, is that what you mean? I suppose I could have, but I had to survive too. I wasn't making much money, and I had rent to pay and car payments and clothes. I couldn't afford to support her too."

"I wasn't suggesting that you should have."

"Well, plenty of other people suggested it, and I

know Laura thought I should. She'd always got whatever she wanted, so she couldn't imagine somebody else not rushing to her side to take care of her."

"What did she do?"

She shrugged. "She had high school friends who took her in, first one and then another until she graduated. Probably seduced all their fathers while she was at it. That's what she did, seduced men. Every boyfriend I ever had, she took. I could have done the same thing to her, but I had morals. Not Laura. She never thought twice about seducing men. She still got some modeling jobs after high school, so it wasn't like she was destitute. And anyway, I had my own problems. I had to support myself, and I had to do it with my brains."

"Unlike Laura."

"You bet, unlike Laura. Not that I wasn't pretty." She looked intently at me. "I'm quite good-looking, you know."

She wasn't, but I nodded.

"I'm not saying Laura was dumb, but she wasn't the brightest bulb on the string either. She didn't have to be, all she had to do was smile pretty and men handed her money on a platter."

She smiled grimly. "And if they didn't, she just helped herself, like she did with Martin Freuland."

"She took money from Freuland?"

She gave a tense laugh and erased the air in front of her face.

"Listen to me! I sound like somebody on a talk show airing the family's dirty linen. All I wanted to ask you was if you know anybody who'll take that cat?"

It took a moment to realize she meant Leo. With a sense of relief, I said, "You're not keeping him?"

"Oh, God, no. I hate cats. Laura was always begging

for one when she was little, but I won that battle. Not that anybody really cared how I felt, but my mother hated cats too, and she put her foot down on that one."

I'm always confused when I hear somebody say they hate any kind of pet. I can understand that a person might not want one, but I can't fathom hating an animal just because it isn't some other kind of animal.

She said, "I hate dogs too. If you ask me, it's plain stupid for human beings to walk behind a dog, waiting for it to pee and picking up its shit. It must give dogs a big laugh to know they've got humans to be their servants."

I said, "I took Leo to the Kitty Haven. That's a boardinghouse for cats." My own voice had picked up its pace as if it wanted to keep up with hers.

"I suppose the Sheriff's Department authorized that too. My God, they must have sent out invitations. Take the cat, come in the house, take her things. If any of her jewelry is missing, I swear I'll file an official complaint."

Stiffly, I said, "Ms. Autrey, nobody will take your sister's jewelry. And Leo couldn't be left in the house after Laura was killed there. Now if there's nothing else I can do for you, it's time for both of us to leave. As I said before, this is not my house, and I'm not authorized to invite strangers into it."

She shot to her feet and stalked to the front door. "And your time is so *valuable*." She laid heavy sarcasm on *valuable*, intent on letting me know that she thought my time was worthless, and slammed the door behind her.

With the echo of the door still reverberating, I deliberately closed my eyes and relaxed my fists, forcing myself to breathe slowly and deeply—a trick my old

shrink had taught me when I wanted to go yank somebody bald-headed.

A little whining noise made me open my eyes. Mazie
and Pete stood looking at me, Mazie with a quizzical
tilt to her head.

Pete waffled his eyebrows. "Holy smokes! That
woman could talk the balls off a pool table."

I said, "She's rabid, absolutely rabid."

"You can tell that, just by listening to her yak, yak,
yak. What the heck was she talking about?"

"She was telling me what a lying narcissistic slut her
sister was."

"The sister that just got murdered?"

"That's the one."

"Man, that's cold."

Like a sloth, I unfolded myself from the sofa arm
and stood a moment looking at Pete and Mazie.

"Pete, if she comes back here, don't let her in."

"Hon, you don't need to tell me twice. I don't like
that woman. Neither does Mazie."

"That makes three of us."

Pete said, "It's a damn dirty thing to go around telling lies about your own sister, even if she hadn't just
been murdered."

I said, "Yes, it is."

But as I went out to the Bronco, I wasn't sure anymore which sister told the biggest lies. Laura had lied
about being married and being pregnant, and she had
lied about her parents. Or maybe she hadn't. Maybe she
had been telling the truth and Celeste was the liar.

Except about the pregnancy. For sure Laura had lied
about that.

But maybe the parents truly lived in Connecticut,
and maybe there truly was a husband somewhere, and

maybe his name was truly Reginald Halston and he was truly a surgeon. I wasn't positive about any of those things anymore.

The only thing I was absolutely positive about was that children don't seduce grown men.

CHAPTER 24

The Camry was gone from Laura's driveway when I left Mazie's house, and a locksmith's truck was behind Bill Sullivan's HAZMAT van. I drove out of Fish Hawk Lagoon and headed south on Midnight Pass Road, but instead of going directly home I turned onto Reba Chandler's street. Reba is a brilliant, gracious, kind woman who teaches psychology at New College. She's also a bird lover, and I've been taking care of Big Bubba, her African Grey parrot, since I was in high school. Back then, it had been a teenager's way to make easy money. Now it's my profession. Funny how life loops back on itself like that.

Reba's house is a cypress two-story with shuttered windows that are always open because she doesn't believe in air-conditioning. The shutters began life a deep turquoise, but they've faded over the years until the color is almost nonexistent. Instead of ringing the bell, I walked along a rock path to the lanai at the back of the house. Big Bubba lives in a large cage out there, and I knew I'd probably find Reba there too.

She wasn't on the lanai but in the yard behind it, where she's put up double-decked bird feeders. She carried two plastic bottles that had once contained water but now were filled with seeds and peanuts. Lots of people who put out birdseed go to all kinds of lengths to keep squirrels and raccoons out of it. They set the feeders on tall poles, surround them with chicken wire, suspend them from high branches, or put cayenne pepper in the seed to burn the squirrels' mouths. Reba just puts out the food and lets nature take its course. I guess psychologists know so much about human depredation they're not fazed by anything animals do.

She said, "Dixie, how nice to see you!"

Reba is probably the only woman in the world who can sound like she's in a receiving line while she's feeding birds.

A young wood stork with a long dark bill and fluffy brown neck feathers stalked to the bird feeder as if he were claiming the best table at a fancy restaurant. Wood storks have such big funny feet, they look like they're wearing tennis shoes. Reba poured peanuts and seeds into the feeder, and a mottled duck waddled forward to join the wood stork. A couple of blue jays swooped down to sort through the nuts, and the wood stork and duck withdrew.

So did Reba and I, hotfooting it to the lanai before the blue jays attacked us. I was annoyed at the thuggish dive-bombing blue jays for scaring the other birds away, but it didn't bother Reba. She doesn't believe in imposing human morals on nature. I don't either, but I still wished the wood storks and ducks had got all the seed first. As Reba has told me more than once, I have a teensy judgmental streak.

From inside the safety of the lanai, we watched as several fish crows flew in and scared off the jays. Fish crows are even bigger bullies than jays. After the crows left with their peanuts, they were replaced by a flock of rose-ringed parakeets chattering like high school girls on a field trip.

Reba said, "I used to get bobwhites, but I never see one anymore. I'm going to have a martini. Would you like one?"

"No, thanks." I figured alcohol right then would make me either throw up or pass out.

"Glass of wine?"

"Thank you, no. I just wanted to ask you something."

"Let me get my martini first. I have better answers when I've had a little vodka."

She scurried into the house, and I went to Big Bubba's cage to say hello.

With their gray feathers, white-rimmed eyes, dark gray wings, and curved bills, Congo African Greys look like prim executive secretaries. But then you catch a glimpse of bright red petticoat feathers under their gray tails, and you know they have a racy side they don't show the world.

I'm a little bit like that myself.

Another thing about African Greys is that they're so intelligent they bore easily, and when they do they're liable to rip out their own feathers.

I'm like that too, except for the feather-ripping part.

Big Bubba tilted his head to give me the one-eyed bird look. He said, "Did you miss me?"

I laughed, because I knew that was something Reba asked him every day when she came home. He laughed too, bobbing his head to the rhythm of his own he-he-he sound.

Big Bubba was a great talker, but not so hot as a conversationalist.

Reba came out with a martini glass in one hand and

a plastic bowl of sliced banana in the other. She set her glass on the lanai table and put the banana in Big Bubba's cage. Then she motioned me to a chair at the table and sat down herself. With her eyes fixed on me, she took a dainty sip of her martini.

"What's wrong?"

It's a mistake to pretend with Reba, so I told her the truth.

"I'm sure you heard about the woman who was murdered in Fish Hawk Lagoon."

"You knew her?"

"I have a client next door to her, and she invited me to dinner a couple of nights before she was killed. I'd only just met her, but I liked her a lot. She told me she had run away from an abusive husband in Dallas. Said he was a sadistic surgeon. She said she was pregnant and didn't want her husband to inflict his sickness on their child."

"Do you think he killed her?"

I shifted uneasily in my chair. "As it turns out, there is no husband. She made the whole thing up. She wasn't pregnant either."

Reba took another sip of martini. "So she lied to you."

"Yeah, and tonight her sister told me some other things about her. She said she'd seduced every man she'd ever known. She also said somebody had called her a narcissist. What is a narcissist, anyway?"

Reba shook her head. "Wait, who called who a narcissist?"

"The sister's name is Celeste. The murdered sister is Laura. Celeste said somebody told her that Laura was a narcissist."

"Somebody who? Her hairdresser? A bartender? A jilted boyfriend?"

"Um, I don't know. She just said somebody."

Reba pulled a toothpick from her martini and nibbled on its olive. "People throw diagnostic terms around all the time without knowing what they mean, but narcissism is a personality disorder marked by grandiosity—a grossly inflated sense of importance or intelligence or talent that has no basis in fact. There's also a sense of entitlement. Narcissists believe they should have whatever they want because they want it. They lie a lot, and they take unfair advantage of people who love them."

"Laura didn't seem grandiose to me. She seemed completely normal."

"But she lied to you, and the lies would have eventually led to more lies, like a miscarriage or a divorce. We don't know if what the sister said was true about her being narcissistic, but lying about a husband and a pregnancy certainly raises a red flag. The truth is slippery to narcissists, even when there's no advantage to them in lying. It's part of their need to control. If they can fool you, they feel powerful."

I said, "I don't know how truthful Celeste is either, because she also said Laura had seduced their father when she was nine years old. Said he went in Laura's bedroom almost every night because she lured him in."

"Oh."

I said, "She was very beautiful. Her sister said she was a child model. The whole family lived on the money she made modeling."

"And the father sexually abused her."

"If what the sister said is true, he did."

Reba said, "If he molested one child, I'd be surprised if he didn't molest the sister too."

With a look of distaste, she took a deep breath and seemed to pull up some invisible page of lecture notes.

"Children have instinctive expectations of love and loyalty from their parents. Sexual abuse is the most basic disloyalty, not only from the parent who inflicts it, but from the parent who allows it."

She took another sip of her drink and set her glass down with a gentle hand.

"The most basic human need is to love and be loved, but we have to be taught how to love by receiving love. Love always includes loyalty. When a child gets neither love nor loyalty from her parents, she grows up with a narcissistic exaggeration of self-love. Even if somebody truly loved her, Laura would have been too emotionally fragile and too involved with herself to seek real intimacy with another person. Instead, she would have focused on being in control so nobody could be in control of her."

I nodded. "Her sister said she took advantage of people."

"She wouldn't have seen it as taking advantage. She would have seen it as being the one in power rather than the helpless one."

"What about what the sister said about her being a slut and seducing every man she knew?"

Dryly, Reba said, "I doubt she had to work hard to seduce them, but narcissism frequently manifests as control through sexual seduction, especially if there has been sexual abuse in the person's childhood."

I swallowed against nausea. "That all sounds terrible."

"Narcissism is a terrible disorder, and it's made even worse by the fact that narcissists are always desirable. That's how they seduce."

"There wasn't anything sexual in my feelings for her."

"Desiring somebody isn't necessarily sexual. We

desire intellectual stimulation from one person, humor from another, spiritual enlightenment from another, all those things are just as seductive as sex."

"Her sister thinks her former employer killed her. He was a bank president, and Laura worked for him."

"According to the news reports, she was stabbed."

"Repeatedly. I was there when the deputy found her, and it was so gruesome that he threw up. Her face was mutilated."

"After she was dead?"

"How did you know?"

"Pathology is magnetic. One pathology attracts its own kind in a different form. Piqueurism is another personality disorder that basically derives from a need to control. A piqueurist derives deep satisfaction from the power of causing terror."

My mouth had gone dry. "There was a man stalking her. He's a nurse who lost his license because they think he may have smothered some old people in a rehab center. Suffocating people would give a psycho a sense of power, wouldn't it?"

Reba drank the rest of her martini and set her glass down with a sharp click.

"Dixie, I hope you're not involved in this investigation."

"I'm not."

"You say that, but you have a way of—"

"Honest, I'm not involved in any way. I thought I would be, because I felt like Laura's murder was something that could happen to any woman, and I wanted to see her killer caught. But it's more complicated than that."

"That may be the understatement of the century."

I stood up. "Thank you, Reba."

"You're welcome."

I told Big Bubba goodbye and left. The last I saw of Reba, she was headed back into the house with her martini glass. I had the distinct impression that our conversation had caused her to need a second drink.

Michael and Paco were gone when I got home, but Michael had left a tomato-and-basil pie on my kitchen bar. The day sat heavily on my shoulders, and only the aroma of Michael's tomato pie kept me from going straight to bed. I poured a glass of Riesling and carried it and the pie out to the table on my porch. A yolk of sun was ankle high above a glassy sea, and the sky was shade-shifting from lambent blue to mango. Pedestrian bird traffic was light on the beach, where a gentle surf was tatting lace edging on the shore. A great egret glided down to my porch railing, pivoted toward the sun, pulled one leg into his skirts and balanced on one foot while the breeze luffed his feathers.

Michael's pie was delicious—puff pastry, overlapping slices of ripe tomato, dark green basil leaves scattered over the top, good Italian olive oil drizzled on with a sure hand, and a light touch of garlic—exactly the light supper I needed after all the heavy information I'd digested. I ate it while I watched the sun slide down the sky and slip below the sea, sending out shimmering banners of gold and cerise.

The egret flew away with a great flapping of wings, and I sat in the draining light and thought about Laura Halston's life. And about her death.

If what her nutcase sister had said was true, Laura had been treated as a sex object from the moment she was born. Used and abused by her father, envied and shunned by her mother and sister, and ultimately left alone when her parents died. At seventeen, no longer able to command large fees for being a beautiful child, she'd had to create a world for herself with no tools except her beauty.

It was hard to condemn her for using sexual seduction to keep from feeling helpless. That's what she'd been programmed to do—it may have been the only thing she knew how to do. I wondered if she had loved Martin, the bank president, or if, as Reba had said, she had never loved anybody because she'd never *been* loved. I had heard Martin tell her she owed him, but he hadn't said what she owed him. Was it love? Had Martin loved her and she had rejected him? Could he have been the one who got satisfaction from seeing her terror as he repeatedly stabbed her?

When I'd had dinner with her, Laura had spoken of Celeste as if the two were close, but Celeste had seemed contemptuous of her sister. Had that been grief talking? Old bitter rancor that had never been expressed when Laura was alive that was now boiling over? Or perhaps Laura had been playing a role for me when she spoke of her sister as if they were friends.

Guidry had said Celeste claimed Laura was the one who had reported Martin to the federal authorities for handling buffer accounts for drug dealers. How did Celeste know that? If Laura had told her, wouldn't that point to a closeness between them? And what had Celeste meant when she said Laura had stolen from Martin? Stolen what?

I thought of Frederick, the nurse, and groaned. Was he just a sick man who preyed on the elderly, or had he been so enraptured by Laura's beauty when they met in the ER that he became obsessed with her and killed her? If Celeste was to be believed, Laura would never have given an out-of-work nurse a moment of her time because he had nothing she would have wanted. But what about Gorgon, the thuggish guy I'd seen at the Lyon's Mane? He probably had gobs of money, and he would have been a challenge to a woman who liked to seduce and control. If, in fact, that's what Laura had liked to do, which nobody knew for sure.

I kept thinking about what Reba had said about their childhood experiences causing Laura and her sister to get kinks in their personalities. But there are millions of people who've been abused as children who don't grow up to be liars and thieves, so what makes one person transcend damage done to her as a child, and another lets it become the central core of who she is?

When our father died, Michael was nine and I was seven. While I drew into a knot of miserable guilt, Michael had spent several months hitting or kicking things. His grades plunged and he went around with a ferocious scowl on his face. Our mother had been too stunned to deal with him, but our grandfather had finally come up with the perfect solution. He got a big football tackle bag and hung it from a tree limb in our backyard. Then he had a talk with Michael about anger. Basically, he told him that anger is a normal emotion and that hitting stuff is a normal action, but that hitting a tackle bag was a lot smarter than hitting walls. Then he gave Michael a pair of boxing gloves and let him be.

After a while, I got so used to hearing Michael thump that tackle bag that I took to hitting it myself, only I used a stick to whack at it. I even saw our mother slam her fist into it a few times. Now I wondered what would have happened to Michael's fury if he hadn't had that bag to hit. Maybe all that frustrated rage would have congealed and turned him into a criminal instead of a courageous fireman.

It was too much to think about. I went to the kitchen

to put away my empty plate and wineglass, and dragged myself to bed. It was only eight-thirty, but my mind had gone blank. I couldn't think anymore about what had happened.

I woke with a start, chasing remnants of a dream that escaped before my eyes were open. My bedside clock said it was quarter to four, time to get up and do my thing. I stretched and yawned, enjoying the rare feeling of being fully rested. Then I remembered why I'd gone to bed so early. Laura Halston had been murdered, and I had learned things about her that I wished I didn't know.

I swung my feet to the floor and realized I'd slept in my clothes. I usually shower first thing when I get home at night, but last night I'd slept in my hairy clothes. Yuk. With the extra few minutes I had, I took a quick shower and shampooed my hair. Toweling my hair, I padded naked to my closet-office and pulled on underpants and shorts and a lightweight long-sleeved knit shirt. I even wore a bra. Pets don't care if your boobs bounce or sag or swing or just lie there, but with all the stuff going on, I thought I might have to deal with men before the morning was over. Men are not as evolved as pets, they are easily distracted by loose bosoms.

I pulled my damp hair into a ponytail, used my remote to raise the hurricane shutters on my French doors, and went out to face the day. A couple of snowy egrets asleep on my porch railing watched me warily as I walked by, but it was too early for them, so they didn't fly away. The sea air smelled of salt and life, the sky was that peculiar creamy pre-dawn color, and the sea glimmered silver white. Down on the beach, a few early gulls waded in the surf's thin foam and searched for goodies. A pelican was asleep on the hood of my Bronco, and a great blue heron dozed on Michael's car. They both took off with a loud thrumming when I got in the Bronco. Maybe they knew what the morning would bring.

CHAPTER 25

Tom Hale's condo was dark when I let myself in. Billy Elliot was waiting for me in the foyer and we kissed hello, with a lot of panting and tail wagging on his part. I snapped his leash on his collar, and we trotted out with our knees pumping like majorettes rehearsing for a parade.

The lobby downstairs was empty, with that gloomy feel that a place gets when it's used to lots of traffic and finds itself deserted. Billy Elliot's toenails made skittering sounds on the marble floor and his leash jingled merrily, sort of livening up the joint. We blew through the double doors and started our usual jog toward the big oval track made by the parked cars in the front lot. Just as we got to the end of the walk and stepped onto the asphalt, a whale-shouldered man stepped from behind a tall stand of cascading firecracker plants.

I jumped and gave a little *whoop!* that immediately changed to a friendly half-laugh, the way people do when they've been startled but they don't want the startler to feel guilty about scaring them half to death. In the next instant, my heart clattered because the man didn't look friendly at all. In fact, he looked menacing. He also looked like one of the mug shots Guidry had shown me—the one of Frederick Vaught, the elder-smothering nurse. If I'd had any doubts, they evaporated when he spoke.

"Dixie Hemingway, I presume. The ailurophile."

I scrambled for the meaning of the word and, thanks to high school Latin, came up with *cat lover*. He had eyes like peeled grapes, and they were bulging down at me with glistening venom.

"Because of you, I have been questioned about a crime for which I haven't a scintilla of involvement. You have besmirched my reputation, ruined my good name."

His breath made low nose-whistles like the distant cooing of mourning doves.

With an effort, I found my voice. "You were involved. You were at Laura's house. You were stalking her."

His smile couldn't have been any more condescending if he'd been giving lessons.

"Oh, the pretensions of those who provide services to others. You know nothing of Laura's life or of my involvement with her. You're a pet sitter. You were not her friend."

My face went hot with anger and embarrassment. Somehow the man had an oily ability to make me feel small and insignificant.

"You were in Ms. Grayberg's room at the nursing unit too. I just want to know why—"

"One of the indices of an inferior intellect is the obsession with the why of things."

My back teeth made grinding movements, as if they had their own obsession of what they'd like to do to this condescending prick.

He said, "Your kind maintains the illusion that life is sacred, that the mere fact of having a breathing body with a beating heart somehow confers the right to continue one's inane existence. That ridiculous worship of oxygenated flesh is an obsession to which I have never fallen prey."

"So you killed Laura because you didn't believe her life was important."

"Why, Ms. Hemingway, you surprise me! You actually understood what I said. Nevertheless, I had nothing to do with Laura Halston's murder, and if you continue to stalk me I shall have you arrested."

"*Stalk* you?" As the words came out of my mouth, I knew he could make a good case for me stalking him. I had asked questions about him at Bayfront and at the nursing unit.

His gaze was diamond hard. "Please don't make it necessary for me to speak to you again, Ms. Hemingway."

With surprising agility for a man his size, he spun away from me and walked rapidly to a minivan that bore evidence of a multitude of minor scrapes and collisions. Either Guidry had been wrong about his driving ability or he'd been reduced to driving an old clunker formerly owned by a mother who did lots of stop-and-go driving.

I pulled Billy Elliot onto the asphalt track and followed him as he did his morning gallop, but my mind was on Frederick Vaught. Something wasn't right about that man, something more than his obnoxious personality and his history of mistreating elderly patients. Whatever it was, it made my skin quiver.

After three mad laps around the track, Billy Elliot slowed to a pace that other dogs would consider a frenzied dash and allowed me to lead him back in the building. I was wheezing and wondering if it's possible for lungs to collapse from running with a speed-obsessed greyhound. Billy was prancing and happily swishing his tail.

Upstairs, lights were on in the kitchen and I could hear a coffeemaker gurgling. I didn't hang around, though. If I had, I might have told Tom about Frederick Vaught accosting me, and he might have felt guilty that he hadn't been downstairs guarding me with big manly muscles. I gave Billy Elliot a quick hug and left him grinning to himself.

I wasn't grinning. I was thinking about Frederick Vaught. I thought about him for the rest of the morning, trying to define what it was that made him so repulsive. I was at a rabbit's house vacuuming up pellets of bunny poop when I realized what it was.

His hands were too clean! With their long thin fingers, his hands looked as if they'd been boiled until all the color had leached out. His fingernails were too pale too, and too well-defined, like an alien's tentacles with little suckers on their tips. Ugh! The thought of being touched by those long bloodless fingers made my spine run cold.

It was near nine o'clock when I cleaned the last litter box of the morning, and I was seriously considering raiding client refrigerators. The tomato pie I'd had for dinner had been too little and too early, and I needed food. But first I popped in the Kitty Haven for a quick hello to Leo.

Marge brought him from his private room and knelt with me to gentle him on the floor. He didn't exactly seem overjoyed to see me, but he did rub his cheek against my hand to mark it with his scent.

Marge said, "He's such a sweetheart. What's going to happen to him?"

I didn't want to tell her that Laura's sister didn't want him. It made him seem like a reject, and I knew there were lots of people who'd love to have him. Besides, it seemed rude to say it in front of Leo.

Instead, I said, "The owner's sister is in town. She's at the Ritz. It will all work out okay."

Marge may have heard the evasiveness in my voice because she didn't ask anything else. I spent a little more time petting Leo and then kissed the top of his head.

I murmured, "Don't worry. I'll make sure you're with somebody as sweet as you are."

When I left the Kitty Haven, I was torn between rushing to walk Mazie and then having breakfast, or eating first and then going to see Mazie. When I'd had that decision the day before, I'd ended up practically crawling from weakness by the time I got food. I knew Pete would have already fed Mazie and taken her outside to potty. He had probably brushed her too, because he and Mazie had come to enjoy him doing that. The only reason for me to go there was to run with her. I decided I would break my own rule and take time for breakfast before I went to Fish Hawk Lagoon, with no harm done.

Besides, I dreaded seeing Mazie's sad face. I dreaded seeing Pete's sad face too.

Before I went in the diner, I called Pete to tell him I'd be a little late. He sounded dispirited.

"I don't think the drops are helping, Dixie. I don't think they're helping at all."

I ended the call feeling as down as Pete sounded. Mazie's depression was like an anvil sitting on all of us.

At the Village Diner, Tanisha waved at me as I headed toward the ladies' room. I ducked into a stall and from the next door cubicle heard a woman with a voice like an ax splitting wood.

She said, "I was married to a man who couldn't get it up unless you twisted his nipples. He would have liked it if I'd attached snapping turtles to them. He left me for a woman who *was* a snapping turtle, so I guess they're happy together."

Another woman laughed, and they both flushed and went to the sinks. When I joined them, they went silent and we avoided one another's eyes in the mirror. I washed my hands, checked to make sure I didn't have cat hair on my shoulders, and left them to continue their observations about love. I swear, if men knew half the things women say about them, they'd probably give up romance altogether.

Judy had already poured a mug of coffee for me, and by the time I was ready for a refill she brought my breakfast.

She said, "You okay?"

I thought, I'm not okay at all. A three-year-old child has just had brain surgery, and I don't know if it was successful. His seizure-assistance dog is in deep depression, and I can't make her happier. A woman I liked a lot has been murdered and her face was mutilated, and the killer is still out there. The truth is I'm scared for myself and for you and for every other woman.

I said, "I'm fine."

She heard the dryness in my voice and did a double-take. But before she could say anything, Guidry slid into the seat opposite me.

He said, "I'll have what she's having, with a side of bacon, extra crisp."

Judy said, "I'd better bring you a double. Dixie steals bacon, especially if it's crisp."

She gave me a quick look that said *You're gonna tell me all about this meeting when he leaves* and swished away to get him a coffee mug, leaving us looking bare-eyed at each other.

I said, "Guidry, do you have a first name?"

I hadn't planned to say that, it just popped out, like an embarrassing belly button.

His eyes narrowed a bit, as if I'd asked him something too personal. "Most people just call me Guidry."

"Your mother called you Guidry?"

His eyes softened. "My mother calls me Jean-Pierre."

He pronounced the first name *Zhahn*, like an American drunk saying *John*, but when you hook that sound to *Pierre*, I knew he wasn't speaking like an American.

"So you're French, right?"

"Have you taken up journalism?"

"Why are you so secretive? Got skeletons in your family closet?"

Oh, God, why did I say that?

He gave me a long look, then firmed his jaw. "My father's a lawyer in New Orleans, heads a big law firm there."

"What about your mother?"

He smiled. "She's always bringing home strangers who need help, feeding them, finding jobs for them, getting them whatever they need to get back on their feet. Used to drive my father nuts, but since Katrina he's been doing the same thing, giving his time to people who need legal help."

Okay, so now I knew why he had a rich man's aura. It was because he had grown up in a rich man's house, with rich parents who had big hearts.

I said, "Did your father want you to be a lawyer too?"

He grinned. "Oh, yeah. And for a while I was. Went to law school, worked in his firm, tried to like it. But after a while we both knew I'd be a much better cop than I'd ever be a lawyer."

There it was again, that reminder that he was a cop, along with the uncomfortable comparison with lawyers. In spite of myself, I thought of Ethan Crane. Why couldn't my perverse body yearn to be close to an attorney instead of a cop?

Guidry said, "Dixie?"

I must have been staring over his shoulder for a while, seeing ghosts, remembering that cops get killed and leave you.

I said, "Do you know what piqueurism is?"

"Why?"

"I talked to Reba Chandler last night. She's a psychology professor at New College. She mentioned the word. It seemed like something that fits with a scalpel stabbing."

I buttered my biscuit and took a bite. Normal people probably wouldn't have been able to eat while they talked about a woman being stabbed to death, but anybody who's been trained in law enforcement has learned to disconnect their stomachs from their hearts.

Guidry reached across the table and took a round of fried potato from my plate.

Ignoring my question, he said, "We talked to Gorgon. He owns the dealership where Laura Halston bought her Jaguar. He says she paid a hundred thousand plus change—in cash. You have any idea where she got that kind of money?"

"She said she drove her Mercedes from Dallas and sold it in Arkansas."

"Yeah, but that was a lie, since she didn't live in Dallas and didn't have a Mercedes."

"What about Gorgon?"

"On the night Laura Halston was killed, Gorgon was with a woman in Naples. She backs up his story."

Judy bustled back with Guidry's plates—one with his eggs and fries, another with a double rasher of crisp bacon. She looked as if she wanted to say something but then seemed to think better of it and left us.

Like Pavlov's dog salivating at the sound of a bell, I automatically raised my head at the fragrance of fried hog fat. I am convinced that heaven is a place where crisp bacon is served around the clock, anytime you want it, and that it won't clog your arteries or go to your hips. I'll bet angels sit around eating BLTs all day long. Probably with fries. Gives me something to look forward to.

Guidry gave me a sympathetic look and moved a couple rigid strips to my plate. I didn't offer any protest. After the last few days I'd had, I damn well deserved bacon.

We ate silently for a while, me taking mincing bites of my bacon to make it last longer, and Guidry chomping down half a slice at a bite. I watched him chew. His lower lip had a teensy sheen of fat on it from the bacon. It occurred to me that I had never kissed a man who'd just taken a bite of bacon.

He said, "Tell me again how you came to overhear Martin Freuland threaten Laura Halston."

The women in Guidry's world probably never ate bacon. Probably didn't eat any fat at all. Skinny anorexic bitches.

I said, "You know that little turtle I found?"

He shook his head, and it seemed to me that he wanted to roll his eyes.

"Well, I found this little box turtle, and I put her by a dock on Fish Hawk Lagoon. While I was there, Laura and that man came walking by on the jogging trail. I could see them through the hedge, but they didn't see me. The man was telling her that he'd see to it that she paid for what she'd done. He said it was the worst thing she'd ever pulled. Then he said, 'You owe me.' She gave him the finger and walked off. He was furious. Got in his car and hauled off."

He said, "You know what he was talking about?"

"At the time, I thought he was her husband and that he was talking about how she'd left him. Now that I know he was her boss, I have no idea. Her sister says she stole from him."

Judy skidded to a stop just then and refilled our cups. She looked at the bacon crumbs on my plate, pressed her lips together to keep from saying anything, and went off to other customers.

Guidry said, "You talked to the sister?"

"She invited herself into the Richards' house last night. She said some nasty things about Laura, what a liar she was, how she had always been a slut and always used men. She also said their father had an incestuous relationship with Laura from the time she was about nine years old. She claims Laura seduced him, which proves Celeste has the mind of a sewer rat. She also said somebody had told her that Laura was a narcissist. That's really why I went to see Reba Chandler. I wasn't sure what a narcissist was."

His gray eyes studied me for a moment. "Are we still on for Saturday night?"

Surprised, I said, "Sure."

"You get something different done to your hair?"

I touched it. "No."

He grinned, as if he found me amusing. His fingertips beat a drumbeat on the table, and then he stood up and put money down. "See you later."

I watched him go and tried to ignore the racket my pulse was making in my ears.

I could understand Guidry's father wanting him to join his law firm, but Guidry was more cut out to investigate crime than handle legal affairs. Ethan Crane, on the other hand, was great at legal problems but would probably suck at being a homicide investigator. I wondered if Guidry's father was more like Ethan than like Guidry. I wondered if Guidry's father would like me, which was really stupid because I'd probably never even meet the man. I mean, why would I?

Judy was beside me almost before he'd got out the front door. "You and that hunky detective got something going?"

"He's not hunky, and we don't."

"Honey, if he's not hunky, I'm the Queen of Egypt. So what was he doing here?"

"Just wanted to ask me about a case he's working on."

"Runaway?"

"Maybe."

"Poor kids, they don't know what they're getting into when they leave home."

Judy walked away with her coffeepot, looking so sad that I wondered if she spoke from experience.

I slid out of the booth and headed for a post-coffee trip to the ladies' room, where Tanisha was lathering her plump hands. I pulled out a brown paper towel from the dispenser.

"Great breakfast, Tanisha. Thanks."

Tanisha said, "I noticed you was with a man this morning. Nice-looking too. 'Course, how a man looks and how a man acts is two different things."

She shook water from her fingertips, and I handed her the paper towel. She looked sternly at me while she dried her hands.

"You know how to tell what a man's really like? You watch how he handles his package. If he's always touching it, like he's gotta make sure it's still there since the last time he checked, then you know he thinks he's got God between his legs. He'll expect you to get down on your knees to it too. If you don't, hoo-ha, he'll get all hurt like you took the Lord's name in vain. You don't want a man like that."

She tossed the wadded paper towel in the basket.

"You want a man that lets his stuff ride easy, acts like he cares more about your stuff than his own. 'Course he don't, 'cause he's a man, but at least he's smart enough to act like he does." She looked intently at me. "I'm just telling you this 'cause I know you don't have no mama. A girl's gotta have somebody warn her about things like that."

"I appreciate that, Tanisha."

Her face creased in a deep dimpled smile. "That man you was with this morning, he's got a big tidy package, but I never seen him touch it once. I was you, I'd keep him around."

Using her big behind to bump open the restroom door, she left me staring after her.

The whimper I made sounded a lot like Mazie's sounds of stress.

CHAPTER 26

Back in the Bronco, I sat a minute to get my act together, then pulled out my cell and made the call to Hal
that I should have made a long time ago. Then I called
Pete and told him what I wanted him to do. When I put
the phone back in my pocket, I felt as if a thousand-
pound load had been lifted from my shoulders.

I was halfway to Fish Hawk Lagoon when I remembered that I hadn't told Guidry about meeting Frederick
Vaught.

At Mazie's house, I parked in the driveway and
looked toward Laura's house. No cars were in her driveway, and I didn't see any sign of Celeste. Maybe she
had got on her broom and returned to Dallas.

Before I went inside, I called Guidry on my cell. My
fist did a victory pump in the air when I got his voice
mail. I love voice mail. I didn't want to *talk* to him, I
just wanted to give him information.

I said, "I forgot to tell you that Frederick Vaught accosted me this morning at the Sea Breeze. I came out
to run with Billy Elliot, and Vaught popped out from
behind a bush. He played the big bad scary monster,
told me to stop asking questions about him, said I'd
besmirched his good name. Like he still has a good

name. He didn't threaten me or anything, but I thought you should know."

Having done my duty, I clicked off and slid out of the Bronco.

A dark sedan slowly passed in the street, the driver looking uncertainly toward Mazie's house as if he didn't recognize it. He may not have known for sure which house he was looking for, but I knew for sure who he was—the big muscled man who wore power like a suit, the man I'd thought was Laura's husband, the man I'd seen her with on the jogging path. The man who may have killed her.

He pulled into Laura's driveway, the car disappearing behind the trees, and I stood staring at the space he'd left. I thought about the locksmith's truck that had been at the house the night before. Ordinarily, if locks are changed following a crime, the new keys are immediately put into the hands of the home owner or a member of the owner's family. But Celeste had left while the locksmith's truck had still been in the driveway the night before, and unless she'd returned she hadn't got the keys.

Martin Freuland surely knew that Laura was dead. If Guidry hadn't questioned him yet, he certainly knew he would be a logical suspect for her murder. So what was he doing at Laura's house? And what had the locksmith done with the new keys? I had an image of him calling Guidry or Celeste and saying, "I put the keys under a rock by the front door," or some such silliness.

I didn't really believe he would do that, but on the other hand, Freuland hadn't backed that sedan out of Laura's driveway yet, so what was he doing? I imagined him standing at Laura's door, staring into the house through the glass panels. Celeste had told Guidry that Laura had tipped off the feds about his work for drug dealers. Guidry had said he was under investigation and could end up spending twenty or thirty years in prison. Maybe Laura had records in her house that implicated him, and he wanted to destroy them.

While I was wondering all that, my feet had gradually moved down Mazie's driveway and turned onto the sidewalk, sort of ambling toward Laura's house as if they didn't really have a destination. I told myself that it wasn't any of my business. I told myself that Martin Freuland hadn't been arrested for Laura's murder, that he was a free man, and that there was no law that said he couldn't go to Laura's door. But my feet kept moving, and when I got to Laura's driveway I turned in and ambled past the empty sedan.

My Keds were careful not to make scuffing sounds, which might have seemed as if I were sneaking up on the man at the door, but it is simply the nature of Keds to do that. Especially when they're careful.

Martin Freuland was bent forward examining the pane of glass closest to the lock. The one that would, if it were knocked out, allow a person to stick a hand in and turn the thumb switch that unlocked the door. Forget new keys, that door would be a snap to open.

I said, "You may not have noticed, but the door is locked."

He jerked upright and spun to look at me, mouth open, eyes wide. He looked like a man who wasn't accustomed to being surprised. He also looked desperate.

Rage began to climb me like a swarm of fire ants. I'd been deceived, tricked, conned, and manipulated. I'd had old murky fears and guilts raise their hoary heads and slash at my sense of safety. I'd been accosted by a psycho nurse who smothered old ladies in their beds, and now I was confronting a corrupt bank president who might also be a murderer. At the very least, he was obviously contemplating breaking into Laura's house.

He walked toward me, his face not sure whether to try for appeasement or defiance. The first time I'd seen him, I'd seen him as a former football player turned orthopedic surgeon. Even knowing he was really a bank president, the form still applied. As Laura had said, the man was big. He wore an expensive charcoal suit with a pale blue shirt and dark tie, the threads of power in any profession.

He said, "You're Ms. Hemingway. I'm told you were one of the last people to see Laura alive."

"Who told you that?"

He made a vague gesture, erasing my question as if it weren't important. "They say you're taking care of her cat. I gave her that cat as a birthday present. I named him Cohiba for the cigar."

I squinted at him, wondering how he knew who I was.

I said, "I know. Laura told me."

His face lit. "She spoke of me?"

"She said the man who'd given Leo to her had called him Cohiba."

"What else did she tell you?"

"Mr. Freuland, I hardly knew Laura."

He looked slightly nonplussed when I spoke his name, then a flash of anger lit his eyes.

"She stole from me. Did she tell you that?"

"I don't know what you're talking about."

"She went in the vault and took it, brazen as always. Waited until the whole city was preoccupied with our George Washington celebration, and then made her move." His firm lips stretched a fraction in an aborted smile. "She was like that. It was one of the things that made her exciting."

"George Washington?"

He scowled, as if my surprise was annoying.

"Laredo has a huge George Washington festival every year. It lasts a month, and half a million people come to it. Carnivals, parades, concerts, marathon runs, cook-offs, all kinds of parties, brings in millions for local businesses. The big finale is the debutante ball on February twenty-second. Elaborate gowns that cost upwards of twenty thousand dollars apiece, lots of spectacle."

"What does that have to do with Laura?"

He looked surprised again. "Laura was like a big sister to the debs. She showed them how to walk, how to do makeup, hair, all that kind of thing. She'd been a model."

I made a stirring motion with my hand, meaning *Get on with it!*

Doggedly, as if he had to tell the story in a particular order, he said, "Every year she'd bring her model's bag to the bank on the morning of the twenty-second. Everybody expected her to do that, she'd been doing it for years, had all the tricks of the trade in that bag. Then she'd leave and spend the day helping the girls."

His jaw tightened, and for a minute he seemed loath to tell me the rest. "This year, she went in the vault and stuffed her model's bag with money. Then she drove to her sister's house in Dallas. I reported her missing, but the police didn't take me seriously. They thought she'd just left me. It took awhile to track her down."

I said, "I don't suppose you told them about the money."

He had the grace to look embarrassed. "It was too complicated to explain."

Some perverse part of me was glad she'd gone to Dallas. At least it made that part of her story true—the part about coming from Dallas. It wasn't much, but it was a teeny truth, and I was irrationally grateful for it.

With an effort, he got his face under control. "I didn't kill her, Ms. Hemingway. I know I'm a prime suspect, but I didn't do it. I was furious at her for stealing from me, but I wouldn't have hurt her."

I remembered what Guidry had said and almost laughed at Freuland's self-pity. The cash Laura stole might have been illegally deposited in his bank by drug dealers. Or it might have been payoff money the drug dealers had given to Freuland as a commission for not reporting them. In either case, I wasn't sure whether Laura had stolen from drug dealers, the bank, or Freuland. Somehow stealing either drug trafficking money or money paid to a corrupt bank president didn't seem as onerous as stealing money honestly earned.

Freuland said, "I have to get that money back. I *have* to. If you know where it is, I'll give you a handsome reward for taking me to it."

My nostrils pinched inward and I took a step backward, the way you do when you've stumbled on something nasty.

I said, "I don't know about any money, Mr. Freuland."

I spun around so fast I almost tripped myself, and stalked away from him. As I walked, I pulled out my cell and punched in Guidry's number again. My fingers didn't even need to think, they'd done this so many times.

This time he answered, with a curt, "Guidry here."

I said, "Martin Freuland is at Laura's house. He says she stole money from the bank vault and he has to get it back. He was examining the glass pane on her front door, and I imagine he'll be inside her house in about ten seconds. He offered to share the money with me if I told him where it was."

Guidry actually chuckled. "People who take bribes

expect other people to take them too. If she took money from the bank vault, it was probably his payoff money."

"He wants it back."

"I imagine he does. I'll send somebody over there. By the way, the Autrey woman has officially named you the person responsible for her sister's cat. Says you can do whatever you want to with him."

"Gee, the woman is all heart."

"Will you take him?"

"I'm not a cat shelter, Guidry, but I'll find a home for him."

"Good. Ms. Autrey says she's going back to Dallas late today."

"So soon?"

"She's already gone through her sister's house and collected the valuables she wanted. I guess she doesn't have any more reason to stay."

"What about Laura? What about her sister's body?"

"The ME won't release it until the criminal investigation is completed. I assume Ms. Autrey will make arrangements with a funeral home before she leaves."

That only meant Celeste would pay the cost of a cremation or a burial and then go home. There would be no memorial service or funeral for her sister, but since Laura had only been in Sarasota a few weeks, maybe that was sensible. But if there were one, I would go, and Maurice and Ruby probably would go too. Also Gorgon, with his diamond rings. Certainly Frederick Vaught would show up and be mournful. It would be a dismal service, but it seemed to me that Laura deserved *something* to mark the fact that she had lived.

As I reached for the doorknob to go inside Mazie's house, I realized that Celeste Autrey had to have been the person who'd talked about me to Freuland. She had probably described me, perhaps described my vehicle as well, so that he immediately knew who I was. It seemed strange that Celeste would buddy up to Freuland since she thought he'd killed her sister, but Celeste was cold enough to sleep on an ice mattress and think it was cozy.

Pete had left the front door unlocked again, but when I went in and saw his face, any lecture I might have given him evaporated. His eyebrows were nearly at his hairline, and his expression was one I remembered Michael wearing as a teenager—defiant and determined and hopeful all at once. I guess men don't ever lose those traits, even in their eighties.

Mazie stood beside him, and it seemed to me that she had the same look. Per my instructions, she was wearing her blue Service Dog vest with its embroidered medical caduceus symbol.

Pete said, "We should have done this sooner."

I said, "We couldn't do it before now. No hospital in the world will allow a dog in ICU, not even a service dog, so we had to wait until Jeffrey was in a room. Even then, we had to have permission. From Hal and Gillis, from Jeffrey's doctor, probably from the hospital."

"You did all that?"

"I got Hal's permission. He's taking care of the rest of it."

I wasn't absolutely sure he could take care of the rest of it, but I was absolutely sure that somehow, some way, Pete and I were taking Mazie in to see Jeffrey.

Pete's smile split his handsome face, and he actually gave a little hop of joy, like a boy. He said, "Then let's go!"

He was practically out the door before he got the words out of his mouth, rushing to the Bronco and getting Mazie secured in a travel crate in the back. We made sure she had water in her bowl, put down rolled towels to protect her from sliding in the crate, and got ourselves in the front.

I took one last look toward Laura's driveway as we backed out, but I couldn't see through the trees. If Martin was still there, I hoped the sheriff's deputies came in time to catch him.

CHAPTER 27

As I got in the driver's seat, Pete scurried to the passenger side. "Don't worry," he said. "I go to the hospital all the time and do clowning skits for the kids. They all know me there. We won't have any problem."

"Uh-huh."

St. Petersburg is about an hour from Sarasota via I-75 north, then over to I-275 and the Skyway Bridge. Before we got to the I-75 on-ramp, Pete said, "Do you mind if I get something to eat? I was too worried to eat before."

I swung into a drive-through lane at McDonald's and waited while he studied the menu.

He said, "I'll have a Quarter Pounder with cheese and fries. And a large Coke. And a pie thing. Apple."

Happiness always perks up my appetite too. I decided to get one of the apple pie things.

I only ate when we were stopped at traffic lights, but the apple pie was gone by the time we hit the interstate. Pete was almost as fast with his burger and fries. After we had done our boa constrictor acts, we rode along in thoughtful silence.

On that stretch of highway, more than half the vehicles were trucks—semis, panels, pickups, or big trucks with hoists and cranes or some other special equipment. Southwest Florida has been under constant construction ever since the new kind of retirees came—no longer in mobile homes but with wads of money from the dot-com boom or hefty executive payouts from bankrupt companies. New highways have been laid, new build-ings erected, old buildings remodeled, all work done by men who drive trucks.

As we met them, passed them, and were passed by them, my mind went off on a little naughty thought trip about those truck drivers. It's what minds do when they're not strictly disciplined. Especially female minds. I mean, let's face it, construction workers, pool men, landscapers, all those outdoor guys have incred-ibly firm butts that you don't see on other men. They also have pelvises that move when they walk. Men who sit at desks all day have flat butts and walk just by bending their knees—their hips don't move at all. It makes a woman imagine the difference in their respec-tive lovemaking abilities, and the truck drivers come off best.

I mused on those high-minded thoughts all the way to the exit to I-275. Then, as we headed toward the Sky-way Bridge, my mind drifted to the memory of Ethan Crane's butt, which was fantastic. Better than Guidry's, to tell the truth, and Ethan sat at a desk all day.

While my mind was wandering down that guilty little avenue, Pete's had different priorities. To get my attention, he made a big to-do of wadding up his pie sleeve and stowing it neatly in the McDonald's bag with his used napkins and empty Coke cup.

He said, "That detective came back again. He asked if I was sure it was Tuesday morning I saw that lady crossing the street, and not the day before. I've already told him it probably wasn't Laura after all, and now he wants to know when I saw some completely other lady. Dumb shit must think I'm too old to know what day it is."

"That's odd."

"Nah, lots of people think you lose your marbles once you pass about ten years older than they are. If they're sixty, they think seventy is old. If they're seventy, they think eighty is old. Personally, I know people in their thirties that are older than me."

"It's odd that Guidry questioned you about when you saw some other woman crossing the street."

We rode along for a while and I said, "You're positive it wasn't Laura?"

"I wasn't up close, if that's what you mean. I thought it was her, but I guess it wasn't."

"Did she see you?"

"She didn't wave if she did. It was so early, she probably didn't think anybody else was out."

The first time I'd met Laura, she'd gone running after nine o'clock. I'd got the impression that she always ran around that time, but I could have been wrong. Lots of runners get up as early as I do and get their exercising done before the sun is up.

After we passed through the tollbooths on the way to St. Petersburg, Pete's brow furrowed and his eyebrows began to climb even higher, and I knew the reality of what we were doing had hit him the same way it did me. We both knew there was no absolute guarantee that Hal had been able to get all the necessary permissions for Mazie to go to Jeffrey's hospital room. Jeffrey was a child. He had just had brain surgery. Mazie was a dog. Some people would think her presence in his room so soon after surgery could be a health risk.

Besides that apprehension, I had other reasons to be tense, reasons that increased the closer we got to the golden girders of the Skyway Bridge. It's silly, I know, but I don't like leaving solid ground. I especially don't like the gigantic roller-coaster feel of the Skyway. By the time we got there and the Bronco's nose began to point toward the sky, I gripped the wheel with both hands. Call it phobia, call it my need to control, but if that sucker collapsed, cars would drop like boulders.

Once we left the Skyway behind and my breath was even, I began watching for the exit that would take us to I-175. Pete watched too, his eyebrows waggling like writhing caterpillars. We found I-175, and after a while took the Sixth Street South exit. The closer we got to the hospital, the higher and twitchier Pete's eyebrows got.

He contained himself until we were turning into the hospital parking lot.

He said, "You didn't really get permission, did you?"

I looked at him the way a mouse coming out of its hole would look at a watching cat.

"Hal promised to clear it with the doctor and the hospital."

Pete said, "I'm like that too. I always operate on the theory that it's better to ask forgiveness than permission."

I said, "I could go in first and talk to the charge nurse."

"I'm afraid they'll say no, Dixie."

"I didn't mean I'd ask if we could bring Mazie in. I'll just talk. You know, as in distract-her-attention-from-the-man-going-down-the-hall-with-a-dog."

"Okay, that's good."

I wasn't sure if it was good or not. But right or wrong, that seemed to be what we were doing.

Pete directed me to a side lot near an unmarked entrance. "This is the wing where Jeffrey's room is. He's on the fifth floor. There's an elevator near the side door that's not as busy as the main one. I've seen people taking therapy dogs up that elevator. I don't think anybody will stop Mazie."

Okay, that sounded good. At least for a moment. Therapy dogs and service dogs go into hospitals all the time, and Mazie was a service dog. But therapy dogs go in with therapists who have been vetted and authorized by the hospital, and service dogs go in as authorized companions of a person visiting a patient. Mazie was a service dog, but she was a companion to Jeffrey, not Pete. The bald truth was that Mazie was going in the hospital simply as a four-legged visitor to see a patient. If the hospital rules didn't allow dogs to visit patients, we were sunk.

I said, "Give me time to go around to the front entrance before you go in."

I don't know why I thought that was a good idea, but it seemed necessary at the time. It must have sounded good to Pete too, because he looked at his watch the way bank robbers coordinate time before they make a big heist.

I parked and nipped around the lot to the front entrance where streams of somber-looking people were leaving and arriving. Inside the lobby, I realized I hadn't asked Hal or Pete for Jeffrey's room number. Feeling as if somebody at the other end of a surveillance camera was probably watching me and calling security, I stopped at a welcome desk.

A grandmotherly volunteer checked Jeffrey's name on her computer. "He's in the Neurology Center on the fifth floor. Room five-sixteen."

I followed arrows to a hall to the Neurology Center, then joined a gaggle of people waiting for an elevator. My palms were sweaty. As the elevator descended, red numbers above the door told us what floor it was on—

now *seven*, now *six*, now *five*—moving, moving, moving. We stared up at the numbers as if our lives depended on knowing when it would get to *one*. When the number *two* flashed, we all tensed like cattle about to stampede.

Inside the elevator, I tried not to think about why the other people were there. Children shouldn't get sick. Childhood should be a golden time of laughter and play, it should not include pain and weakness.

At the fifth floor, I left the elevator and walked briskly down a long hall toward a nurse's station. The sound of crying babies and toddlers floated on the air, and several nurses wearing bunny-printed smocks hurried past me, their rubber-soled shoes not making a sound. From one of the rooms, a woman in a dark leather recliner lifted a hand to wave at me as I passed. A hospital crib was hidden behind a drawn curtain, and I got the feeling the woman had been keeping lonely vigil for a long time.

More bunny-printed smocks were at the nurse's station, every person serious and intent. It looked as if five or six corridors met at the station, and from their vantage point, they could see down every one to the elevator at the end. More than likely, some of their computer monitors showed every person who got off those elevators. They were people who saved kids' lives, good people who shouldn't be tricked.

A man with calm eyes and a metal patient record tucked under his arm watched me approach the stand. I figured he could see right through my skin into my brain.

I said, "Look, here's the thing. I'm here to see Jeffrey Richards, and my friend is coming up the elevator in a minute with Jeffrey's seizure-assistance dog. Her name is Mazie, and she hasn't left Jeffrey's side since they've been together. Jeffrey had surgery three days ago, and he and Mazie miss each other desperately. So we brought Mazie to see him." For emphasis, I said, "She's his best friend!"

He looked over my shoulder and smiled. "Would that man be your friend?"

I turned to see Pete and Mazie coming toward us. Pete seemed to be pretending to be blind. Even Mazie seemed in on the act, walking in front of him as if she were leading.

"That's Pete Madeira and Mazie. Pete's a clown."

"Come on, I'll take you to Jeffrey's room."

I motioned to Pete, whose strained face broke into a smile when he realized we seemed to have permission. We followed the man down the hall to a closed door. With a light tap, the man pushed the door open, and we all filed in.

Standing beside Jeffrey's bedside, Gillis looked frazzled and exhausted, but ten years younger than she had four days ago. Knowing Jeffrey had come through the surgery and was back to consciousness must have been a tonic for her. When she saw us, she blinked in momentary surprise, then gave a choked sob. Hal wasn't there. He must not have told Gillis that we were coming.

With his head swathed in thick bandages and his tiny body in a miniature hospital gown, Jeffrey looked like a pale alien child. The top sheet on his bed had been folded down, so his little bare legs stuck out from his hospital gown. I had a quick flash memory of Christy's lifeless body and jerked my mind away.

Hal had told me that Jeffrey slept a lot, and he was asleep now, but frowning and fretful.

Mazie broke free of Pete's hold and in one bound was on the bed beside Jeffrey. Gillis put out a protective hand, but she needn't have worried. Mazie stepped with exquisite care to look down into Jeffrey's slack face. Then, turning cautiously, she stretched out on the bed close to Jeffrey's legs.

Jeffrey smiled, and as one person we all exhaled the breaths we'd been holding. Jeffrey's eyes were still closed, but he no longer frowned or whimpered. The man with the patient record under his arm stepped forward and touched fingers to one of Jeffrey's wrists. He had a kind face.

To Mazie, he said, "Good job, Mazie."

Gillis said, "Dixie and Pete, this is Dr. Travis, Jeffrey's surgeon. But I guess you know that since you got permission from him to bring Mazie in."

Pete and I avoided each other's eyes.

Dr. Travis grinned. "Hal talked to me. Maybe it would be better if you wait in the visitors' lounge and let Mazie and Jeffrey be alone for a while."

By *alone*, he meant with Gillis, who could not have been dislodged from Jeffrey's side with a crowbar. Pete and I trailed out into the hall and found the visitors' lounge, where we each took one of the leather recliners lined up along the wall and stared straight ahead. Pete's eyes were blood-rimmed, and my own felt as if the inside of my lids had been scraped with emery boards.

Guilt was once again wrapping its slimy body around my neck. I had been so preoccupied with Laura's murder that I'd failed to pay attention to my job. Even if nobody else had thought of it, I should have known to bring Mazie to see Jeffrey the minute he'd been put in a floor bed. I was a pet sitter, not a detective, and I should have put all my energy into making sure Mazie's needs were being met instead of running around asking questions that were Guidry's job.

Pete said, "Ever since I met that kid, I've been afraid

something would go wrong with his surgery. I wish I hadn't done that. All that fear probably made Mazie afraid."

I guess guilt always tries to come along for the ride with everybody.

I said, "Mazie would have been worried and stressed no matter what you were thinking."

I remembered Pete telling me once that his own daughter had died. I didn't know how old she'd been, but the loss of a child at any age is devastating, and I felt a new kinship to him. Every parent who's ever lost a child has a link of sadness that nobody else can ever understand.

The room was quiet, the only sounds a distant *ping* of elevator doors and the hushed voice of a woman speaking on the hospital's PA system.

I leaned my head against the recliner and closed my eyes. The next thing I knew, Hal Richards was kneeling beside me and saying my name.

Like Gillis, he looked haggard with fatigue, but younger. "Thank you for bringing Mazie. I'm sorry I wasn't here when you came. Gillis and I are taking turns sleeping, and I was at the hotel. It was a brilliant idea to bring Mazie, I don't know why I didn't think of it."

Pete said, "Mazie needed to see her boy. She didn't know what had happened to him."

Hal nodded somberly. "Jeffrey needed Mazie too."

I looked at my watch and saw that two hours had passed since we'd left Mazie in Jeffrey's room.

I said, "We should go now."

With creaking sounds from the chair and his knees, Pete got to his feet and headed toward Jeffrey's room. I followed, with Hal walking beside me. Pete opened the door and we all stopped to look at Mazie and Jeffrey. He was sleeping soundly, and she had moved so she covered both his legs like a blanket. When she saw us, she lifted her head as if she knew her time with Jeffrey had ended.

Hal said, "Hi, girl."

Mazie's tail wagged, and Hal went over to stroke her head.

Meeting his wife's eyes over Mazie's head, Hal said, "Pete and Dixie are going to take Mazie home now."

Pete said, "If it's okay, I could bring her back tomorrow."

Gillis gave him a radiant smile. "That would be great, Pete."

Hal lifted Mazie and set her on the floor. Pete took her leash, and we all said awkward goodbyes. Silently, Pete and I went down the hall with Mazie walking between us. At the elevator, Mazie whined and strained against the leash when Pete led her inside.

He said, "She wants to stay here."

As the elevator descended, Pete and I met each other's eyes. Something about this visit hadn't gone right, and we both knew it.

We made it all the way to the parking lot before Mazie jerked away and tore back to the hospital.

CHAPTER 28

Streaking to the side door where we'd come out, Mazie ran full out and determined. She had her mind set on going back to Jeffrey, and she wasn't waiting for any human to go with her. Pete and I ran to catch up. At the door, we met Hal.

He said, "Jeffrey's crying again. Worse than before."

Pete and I met each other's eyes, both of us afraid the seizures had returned.

At Jeffrey's floor, Mazie scrambled forward the minute the elevator doors opened, moving ahead so strongly that Hal had to run while he vainly tried to slow her to a walk. Jeffrey's door was open, and we could hear him crying before we got there. It was the same droning sound I'd heard him make before, the same sound Mazie was accustomed to hearing when he was on the verge of a seizure. Jeffrey's legs were kicking, and his face was grimly twisted like an old man's. Dr. Travis was beside the bed, and the room seemed to contain a lot of other people wearing bunny smocks and anxious looks.

Mazie jerked away from Hal and leaped onto Jeffrey's bed and settled her body against his side. Abruptly, the crying stopped, Jeffrey's legs went still, his eyes closed and his face became calm. Everybody in the room smiled.

The only one who didn't seem happy was Mazie. Pulling herself up on her elbows, she cocked her head and stared into Jeffrey's passive face with an odd fierceness.

A couple of nurses whispered to each other that she was checking him out to make sure he was okay, but I didn't think so. Something else was going on in Mazie's mind, but I wasn't sure what it was. Hal and Gillis exchanged a look, and I knew they also thought Mazie had some perceptive knowledge the rest of us didn't have. Whatever was causing Mazie's determined study, it gave her the invigilating look of a scientist inspecting a new find.

My own body hairs suddenly stood upright with a realization. Seizure-alert dogs recognize a change in body odor that presages a seizure, but maybe people with seizure disorders *always* have a unique odor that only dogs can detect. If that were true, and if surgery had removed the cause of Jeffrey's seizures, there would have been a subtle change in his normal odor. To Mazie, that would be extremely puzzling because it would mean Jeffrey was no longer the same Jeffrey she knew.

As if she had come to a firm conclusion, Mazie got to her feet and stood on the bed with her legs braced beside Jeffrey's feet. Lowering her head, she put her nose to his toes and licked them.

Jerking his feet away, Jeffrey's eyes flew open and he giggled. "Stop it, Mazie!"

Beside the bed, Gillis covered her face with both hands and sobbed quietly. Hal moved to put an arm around her shoulders, his own eyes wet. They didn't need to say that they'd had secret fears that Jeffrey would never laugh in his old way again. It had taken Mazie to harmonize the Jeffrey who'd had seizures with the Jeffrey who didn't.

With an ear-to-ear grin, Dr. Travis said, "I think Mazie should stay here with Jeffrey."

I felt like telling him that it didn't take a brain surgeon to figure that out. Instead, I almost gave myself whiplash from nodding.

Leaning to give Gillis a quick kiss, Hal said, "I'll just walk to the elevator with Pete and Dixie."

In the hall, Pete put a fatherly arm around Hal's shoulders. "The boy's going to be fine, just fine."

I managed to make some squeaky sounds of agreement, but I was afraid I'd blubber if I tried to talk.

By the time we'd got to the elevator, we'd decided that Pete and I would go to a pet supply store, get the things Mazie would need, and bring them back to the hospital before we headed back to Siesta Key. For the rest of Jeffrey's hospital stay, Mazie would spend part of her time in the hospital room and part of her time in the hotel with Hal or Gillis. When it was time for Jeffrey to come home, either Pete or I would go back and help transport Mazie.

Pete and I sort of floated out to the parking lot, grinning like idiots and wishing somebody would ask us why just so we could tell them that Jeffrey was okay.

I used my cell phone's convenient locator service to find a pet supply store, and we were walking its aisles within fifteen minutes. We got a water bowl, a food bowl, a bag of kibble, some doggie treats, and a sleeping cushion. As we went down the aisle toward the checkout counter, we passed the store's cat-food section, and I noticed a box of cat food like the one Laura had set out on her counter as a reminder. Something about that box of cat food set off little clanging bells in my head, but I didn't know why.

The checker totaled up our purchases with a cheerful pinging sound, and I paid her and pocketed the receipt. Pete picked up the bags and we headed for the parking lot and the Bronco. At the hospital, I waited in the parking lot while Pete hustled in the doggie supplies to Hal. When he came out, he was almost bouncing.

"Jeffrey's sitting up. Not in a chair, but they've got his bed cranked up and he's talking. Mazie is lying next to him, and he's got a grip on her like he's afraid she'll leave him. The doctor says he'll send him some real food pretty soon. All he's had so far is clear soup and Jell-O. They always give you Jell-O. The Jell-O company must make a mint off hospitals."

I laughed. Pete laughed. We would have laughed at the Jell-O itself if we'd seen it. We were high on sheer happiness. We didn't look ahead. All that mattered was that Jeffrey was alive and alert and that he was going to eat real food. Life is really very simple when you narrow it down to the things that really matter. I was so elated that I forgot to be nervous when we went over the Skyway Bridge.

After we'd passed the tollbooths, Pete turned in his seat and faced me.

"I'm not going to work for you anymore, Dixie. I can't take another case like this one."

I couldn't blame him. He'd expected a calm week or two, and he'd had emotional chaos.

I said, "I'm sorry it's been so trying."

"I've been thinking about that cat. What's going to happen to him?"

"Celeste has given me authority to find a home for

him. She's going back to Dallas and she doesn't want him."

"Could I take him? I think we'd get along just fine."

I smiled to myself. Pete would probably play saxophone for him.

In the interest of full disclosure, I said, "He has a long tail that he leaves in doorways. You'd have to be careful that he didn't trip you."

"Honey, I've worked with circus monkeys that had tails so long they could wrap them around your waist. They were always leaving their tails looped around too, that's just their sense of humor. That's not a problem for me."

"Then you've got yourself a Havana Brown named Leo. As soon as you're ready for him, I'll bring him to you."

"Do you think it would be okay if I changed his name? I worked with a guy named Leo one time, and he was a bad apple."

I laughed. "A lot of cats start out with one name and end up with another. Leo's first name was Cohiba."

"Well, that's dumb. I was thinking more of Percy. Like P-U-R-R-C. I always kind of wanted a cat named Purr-C, spell it like that."

We didn't talk much after that, both of us caught in our own thoughts.

Back on Siesta Key, I drove to Mazie's house to drop Pete off so he could clean the house, wash his sheets, and generally erase all signs that he'd been there. Home owners are glad to have somebody watching things when they're gone, but they don't want reminders of you when they return.

I was tired and sticky and unshowered, and my eyes felt like boiled tomatoes. I was also hungry. Nevertheless, it was time for my afternoon rounds.

Before Pete got out of the Bronco, he said, "Do you think you could get that cat today?"

I stared at him. *"Today?"*

"Well, I've been thinking, that cat hates being cooped up, that's why he runs away so much. So he must really hate being in a cat hotel, all squeezed in a tiny little room. If I were him, I'd want to get out of that hotel and move to a new house."

Pete lives in an old Florida cracker house tucked away on one of Siesta Key's tree-lined streets. It has a front porch where a tranquil cat could sit and watch the world go by, and a quiet garden where a contented cat could have fun chasing butterflies and birds. Leo had been neither tranquil nor contented at Laura's house, but now that I knew more about the fireworks that had been going off inside her mind, I had a feeling he might have a personality change when he was with Pete.

I said, "When I've finished with my last call, I'll go to the Kitty Haven and get Leo and bring him here."

"Purr-C, not Leo."

He looked toward Laura's driveway and frowned. "Who's that next door?"

I looked too and did a silent groan. The locksmith's truck was at the curb, and Celeste's rented Camry was in the driveway.

I said, "That's the car Celeste drove."

We both stared at the Camry.

Pete said, "Maybe now's the time to ask her about me taking the cat."

"We don't need her permission for you to take Leo. She's given me authority to find a home for him. It's none of her business who gives him that home."

Pete lifted one of his woolly eyebrows at my snarkiness. "Whatever you think."

I sighed. "I just don't want to talk to the woman."

"Don't blame you, but maybe she's not such a pain in the patootie when things are going okay. It must have been a terrible thing for her to have to identify her sister's body."

I knew he was right. Of all people, I should have been more sympathetic to Celeste Autrey. I had been the one who had gone apeshit in front of a bank of cameras at Todd and Christy's funeral, and I had been the one who had been fueled by consuming rage for a long time after their deaths. I hadn't been such a sweet person either, and I didn't have any business being so judgmental about Celeste's attitude.

I said, "I'll talk to her, but I'm not going to mention who's taking Leo."

Pete patted my shoulder. "You're a good girl, Dixie."

As he walked to the house he gave me a backward jaunty wave, and for a minute I wasn't seeing his tall elegant frame but Laura's body, flipping Martin a backward finger as she left him. Martin had said he'd been furious at Laura, but that he wouldn't have hurt her. But from what I'd seen of Martin Freuland, he would say anything that served his purposes and do anything he thought he could get away with.

CHAPTER 29

I eased out of the driveway, drove the short distance to Laura's house, and pulled behind the locksmith's truck at the curb. As I walked up the driveway, I saw Celeste and the locksmith in front of Laura's front door, and from the way they were glaring at each other, it didn't seem like a friendly meeting. When Celeste saw me, color rose in her face and her eyebrows drew together in a furious frown.

"Oh, this is perfect! The pet sitter has come to join the party! I suppose the Sheriff's Department sent out a special invitation to you. Did they give you a key to the house too? They won't give me one, but they'll give one to anybody who lives in this godforsaken dump! I couldn't even go through my sister's house by myself, had to have a deputy watch while I got her jewelry and some of her clothes. She was my sister, you know, and we were close—even with all I had to put up with, we were close. I didn't take anything she wouldn't want me to have. Not that I don't have nice things of my own, because I do, but there's no point in leaving these things here. In any civilized town, the neighbors would have helped me carry things, but not here. Here the cops keep the keys to my sister's house from me."

The locksmith heaved a huge sigh. "Ma'am, as I've told you probably a hundred times now, the cops aren't keeping the keys from you, I am. You can have the keys as soon as you pay me for changing the locks. You're the one who ordered the change, you're the one who has to pay for it. As soon as you pay me, I'll give you the new keys."

"I'm not paying you for something I have the right to have. It's my sister's house. I had the right to have her locks changed."

"Yes, ma'am, but I have the right to be paid for changing them. You've made three appointments to get the keys, and you missed all of them. Now you want the keys for free. Sorry, not gonna happen."

Whirling to me, Celeste said, "And exactly what is your purpose here?"

Mildly, I said, "I just came to tell you I'd found a good home for Leo. I thought you might want to know."

"That *cat*? You think I care about that stupid *cat*?"

"He was your sister's cat, so I thought you might."

It didn't seem like a good time to tell her that the Kitty Haven charged fifty dollars a day for boarding a cat. Legally, the charge should go to her sister's estate. In reality, I would pay it.

Even allowing for the shock of learning that her sister had been brutally murdered, Celeste's behavior was bizarre. She was not a stupid woman. If she were Laura's legal heir, she surely knew she had a right to everything in her sister's house, no matter when she returned to Dallas. But she must also know that the house was devoid of art and had extremely modest furnishings. Any valuables would be jewelry or furs, which Celeste had apparently already taken.

She said, "You think I'm a selfish bitch, don't you? Both of you think that."

Neither the locksmith nor I answered, at least not out loud.

With her face the color of new radishes, Celeste dived into her handbag and took out a leather wallet. As if she were thumbing out playing cards, she slipped some bills from the wallet and flung them at the locksmith.

"Here's your money."

The money fell to his feet and he left it there while he pulled a small paper packet from his pocket. "Here's your key."

She held it on her open palm. "Just one?"

"One comes with the lock change. You want more, you pay for more."

Her head jerked backward, and in the next instant she spat at him and threw the key against his chest.

"Take your damn key and to hell with you!"

Brushing past me, she stomped to the Camry and got in with a loud door slam. When she pulled out, she came within inches of hitting both the truck and my Bronco on the street, and left with a loud revving of her engine. The locksmith waited until she was out of sight before he picked up two hundred-dollar bills at his feet.

He said, "That woman is a nut."

I couldn't disagree.

He said, "You want this key?"

I shook my head. "I'm just the pet sitter. I've got the cat that belonged to the woman that was killed here, that's all."

"She left a cat?"

"A Havana Brown. Beautiful cat. I've found him a good home."

He handed me the key. "You might need something for the cat."

I didn't want the key, but I could see his quandary.

He'd changed locks on the house and been paid for it, and he felt duty bound to leave the new key with somebody, even if the somebody was just me.

I said, "I'll give it to Lieutenant Guidry. He's handling the murder investigation."

"Okay, that'll work."

He stuffed the bills Celeste had thrown at him into his pocket and went out to his truck. I followed him. I had been tired and sweaty and hungry before, now I was tired and sweaty and hungry and totally disgusted with Celeste Autrey.

The locksmith had been only half right. Celeste wasn't just a nut, she was a vicious nut. She and Laura must have been two halves of one disturbed whole, but while Laura had been disturbed and sweet, Celeste had soaked up all the bitter.

CHAPTER 30

My voice was hollow with weariness when I called Guidry.

I said, "I spoke to Celeste Autrey a few minutes ago. She was at Laura Halston's house with the locksmith. Outside the house, actually, because she refused to pay for having the locks changed, so he refused to give her the new key. She finally threw money at him and he gave her the key, but she was so mad that there was only one key that she spit at him and threw it back. Then she left, and he gave the key to me. What do you want me to do with it?"

"She spit at him?"

"Like an adder."

"Why'd the locksmith give you the key?"

I sighed. "I don't know, Guidry. Probably because I was there and he was fed up with the whole business. He'd been paid for changing the locks and making the new key, so he wanted to be rid of it. Good thing Martin Freuland wasn't there, he would have given it to him. Did you pick Freuland up?"

"Can't pick a man up just for being outside a house, Dixie. I sent some deputies over to suggest to him that loitering outside a dead woman's house could be construed as suspicious behavior, so he left."

"What about Vaught? I've been thinking about him. The man's hands are too clean. Freuland has more reason to want to kill Laura if she stole money from him, but Vaught's hands look more surgical, like they'd know how to use a scalpel."

The line was silent for a long moment, then Guidry's voice came back almost as heavy with fatigue as mine.

"Dixie, I never told you Laura Halston was stabbed with a scalpel."

My tired brain started gathering all the information it had collected to tell him that of course the killer had used a scalpel. For starters, there was her sadistic surgeon husband who threw scalpels at the ceiling for fun.

An icy trickle of reason slid down my neck, and my entire body went cold with shame. The husband had been one of Laura's lies, and I was an idiot. Not only had I fallen for the lie when I first heard it, I'd continued to operate as if it were true even after I'd learned it wasn't.

I said, "Oh."

"Does anybody else know you have that key? Anybody besides the locksmith?"

"You do."

"Don't mention it to anybody, okay? I'm a little tied up right now, but I'll call you later and pick it up."

"Okay."

He must have been surprised at my unaccustomed meekness, because he actually said "Goodbye" before he clicked off.

I sat there with my phone in hand and wondered how I could have been so stupid. But I knew the reason. Laura had been a master at pulling people into her fantasies. Unlike her sister's, Laura's dishonesty had been laced with warmth and generosity and humor. She'd made people *want* to believe her, and once they believed, they protected themselves from feeling like fools by continuing to believe.

For the first time, I felt a touch of sympathy for Martin Freuland, whose huge ego and lust for power would have made him a perfect mark for a woman of Laura's talents. Even the town had been a perfect venue for her heist. A city in which the predominantly Hispanic residents throw a monthlong celebration every year in honor of George Washington is a world where fantasy rules. In such an atmosphere, it wouldn't have seemed incongruous to Freuland to allow his lover access to his bank's vault. After all, he believed in her. He believed she was mentor to the town's debutantes, and he'd thought the model's bag she carried on the day of the debutante ball was admirably philanthropic.

I wondered how long she had plotted and schemed before she carried her model's bag into the bank vault and filled it with stacks of Freuland's ill-gotten money. I wondered how long it had taken Freuland to realize he'd been had. It had been an almost perfect crime. He couldn't charge her with theft because the money had been given to him as a payoff for taking deposits from drug dealers. All he could do was report her missing, which must have seemed something of a joke to the city's police.

I doubted he had understood right away—or that he'd been willing to admit to himself—that what she'd done had been premeditated. Laura would have pulled him in as skillfully as she'd pulled me in. She would have made him believe she was in love with him, and even after she left he would have continued to believe it. More than likely, he had chosen to believe that Laura had put money in her model's bag and driven to Dallas as a spur-of-the-moment thing, a momentary lapse of ordinary good sense.

I might have thought that too, but she had taken Leo with her. Leo had either been in her car when she went in the bank with her model's bag, or she'd gone home and got him before she drove away. Laura had known exactly what she was doing when she took that money. Furthermore, she hadn't been afraid of Freuland. Not then, and not when he found her and confronted her. She had walked away from him, and the flippant finger she'd shot him hadn't looked the least big frightened.

Had she underestimated his capacity for violence? Perhaps she went too far when she reported his illicit dealings with his drug-dealer depositors. Perhaps he would have forgiven her for stealing his money, or at least not killed her for it, but killed her for being disloyal to him.

On the other hand, maybe he hadn't been the killer at all. Maybe the creepy nurse Vaught had killed her because she'd rejected him. His sickness was a desire to control, to humiliate, to create terror in helpless victims. The police suspected he'd smothered elderly people in nursing homes, but he could have committed other kinds of murders that nobody knew about. Homeless people, children, mentally ill people, unwary women are killed every day and the killers are never found. Frederick Vaught could be a shadow killer who'd gotten away with crimes simply because he chose helpless victims in private places.

With that gloomy thought, I backed out of Mazie's driveway and headed for Tom Hale's condo. I was a pet sitter, and it was time for my afternoon rounds, beginning as always with Billy Elliot.

When I let myself into Tom's condo, he and Billy Elliot took their eyes off the TV and looked up at me with mild welcome. Then they both widened their eyes a bit, and it seemed to me that Billy Elliot's nostrils pinched together. I know for sure he pulled his head back a bit.

I said, "I look like hell, don't I?"

Tom said, "Maybe not hell. More like heck. Why are you so . . . ah . . ."

"Sweaty. The word is sweaty, Tom, plus rumpled, plus hairy, plus I don't know what-all."

"Yep, that would be the word. So why are you?"

I sighed and lowered my rump to the arm of the sofa. "Pete Madeira and I drove to St. Pete this morning and took Mazie to see Jeffrey."

Tom's face was blank, so I dragged an explanation from my basket of words.

"Mazie is a seizure-assistance dog. Jeffrey is a little boy who just had brain surgery to stop his seizures. Mazie was becoming too despondent away from him, so we took her to the hospital. Which means that I didn't get to go home and take a shower or nap. Well, I napped a little in the hospital in a chair, but it's not the same."

"She's one of those dogs that signal a person when they're about to have a seizure?"

"No, that's a seizure-*alert* dog. Jeffrey's too little to have that kind of dog. Mazie's a seizure-*assistance* dog, which is different. She doesn't alert him to a seizure, but she stays close to him when his balance is off from the medication, and she distracts him when he's unhappy and frustrated."

"Dogs are so great."

I got Billy Elliot's leash and led him into the hall and to the elevator, where he moved as far from me as he could get.

I said, "If you hadn't had a bath lately, you wouldn't smell so hot either."

He pretended not to understand, but when we got to the parking lot, he ran at a slower speed than usual, which I appreciated. By the time I got him back upstairs, I'd made up my mind to go home and take a quick shower. When dogs make a point of standing upwind from you, it's time to attend to your personal grooming.

My apartment is only about half a mile from Tom's condo building, so if I hurried, I could shower and change clothes without losing more than half an hour. I didn't even try to avoid alarming the parakeets when I tore down my curving drive, just let them have hysterics in the air. They like to do that, so I didn't feel bad.

Paco's car was in the carport, but his Harley was gone, which meant that he was out impersonating some road-calloused biker, which meant that some drug dealer or gang leader was under scrutiny. I took the stairs two at a time, using my remote to raise the aluminum shutters as I went. Inside, the apartment was fusty and warm, but I didn't turn on the AC because I'd only be there a short while. Peeling clothes off as I went toward the bathroom, I felt a renewed energy just from anticipation of a shower. Next to telephones and Tampax, warm water piped to a shower has to be the greatest invention of modern man.

I didn't indulge myself, just stayed in long enough to scrub down one side and up the other, letting the water fall hard on my hair but not actually shampooing it. Well, I may have run a teensy bit of shampoo through it and rinsed it out, but it wasn't a true shampoo with huge lather or anything, and I only used a dollop of conditioner so it wouldn't fan out from my head like a sunflower.

Out of the shower, I ran a comb through my hair, brushed my teeth, smeared on some moisturizer with sun block, and ran a quick slick of lipstick over my mouth. As I ran to the office-closet still damp, I gathered my wet hair into a ponytail. It didn't take five minutes to pull on underwear, clean shorts, a T, and lace up clean Keds. A new and better-smelling woman, I was halfway to the front door when I remembered the key to Laura's house, and ran back to the bathroom to fish it out of the pocket in my dirty shorts.

As I raced back toward the front door, a very large man dressed head to toe in black loomed in the doorway between my bedroom and living room. Except for his eyes and lips, his head and face were entirely covered by a dark ski mask, and he wore leather driving gloves on his hammy hands.

I came to a thudding halt with about a million thoughts running through my mind. One was that in my haste I'd left the front door unlocked and the shutters up. So much for the lecture I'd given Pete about keeping doors locked because a killer was loose. The other was that my .38 was six feet away in its special case inside a secret drawer on the wall side of my bed.

Through a slit in the mask thin as a mushroom gill, he said, "No doubt my presence is unwelcome, but it would behoove you to eschew any thoughts of escape. I assure you I have taken every precaution to complete the task for which I came."

Oh, Jesus, it was Frederick Vaught.

There have been a few times in my life when some wisdom I didn't know I had takes over. This was one of them.

With a nervous giggle, I said, "Oh, my gosh! You scared me half to death! Richard put you up to this, didn't he? I swear, that boy will do anything for a practical joke. When he gets here, I'm sure the two of you will have a big laugh at how high I jumped."

The eyes outlined by the ski mask's holes wavered slightly.

I said, "For a minute there, I thought you *were* Richard, all dressed up to scare me. But he's bigger than you. And excuse me for saying it, but he's in better shape too. Probably from his wrestling. Or maybe it's just that he climbs utility poles all day. Being a lineman builds muscles."

Vaught's eyes shifted with uncertainty. I didn't blame him. I was almost beginning to believe in a lineman named Richard myself.

Tilting my head to one side, I said, "If I were you, I'd take the mask off now. A joke is a joke, but Richard's a good friend of my brother's, and my brother will be royally pissed if he thinks you overdid it making like the bogeyman with his little sister. I mean, my brother has a sense of humor as good as anybody's, but he's not going to think this is funny."

Vaught gave a quick look over his shoulder and then fled through the living room and out the open front door. I already had my cell phone out and was punching 911 when I heard a car door slam. I sprinted to close the French doors and lower the shutters as the operator answered.

Crisply, I gave her my name and the address. Crisply, I told her an intruder wearing a ski mask had come into my apartment. Crisply, I told her he had already left the scene, and I promised I would remain there until officers came to investigate. I was calm, cool, collected. It was amazing.

While I waited, I went to the bedroom and pulled my bed from the wall. I opened the drawer built into my bed and looked at the guns nestled in their specially built niches. I no longer have the SigSauers issued by the Sheriff's Department because they had to be returned when Todd was killed and I was put on indefinite leave. But I have Todd's old backup guns and my own. I took my favorite, a Smith & Wesson .38, from its niche. I dropped five rounds into the cylinder and another five in a Speed Loader to put in my pocket. My hands were trembling, a peculiarity I noted from what seemed a far distance, as if I were watching somebody's hands on a movie screen.

The doorbell rang, and I marched to the front door to peer through a slit in the hurricane shutters. I wasn't taking any chances. I was cool. Deputy Jesse Morgan stood on the other side of the door, his diamond stud glinting in the afternoon sunlight. His face was as impassive as ever.

I raised the shutters and opened the French door. I said, "Deputy Morgan, we have to stop meeting like this."

Then I burst into convulsive sobs. I don't know which of us was more surprised.

CHAPTER 31

Deputy Morgan said, "Miz Hemingway?"

I erased the air with the flat of my hand, denying what I was doing even as I did it.

Snuffling like a kid, I said, "I don't know why I'm crying, I'm not hurt."

"You reported an intruder?"

"His name is Frederick Vaught. He's a suspect in the Laura Halston murder. He was stalking her. He used to be a nurse, but he lost his license for abusing elderly patients. He may have killed some of them."

While I leaked tears, Morgan pulled out his notepad and wrote the name. "You've had contact with him before?"

"He was waiting outside the Sea Breeze when I ran with a dog this morning. He told me to quit asking questions about him."

"You'd been asking questions about him?"

"I overheard him talking to a patient at the Bayfront nursing unit, and I asked who he was. Lieutenant Guidry knows all about it."

Morgan took in the information about Guidry and nodded.

"And this guy, Vaught, he came in your house?"

I snuffled some more and pointed toward the door into the bedroom, where my bed was still pulled away from the wall.

"I was running out, and he just stepped into the doorway."

"He threaten you?"

"He said it would behoove me to eschew any thoughts of escape, because he had taken every precaution to complete the task for which he came."

Morgan looked up from his notepad.

I said, "He talks like that. Like a dictionary. That's how I knew it was him."

"You didn't recognize him?"

"He was wearing a ski mask. Also gloves."

My voice quivered when I said the part about gloves. Laura's killer had worn gloves.

"But you didn't see his face."

"Trust me, that man was Frederick Vaught."

Morgan studied me for a moment. "How'd you get rid of him?"

"I pretended to believe he was pulling a prank, that it was a big joke that somebody named Richard had put him up to. I said Richard would be here any minute, and that Richard was a good friend of my brother's."

"And he believed that?"

"I guess he did, he ran out."

For some reason the tears came back then, and I stood there for a minute and bawled like an idiot while Morgan looked extremely uncomfortable.

When I could speak, I said, "I don't know why I'm crying."

In about three strides, Morgan walked over to my breakfast bar where a roll of paper towels stood. Tearing off a towel, he came back and handed it to me.

"Sure you do. That was a close call. If you hadn't

played it right, no telling what would have happened. That was a smart thing you did."

Shakily, I mopped my face and blew my nose. "Thanks."

"Are you going to be home for a while?"

"No, I have rounds to make. My pets. Dogs, cats, you know."

"Oh, yeah. Okay, I'll put out an alert about Vaught and I'll contact Lieutenant Guidry. I imagine he'll want to talk to you about it."

"I imagine he will."

"These calls you're going to make, are all the houses empty? I mean, except for the pets? No people?"

I knew what he was getting at. If Vaught was determined to get me, he could follow me and surprise me inside a pet's house.

I said, "I've got my thirty-eight now. Until Vaught is picked up, I'm carrying it with me."

He nodded and closed his notepad. "I'll just wait until you leave."

I knew what that meant too. Vaught could be lurking nearby waiting for me to come out.

Together, Morgan and I went down my stairs to the carport, and Morgan waited until I was in the Bronco. I drove out first, with Morgan following me. In my rearview mirror, I could see him talking on his phone.

For the rest of the afternoon, I was hyperalert for Frederick Vaught. At every pet's house, I locked the door behind me when I went in and I was extra cautious when I left. Even in ordinary circumstances pet sitters have to be vigilant for creeps hiding in the bushes, but in this case I had even more reason to take care, and I knew who the creep was.

Even on edge and watching for Vaught to pop up in front of me in his freaky monster getup, I was still acutely aware that breakfast had been a long time ago. Maybe fear makes me hungry, but I kept thinking about what I could eat for dinner without having to go to a lot of effort to get it. Michael was on duty at the firehouse, so he couldn't feed me, and I had no idea what Paco was doing.

By the time I was playing with the last cat on my schedule, I was having visions of platters of food set in front of me. The food on the platters was indistinct, but there was a lot of it and I knew it would be delicious. That's the good thing about visions, you don't have to be specific about the details.

I was just telling the last cat goodbye when my cell phone rang.

It was Michael, with a curious sound to his voice. "Are you near a TV?"

"I'm at a cat's house."

"Turn on the TV quick, Channel Eight."

He sounded so urgent that I obediently went to the TV set, punched it on, and found the channel. With the phone at my ear, I looked at a close-up of a young news reporter holding a microphone close to her ruby-red lips. Under the shot on the screen, a hyperventilating banner told us we were watching a special news bulletin. To prove it, the young woman was gushing that viewers were seeing a once-in-a-lifetime event.

The camera pulled back to show another person standing beside her, and I made the kind of sound you make when somebody punches you in the stomach. The other person was Frederick Vaught, but without his ski mask and gloves.

On the phone, Michael said, "That guy claims he killed the woman you knew."

I couldn't answer. All I could do was breathe.

On-screen, the reporter was trying her best not to

sound too perky, given that it was a murder she was talking about, but it was a stretch for her.

Shoving the microphone into Vaught's face, she said, "Without going into any detail about the manner in which you killed Ms. Halston, would you repeat the main point of what you've told me?"

Vaught stared directly into the camera and spoke in a deliberate monotone. "I had a romantic relationship with Laura Halston, and we had a lover's quarrel. In a moment of passion, I stabbed her. I feel incalculable remorse for what I've done, and I therefore make a full confession in a vain attempt to expiate my crime."

There was a disturbance off camera, with sounds of raised voices. The camera swung to a uniformed deputy with about thirty pounds of guns and radios and flashlights dripping from his belt. He seemed to be seriously contemplating a crime of his own.

Stepping to the reporter, he said, "Ma'am, this interview is over."

Widening her eyes in mock innocence, she said, "Mr. Vaught called the press conference, officer."

Another officer must have persuaded the cameraman to aim his camera away, because the screen went dark while a muffled voice read Vaught his Miranda rights. I imagined Vaught was being handcuffed at the time, and that he was enjoying it immensely.

Every crime brings out mentally deranged people who confess their guilt. Some of them may actually believe they committed the crime, others just want the momentary attention. Vaught was either crazy enough to believe himself actually guilty, or crazy enough to enjoy the limelight of TV interviewers and cameras.

Michael said, "What do you think?"

"In the first place, Laura Halston wouldn't have touched Frederick Vaught with a ten-foot eyebrow pencil, so that stuff about being her lover is a lot of hooey. In the second place, Vaught is crazy. I'm talking bona fide mentally ill, like he should be locked up. He came in my apartment today dressed up like some geek version of Darth Vader."

Michael's voice sharpened. "He came in your apartment?"

"It's okay. I got rid of him, and I called nine-one-one. There's been an alert out for his arrest."

"Well, now they've got him."

"And he's having his fifteen minutes of fame. They'll find out he's lying and let him go."

"Couldn't he be telling the truth about killing her and lying about the reason? Maybe he killed her because she wouldn't have anything to do with him."

I said, "Huh," because he had a point. I would never believe Frederick Vaught had been romantically involved with Laura, but he could have killed her in a frustrated rage because she rejected him.

Michael said, "Call me before you go home tonight, okay?"

That's my big brother, always concerned about me, always wanting to protect me. I promised I would call him, knowing he would get in touch with Paco if he could, knowing they would join forces to keep the big bad world away from me. We're a family, and that's what families do.

Knowing that Vaught was in custody made me less wary, but it didn't make me less hungry. Streetlights had come on, and early-bird diners were already headed home with leftovers packaged in little square Styrofoam boxes. I would have paid a dollar and a quarter for one of those little boxes.

Thinking Pete might be starving too, I called him before I went to the Kitty Haven to get Leo.

He said, "Thanks, Dixie, but I heated a can of soup earlier. After I get Purr-C home, I'll just have a bowl of cereal or something."

"I'm picking him up in a few minutes."

"Okay, that's good. I forgot about the sheets from my bed, but they're in the washer now. It'll just take awhile to dry them and put them back on the bed, and then I'll be ready. But I don't think you should bring Purr-C in here. I wouldn't want Mazie to come home and smell cat in the house."

It wouldn't have been ethical to take a pet into another pet's home in any case, but it was thoughtful of Pete to consider how Mazie would feel. I told him I'd get Leo, aka Purr-C, and be there in half an hour.

I wished I had a chunk of cheese or an apple or at least some crackers. I rummaged around in my bag and found a box of breath mints and ate a few. They weren't very nourishing, but they gave me something to chew.

At the Kitty Haven, I took the .38 and the Speed Loader from my pocket and stashed them in the glove box. With Vaught in custody, I didn't have to go around armed like a vigilante. Besides, I don't like to take a gun inside a gentle place like the Kitty Haven. I got one of my emergency cardboard cat carriers from the back of the Bronco and took it inside. Marge had gone to her own apartment in the back, and a nighttime assistant was lolling on a velour sofa in the front room with a few cats piled on her. The TV was on with the sound turned low, and the cats were as slow to take their eyes off the screen as the human.

I said, "Sorry to interrupt, but I'm here to pick up Leo."

Disengaging herself from the limp cats, the young woman rose with feline grace.

"Last name?"

"His owner's name was Halston, but Marge may

have registered him under my name. I'm Dixie Hemingway."

She looked at me with more interest. "I've heard of you."

I swung the cat carrier. "I'm in a bit of a hurry, so I'll settle up the charges with Marge later. I know where Leo is. Do you mind if I go on back and get him?"

She looked a little flustered at so much decisiveness in one sentence, but opened the door to the private cat rooms and followed me to Leo's quarters.

Setting the open carrier on the floor, I said, "Good news, Leo. You're going to a new home."

I opened the screen door and lifted him, taking a moment to stroke him before I settled him in the carrier. He hunched low to the floor, looking up at me with suspicious eyes.

The attendant said, "He's been very quiet. I think he's sad."

"He'll be happier now."

"His owner got killed, didn't she?"

I gave her the look I give dogs who lift their legs on the furniture, and closed the cat carrier.

"Tell Marge I'll stop by in the next few days and pay her."

The attendant blushed, undoubtedly hoping I wouldn't mention her tactless nosiness to Marge.

The cats in the velvety front room languidly flipped their tails as Leo and I went out the door. While Leo had considered his time there a jail sentence, the resident cats believed themselves in paradise. I know humans who feel one way or the other about their own situations.

It was almost eight when Leo and I got to Mazie's house. While Leo waited in the Bronco, I rang the bell. Pete was slow getting to the door, and when he opened it his hair was standing upright as if he'd been in a whirlwind.

He said, "I'm just finishing up. Had a heck of a time getting the sheets on the bed. Those king-size mattresses are big as a circus ring."

"Leo's in the car. Can you use a hand?"

"Purr-C. No, no, I'm almost done. My bags are packed and in the car. I just have to gather up some last-minute things, get my saxophone, make a last check to be sure I haven't forgotten anything."

I said, "I'll wait with Purr-C." I was sort of looking forward to seeing how Leo would react when he found out his name had been changed.

"Dixie? Did you think to get food for him?"

I did a slow pivot to look at him. If he hadn't looked so cute, with his white hair sticking up like a Smurf's and his bramble eyebrows hovering above the kindest eyes in the world, I would have yelled at him. I'd been up since 4 A.M. with only a catnap in a hospital lounge, I'd driven over the Skyway Bridge to St. Petersburg, I'd shopped for supplies for Mazie, I'd been damn near attacked by a man who might be homicidal and who was definitely crazy, and I'd picked up Leo at the Kitty Haven, all without any food since nine o'clock in the morning, which was damn near twelve hours ago unless you counted the piddling little apple thing I'd eaten in the car on the way to St. Petersburg, a little apple thing I wished I had right then, and he wanted to know if I'd remembered to get cat food as well?

With what I thought was admirable mildness, I said, "No, Pete, I didn't."

"Well, I guess I can stop on the way home and get some. But I hate to leave him in the car by himself while I'm in the store, and I don't want to take him home first and leave him by himself because he won't know what's going on. Do you think you could go pick up some things for him now? While I finish up inside? I'd go but I don't know what brand to get. That's one of the things I'll have to learn."

Like a lazy shark, the memory of the box of cat food on Laura's counter swam across my cortex, the box she had set out to remind herself to buy more. That was the brand Leo liked, but Laura had died before she could replace it. If she had lived long enough to buy another box, I could have simply used the key the locksmith had given me and gone in her house and got it. Got the box of cat food, got Leo's food and water bowls, got his toys, got the cat treats I'd seen in Laura's kitchen cabinet.

It's a wonder an orchestra didn't pop up by the driveway right then with a rousing rendition of "The William Tell Overture," because remembering the kitty treats made me remember the two whopping twenty-pound bags of organic cat food that had been in the cabinet with the treats. Forty pounds of dry cat food would be like money in the bank for a retired clown on a fixed income, and it would be a steady source of meals for Leo.

I said, "There's cat food at Laura's house, and a lot of other things you'll need. I'll get it while you finish making the bed."

He looked anxious. "Is that all right? To go in her house?"

I shrugged. "It's Leo's house too, and Celeste officially gave me authority to find a home for him. As far as I'm concerned, that includes handing his food and toys over to his new owner."

"Well, if you think it's all right."

From the Bronco, Leo made a loud and indignant yowl. It was the first sound he'd made, and both Pete and I hurried to the car to see what had provoked him. He was poking his paws through the air holes in the carrier, and from the low growling noise he was making, I didn't think he was going to be quiet much longer.

Pete said, "I don't want him to think I'm keeping him locked up in here. That's not a good beginning for us."

I grunted and reached inside the Bronco for the carrier.

I said, "I'll take him with me."

"Well, maybe that's good. He can say goodbye to his old home before he moves to his new one."

I grunted again. I was too tired and too hungry to speak. As I trudged down the sidewalk to Laura's house with the cat carrier in my hand, a neon sign inside my head was flashing *Will This Friggin' Day Never End?*

CHAPTER 32

Laura's house looked smaller in the dark. Security lights on each side of her front door cast glittering reflections on the glass panes, but dull grayness lay behind the glass. As I unlocked the door and pushed it open, I had a momentary apprehension that a passing motorist might see me going in and think I was an intruder.

Out of habit, I locked the door behind me, but I didn't switch on a light. I might have had every legitimate right to be there, but I didn't want to call attention to it. An observer looking through the glass-paned front door and seeing me inside might get suspicious and call the cops, and then I'd have to explain the whole business. I was in no mood to explain myself to anybody.

The house had the strange neutral feel that a place gets when its life odors have been eradicated. Crime-scene cleaners not only remove all traces of blood and body fluids, they destroy all possibility of bacteria and odor with a pall of ozone, then cover up the ozone with a spray that smells like cherry-flavored cough syrup.

As I walked through the shadowy living room, Leo made a noise that seemed to end in a question mark.

I said, "I know it smells different, but this really is your house."

At the end of the living room, where it made an L to a dining area next to the kitchen, I turned the corner and set Leo's carrier on the bar between kitchen and dining area. Out of sight of the front door, I felt safe to flip on overhead kitchen lights.

Leo whined and scrabbled at the roof of his carrier.

I said, "We'll just be a minute, and then you're going home with Pete. You'll like him, he's a sweet guy."

While Leo growled and pushed at the carrier's top, I searched for his food and water bowls. I found them in the utility room between kitchen and garage, where somebody had neatly stacked them on the dryer. I carried them to the bar and put them down beside the carrier. As I did, it occurred to me that it was going to be awkward, to say the least, to carry the bowls, two twenty-pound bags of cat food, and the cat carrier.

I said, "Damn, I should have brought the Bronco."

Okay, no big deal. I'd just have to take Leo back to the Bronco and drive to Laura's driveway, then come in and lug out the bags of cat food and the bowls. Except I'd have to let Pete know what I was doing so he wouldn't get anxious when I left in the Bronco. I rolled my eyes. Sometimes it's a real pain in the butt to play well with others.

With a plan in place, I went to the pull-out cabinet where I'd seen the bags of cat food. Sure enough, there they were, each weighing twenty pounds. There were also several jars of vitamins, along with a bunch of twenty-ounce bags of sun-dried bonita treats. Laura had definitely believed in having plenty of stuff on hand, which was good. Cats love those fish flakes, and Pete would be glad to have them. They made a rather large heap when I piled them on the bar next to the carrier. They were also too slippery to carry by hand, so I went looking for a bag to put them in.

While I was exploring the cupboards in the utility room, Leo popped open the top of the carrier, leaped to the floor, and streaked out of sight.

Under my breath, I said, "Shit."

I had failed to take into consideration that Havana Browns are strong muscular cats, not to mention smart. Leo had used his brain and his muscles to open the carrier, which made him a lot smarter than me. Furthermore, every cat has its favorite hiding place, and Leo was bound to have his. Now, lucky me, I'd have to coax a stressed cat out of its hiding place.

I found a stash of plastic grocery bags and filled one with the packets of bonita flakes. Leo's food and water bowls went in another bag. I didn't intend to take Leo's litter box. I had plenty of temporary boxes in the Bronco and Pete could use some of them until he got a permanent one. All I had to do was get the bags of dry food out and persuade Leo to play nice with me.

Back at the pull-out cabinet, I leaned down and lifted one of the bags. That sucker felt like a lot more than twenty pounds, but I was so tired a five-pound weight would have seemed heavy. I carried it to the bar and plopped it beside the carrier. I looked again at the description of the contents printed on the bag. Chicken and lamb nuggets, it said. Twenty pounds, it said, but I could have sworn it was a lot heavier. It was also oddly rigid. Dry cat food is usually packed a bit loosely to allow for the contents to slosh around and not break through the bag. When you set it on the floor, it sits with a certain relaxed slump, like a woman sits when she doesn't care if she bulges in spots.

I started to get the other bag from the cabinet, then turned back to check the first bag again. The top inch had been neatly folded over and stapled. That seemed peculiar, because it seemed to me that most bags of cat food were glued at the top. But maybe they weren't. Maybe some were glued and some were stapled, and what difference did it make? It didn't make an iota of difference to a cat, and it shouldn't make any difference to me.

I got the other twenty-pound bag, and as I lifted it out I had an image of Laura Halston lifting her model's bag after she'd stuffed it with money from Martin Freuland's bank vault. The image was so clear and so sudden that I went to my knees with the shock of comprehension. With the bag between my knees, I examined the stapled top. The staples had been driven in with careful exactness, but they didn't appear to have been done by a machine. Some human had laid those staples in that folded-over top, and the human had probably been Laura Halston.

I stood up and got a table knife from a drawer, then knelt on the floor and gently used the knife to pry the staples out. Carefully unfolding the bag's top, I peered inside. It took a moment to recognize what I was seeing, because I'd never seen anything like it. Two rows of brown paper bands, each band imprinted with $10,000, each wrapped around a stack of hundred-dollar bills. Six bands in all, holding sixty thousand dollars, and that was just the top layer. I sat down on the floor and pulled out one of the stacks. It was surprisingly thin, not even an inch thick. The bag itself was about twenty inches tall. I did some fast arithmetic and came up with around a million dollars in the bag. And there were two bags, which meant Laura had been hiding around two million dollars in plain sight in her kitchen.

I said, "Son of a gun."

As if in response, a cracking sound came from the living room. My first thought was that Leo had become so agitated at the strangeness of his home that he'd knocked something over. My second thought was that somebody had knocked out a glass panel in the front door so they could unlock it. My third thought was that I had left my .38 in the Bronco.

With the bag of money on the floor between my outstretched legs, I began scrambling to get upright. I was on one knee, with one foot on the floor, when the bag tipped over and spilled bundles of hundred-dollar bills onto the floor. Dimly aware of the puddle of money on the kitchen tile, I was frantically sorting through my options, which were more or less limited to running to the back door and hoping to escape through the garage, or climbing into one of the kitchen cabinets.

Martin Freuland came around the living room's L and stood on the other side of the bar separating the dining area from the kitchen. He held a .9mm Glock in his hand, and his face registered a curious shock when he saw me.

He said, "Oh. It's you."

There were so many unspoken assumptions in those few words that I couldn't think of a response. Obviously, he had known somebody was in the house, and obviously he had expected it to be somebody else.

His gaze swung to the money on the floor, and he nodded. "I knew it was here."

Still on one knee, I said, "Was it really worth killing for?"

His smile was like a barracuda's. "It will be, yes."

That was when I realized he meant killing *me* would be worth it.

I said, "I was talking about killing Laura. You said you didn't, but you did."

He moved the Glock back and forth like a head shaking. "You're very naïve about the way the real world works. People like me don't kill people like Laura. We pay other people to do it for us."

"Vaught?"

He frowned and spoke louder. "I said we pay other people to do it for us."

Help me Rhonda, we were doing a "Who's on First?" routine.

I said, "A man named Frederick Vaught has confessed to killing Laura. Is that who you paid?"

He actually laughed, an easy relaxed chuckle. "I don't know who the hell you're talking about."

I wasn't as naïve as Freuland thought. I knew about paid killers, knew how easy it is for somebody in Freuland's position to hire somebody whose morality is measured in dollars. But professional killers simply do their job and leave. They lay a bullet in a precise location, or they surprise with a wire garrote around the neck or a swiftly driven blade between the ribs. They don't hang around and slash the dead victim's face in mad fury. Only killers with personal vendettas to settle do that. If Freuland hadn't killed Laura himself, he had paid somebody with personal history with her to do it.

A wave of dizziness swept over me as I realized how a thing can happen in one place, and the entire universe shifts to make space for the fact of it. A man accepts two million dollars from drug dealers who've made millions more from selling hopelessness to other men, and hundreds of miles away a gap in time appears, a cosmic breath is held until a woman is finally stabbed to death in her shower, a death that no longer has anything to do with the two million dollars, but is about a child knowing her father is in her sister's bedroom doing something shameful, and she is stunted, maimed, soul-stained with jealousy because it means her father loves her sister best.

I said, "Was mutilating Laura's face part of what you paid Celeste to do?"

If I'd had any doubts that he was telling the truth about not being the killer, they were dispelled by the shock in his eyes.

"Mutilating her face?"

"Her face was so cut up that the deputy who found her body threw up. Think about that, Mr. Freuland. Think about how lovely Laura was, and how she looked when Celeste finished with her."

A faint sheen of perspiration glistened on his forehead. "I didn't know."

"Well, that's the problem with having somebody killed, isn't it? You can't control all the details of how they'll do it."

For a moment, we looked into each other's eyes with the stark rawness that can only happen when one person is about to blow another person to smithereens. He may have paid Celeste to kill Laura, but we both knew he fully planned to kill me himself. I had to stall him, had to keep him talking until . . . until what? Until Pete wondered what was taking so long and came to investigate and got killed too? I couldn't let that happen, but I wasn't ready to give up.

I said, "You expected to find Celeste here tonight, didn't you?"

"She thought she could outsmart me and take all the money for herself. We'd gone all through the plan, all she had to do was show up, tell Laura she'd come to visit, act friendly, like a sister, and then take her by surprise and punish her for what she'd done. The bitch spent the entire night here searching for the money but she couldn't find it."

Of course she didn't. Celeste had never had a cat, and it wouldn't have occurred to her that it was odd for a person to have forty pounds of cat food stored for one cat.

Now I knew who it was that Pete had seen. It had been Celeste, dressed in Laura's clothes. That's why Guidry had questioned him so closely about the time, because Laura had been killed hours earlier.

"I suppose you'll kill her too, when she comes back?"

He gave me that smile again. "That won't be necessary. I'll be long gone when she shows up, and all she'll find is your body."

"The cops will think she killed me, and she'll tell them it was you."

He shook his head. "She can't afford to implicate me because she knows I'll tell them she killed her sister. And the police have no reason to believe she killed Laura. No, they'll think the same person who killed Laura killed you, some unknown maniac."

I had to agree that it was a fairly tight plan.

I had never imagined the end of my life happening this way. Even though my husband had died at thirty, and my child at three, I still thought of death as something that happened to old people, an inevitable closure to a long full life. But now here I was with a man who seemed determined to make my death as premature as Laura Halston's.

I said, "Could you just tell me why? Why did you want Laura killed? And don't tell me it was because of the money she took, or because she reported you to the feds. That would make you bitter, but it wouldn't make you a killer."

I didn't need to ask why he planned to kill me. We both knew the answer to that.

For a long silent moment, I thought I might have

gone too far, and that the next instant might be my last. But then Martin spoke in a tight voice.

"She treated me like a fish, reeling me in one minute and letting me flap at her feet, and then throwing me back."

"Why? Because you were too little to keep?"

He wagged the gun at me like a head tut-tutting, and I bit my lower lip. I've never been good at keeping my mouth shut when a good line pops into my head.

"She liked keeping me on the hook. Wanted me to dangle there in case one of her other men got away. Then she'd have me in reserve. On ice, so to speak."

I thought of how TV psychologists act, and drew my eyebrows together in a way I hoped looked sympathetic. "That must have been painful for you."

He was too smart for that. Walking around the bar, he came toward me with the Glock pointed at my forehead. "It's time to end this charade."

I wish I could say I kept my cool, but I didn't. My heart was hammering in my ears, and all I could think about was not letting him see how terrified I was. If this was going to be my last moment, I didn't want it to end with my humiliation.

He was breathing heavily, gathering the will to pull the trigger.

In my head, I heard Todd's voice. "Use your feminine weakness, Dixie. It's your ultimate weapon."

Like being hit by lightning, I got the meaning in a flash. Freuland's need for power made him especially vulnerable to a helpless woman at his feet.

Rolling to the floor, I stretched on my back, put my hands over my face and blubbered that I didn't want to die.

He came closer, his feet shuffling beside me. When he spoke, his voice oozed satisfaction.

"I see you understand the situation."

I bobbed my chin up and down and bawled. "Uh-huh, I do."

"I thought you would. You seem like a smart woman. Too bad you had to stumble onto the money."

Crying louder, I spread my fingers and looked through them. The overhead fluorescents bathed us both in cold light.

Straddling me, he leaned over with the Glock aimed between my eyes. I opened my mouth wide and howled like a little kid.

At the same time, I jerked a knee to my chest and drove my foot into his big bull balls.

CHAPTER 33

A .9mm Glock going off in an enclosed kitchen makes an extremely loud roar. So does a large man with badly bruised gonads. Dropping his gun, Freuland folded to the floor in a fetal position, and I scrabbled for the Glock.

Panting, I got to my feet. With my knees shaking so violently I had to lean on the counter for support, I covered Freuland with the Glock while I used my free hand to pull out my cell phone. Fingers trembling like a drunk's, I punched in Guidry's number. Mercifully, he answered on the first ring.

My voice seemed to have forgotten how to work. All it could do was make choking noises.

He said, "Dixie?"

I gasped, "I'm at Laura's—"

That's all I got out before several shrieks like banshee fury sounded in the living room, so loud that Guidry heard them.

Guidry said, "What? What's happened?"

There was another scream, a curious thunking sound, then a sound like a heavy object hitting the floor with a dull thump. Then utter silence.

Guidry said, "Dixie?"

Freuland lay mewling and puking on the floor, out of commission for two or three minutes at least. But somebody else was in the house, possibly with accomplices outside.

Guidry's voice rose. "Dixie? Answer me! Dixie!"

In the stillness, his voice was so loud it echoed.

Putting my lips close to the mouthpiece, I whispered, "Somebody's here."

Freuland retched and groaned. I pointed the Glock at him while I kept one eye on the bar where Leo's supplies sat next to the sack containing a million dollars.

At the edge of the bar, a silver glint extended from behind the wall, then withdrew. My first thought was that it was a gun barrel. My second thought was that it was the blade of a knife. Then I realized what the shrieking sound had been—Celeste had stepped on Leo's tail and they'd both screamed. I didn't want to think about the implication of the thudding sound hitting the floor. I didn't want to think about the implication of the tip of that knife blade, either, but the fact was that Celeste was in the house and she was slipping toward me with a knife in her hand.

Once again, I had been duped by one of the sisters. Celeste had made a big show of refusing the key the locksmith had made, and another big show of telling Guidry she was returning to Dallas. And all the time she'd known she could easily knock out a pane of glass and get in the house without the key. She had either expected Freuland to come looking for the money she hadn't been able to find, or she'd thought she'd give it another search herself. In either case, she had made me a witness to the fact that she didn't have a key, and she would have known that I would tell Guidry.

Guidry yelled, "Dixie! Talk to me!"

I put the phone on the counter because I needed both

hands to hold the Glock. I had to watch Freuland, and I also had to be ready to stop Celeste. The knife blade re-appeared, slowly edging forward. Bright, shiny, silver.

Guidry barked, "I'm on my way!"

The silver object went still, and Pete's voice said, "Dixie?"

I swear I think my ears wiggled a little bit in disbelief.

"Pete?"

With saxophone in hand, Pete stepped behind the bar so I could get a good look at him. His fuzzy eyebrows were lowered like a mastiff's, and his jaw was clenched in a way I'd never imagined Pete capable of. He didn't look like a sweet octogenarian clown, he looked like a man who would as soon kill you as smile at you.

With a glance at Freuland groaning on the floor, he said, "Looks like you've got him under control."

I picked up the phone. "It's okay, it's Pete. I thought it was Celeste Autrey, but it's Pete."

Looking like himself again, Pete said, "Celeste is in the living room."

For the second time that evening, I was struck speechless. While I gaped at him, he said, "Don't worry, she's asleep."

Oh, shit, it must have been Celeste's body I heard hitting the floor.

Guidry said, "Talk to me!"

I said, "I've got Martin Freuland covered, and I need backup. Freuland came to get his money, and he tried to kill me. But he didn't kill Laura, Celeste did." Weakly, I added, "Celeste is here too."

Guidry said, "I'm two minutes away, and some units are even closer."

As he said it, a loud rapping sounded at the front door, and a voice yelled, "Sheriff's Department!"

Pete sidled away and hollered, "Come on in!"

I heard a man say, "Sir, what's going on here?"

I yelled, "Freuland's in here!"

A deputy rounded the corner from the living room and in one sweep took in the bullet hole in the cabinet, the Glock in my hand, and Freuland's agonized writhing.

Still quivering, I handed the gun to him and crossed my arms over my chest.

"This man tried to kill me with this gun. His aim went bad when I kicked him in the balls."

The deputy winced. "Lieutenant Guidry is on his way."

In the living room, the other deputy said, "Sir, what's the story with the woman?"

Pete said, "Wait, I haven't explained that to Dixie yet."

He popped back into view behind the bar with his saxophone tucked under one arm and Leo cradled against his chest. Leo looked surprisingly contented.

"Dixie, I didn't get a chance to tell you what happened with Celeste. I was on the way to my car to put my saxophone in there and I saw her cross the street from the hedge where the jogging trail is. For a minute I thought it was Laura, and then I remembered Laura was dead. That's who I saw Tuesday morning! She looks like Laura when she's got on all that jogging stuff. Anyway, she ran in behind the trees so I knew she was coming in here. I don't trust that woman, and I didn't like the idea of her coming in on you like that, so I came down to see what she was up to. The front door was open, and she just came in. When I got to the door, I could see her in the living room, and she had a big knife in her hand. She looked like she was planning something bad with that knife, so I snuck up on her real quiet."

The deputy and I stared at him with big round eyes.

The deputy said, "And then?"

In the living room, Guidry's voice barked a question, and we all looked toward the sound. He spoke a minute to the living room deputy and then came to stand beside Pete.

I turned to face him in all my snotty, tangled, smeared glory, and gave him a megawatt smile. I felt a little bit like a director of a play announcing the characters and their roles. There in Laura's kitchen we had a big moaning man in a thousand-dollar suit rolling on the floor and clutching his genitals with both hands. We had two million dollars bundled in neat packages like Hershey's chocolate bars. We had a long-tailed cat who had exacted feline revenge by tripping his owner's killer. Last but by no means least, we had an octogenarian who had cold-cocked a killer with his saxophone. And we had me, girl pet sitter, size six, thank you very much, five-foot-three inches tall, who had just felled the big man in the suit.

I said, "Celeste Autrey murdered Laura Halston. She stabbed her to death and then mutilated her face." I pointed to Freuland. "And he paid her to do it."

Freuland shuddered and tried to roll to a sitting position. Guidry was instantly beside him, one hand helping him sit up, the other putting a handcuff on one of his wrists. As he cuffed the other wrist, he Mirandaed him, his voice even and deliberate.

In a dramatic show of indignation, Freuland jerked his torso away, but he was still so groggy from my kick that he toppled over and landed with his head pillowed on a bag of money. It seemed a fitting support.

EMTs were suddenly in the house to get Celeste. Still holding Leo in his arms, Pete stepped away from the bar to watch them haul her away, while Guidry motioned the deputies to help Freuland to his feet. Freuland's face was pasty, with beads of sweat dripping on his silk suit. In minutes, they were all gone except for Pete and me and Guidry and the first deputies who'd arrived.

One of them said what I'd been dreading. "Lieutenant Guidry, we were just getting a statement from this gentleman when you came. He followed the woman into the house and stopped her."

Guidry said, "Stopped her?"

Pete drew himself as tall as possible and tilted his chin toward Leo.

"This here's my cat. Name's Purr-C. He was supposed to be in a carrying case"—here he gave me a stern look—"but I guess he got out. Anyway, I was behind Celeste and she had that knife up, and she was listening to Dixie and that man, and it seemed to me that she didn't plan anything good for either of them."

I realized I'd stopped breathing, and forced myself to inhale.

Pete said, "There was a big blasting sound, and a man hollered real loud. I knew he was hurt, but I didn't know what had happened to Dixie. I started running to see if she was all right, and then Celeste stepped on Purr-C's tail. Now, I don't know if you're familiar with cats, but when a cat's tail is stepped on it makes a horrible noise, yowling and screeching like nobody's business, and that must have startled Celeste because she commenced yowling and screeching too, and with all that screeching and her with that knife in her hand, I thought it would be best if I put a stop to it."

I felt light-headed. Pete had been such a gentle man when I first met him.

The deputy said, "Sir?"

Touching the side of his neck, Pete said, "So I just tapped her with my saxophone."

Guidry said, "You knocked her *out*?"

"But not hard. See, I was a clown for a long time with Ringling, and you learn a lot of things when you're a clown. Some little-town bullies think killing a clown would be better sport than killing deer or grizzlies, so clowns have to learn to protect themselves." With a note of pride, he said, "I know sixty-six places to tap a person and put them to sleep."

We all went still. I was sure every person in that room believed that tapping a person in some of those sixty-six places would put them to sleep for good.

Pete seemed to know that we knew that, because he rushed to reassure us. "She'll sleep for about an hour is all, then she'll wake up yakking like always. If I was you, I'd make sure she's tied down before she wakes up. That woman is a she-devil for sure. She gets ahold of a knife, she'll slit your throats and tell God you cut yourself shaving."

For a moment, nobody spoke. What do you say to an octogenarian who has just used his saxophone to put a murderous woman to sleep?

Guidry recovered first. "Good job, sir."

To the deputies, he said, "Radio the EMTs to make sure that woman can't get access to a knife."

When he turned to me, he had a glint in his eyes that I couldn't exactly define, but it looked a lot like admiration. Like Pete, I drew myself a little taller.

Strength is where you find it, and Pete and Leo and I had plenty of it.

CHAPTER 34

When Guidry first saw me in my new black dress and my new high heels, he quirked an eyebrow. "You clean up good, Dixie. I like that neckline."

A blush began somewhere south of my navel and traveled upward. Resisting the urge to grab the front of my dress and hoist it higher, I made an inarticulate gurgling sound that intended to be words and failed.

Guidry in evening clothes made me feel like a yokel at her first visit to an art museum. All men look dashing and sophisticated in black dinner jackets, but Guidry looked as if the style had been created for him. His trousers fell in that easy straight way that bespeaks fine fabric and expert cut, the jacket lay on his shoulders in a perfectly fitted caress, and the collar of his crisp white shirt rose like a tribute toward his firm jawline.

I was still in something of a daze from the hectic week. Pete and Purr-C were happily settled in Pete's house, with Purr-C cozying up to Pete as if he'd been with him forever, and not seeming to remember any of his former names.

As Pete had predicted, Celeste had been unconscious for about an hour and then woke up howling mad in the county jail, where she would be held without bail.

Martin Freuland was also in the county jail, his arrogant personage the source of a hot tug of war between federal, Texas, and Florida lawmen. No matter who got him first, he would face a mountain of charges from the others, and it wasn't likely that he would be a free man for a long, long time. Maybe never.

Frederick Vaught was still in the county jail too, but since he was only guilty of being weird, he would probably be released. He should have been incarcerated in a mental hospital, but since our society no longer protects the public from the insane, he would be back on the streets. At least until he commits a crime for which he can be locked up.

The Humane Society gala was held in the ballroom at Michael's on East, an upscale restaurant and convention center tucked behind a shopping center on the Tamiami Trail. There was music, there were beautiful people, there was good food. Before we sat down to eat, there was a mingling hour, with cocktails.

Guidry raised his gaze from my chest and said, "You want a drink? They have cheap white wine, cheap red wine, and something in a punch bowl that I think is supposed to be Sangria."

"White, please."

He disappeared into the crowd, leaving me to continue chasing the same question that had been racing through my mind since Thursday night. How could I have liked Laura Halston so much? How could I have felt such a strong connection to her? Not just when I first met her, when she'd been bright and funny and warm and sympathetic, but after I'd learned that she was a liar and a thief. Even then, I'd felt empathy for her.

Millions of people fall under the spell of skilled con artists—that's why they're called *artists*—but my attraction to Laura had been more than a rube falling under the influence of a slick charmer. It hadn't been sexual, that much I knew. I'd enjoyed her beauty, but I hadn't wanted her in a sexual way. And while it was true that I was nostalgic for woman talk and woman confidences, that wasn't the whole story, and I knew it.

I caught a glimpse of Guidry threading his way through the crowd with a wineglass in each hand, and in the next moment I had a clear-eyed look at myself. I'd been drawn to Laura Halston for the same reason I was drawn to Guidry. We each had come to it from different places and by different routes, but all three of us were attracted to the edge of danger.

It was a sobering thought, but not nearly so sobering as the knowledge that flirting with danger was an integral part of who I was, and I doubted that I would ever change.

Guidry emerged from the crowd and sauntered toward me, graceful, bright, funny, honorable, a great-kissing cop. I watched his approach with a sense of fascinated inevitability, knowing I was lost but unable to save myself.

Turn the page for an excerpt from

RAINING CAT SITTERS AND DOGS

the next Dixie Hemingway mystery from Blaize Clement and St. Martin's / Minotaur Paperbacks!

Every now and then you meet somebody you like on sight, even when everything about them says they're bad news. Jaz was like that. The first time I saw the girl, she was sobbing hysterically and rushing across Dr. Layton's parking lot with a towel-wrapped bundle in her arms. A large man trailed behind her with reluctance.

She looked about twelve or thirteen, with beginner breasts making plum-sized bulges under a stretchy tube top, and the thin, coltish awkwardness of adolescence. She had cocoa-colored skin and a long mop of tangled black curls. Her cut-offs were frayed and had the mulled look that clothes get when they've been slept in.

The man was around fifty, with pale jowels beginning to sag, and graying hair that looked more mowed than barbered. He wore a navy blue suit and a paler blue tie, both too unwrinkled to be anything except polyester. With his pulled-back shoulders and drip-dry shirt taut across his chest, he looked like a junior high school principal who had learned too late that he hated kids.

I'm Dixie Hemingway, no relation to you-know-who. I'm a pet-sitter on Siesta Key, an eight-mile barrier island off Sarasota, Florida. I used to be a deputy with the Sarasota County Sheriff's Department, but something happened almost four years ago that caused me to go howling mad-dog crazy for a little while, so I left with the Department's blessing. I'm still a little bit tilted, I guess, but not more than the average person. Like they say, a person who's totally sane is just somebody you don't know very well.

Now that I'm more or less normal, I have a pet-sitting business that I enjoy, and I end every day feeling like I matter to the world. Some people might not think it's a big deal to make sure pets are groomed and exercised and given sparkling clean food and water bowls, but it's a big deal to the pets. And to me. I mostly take care of cats, with a few dogs and an occasional rabbit or hamster or bird. No snakes. I refer snakes to other sitters. Not that I'm snake-phobic. Not much, anyway. It just gives me the shivers to drop little living critters into open snake mouths.

I had come to the vet's that morning to pick up Big Bubba, a Congo African Grey parrot who had seemed under the weather when I'd called on him the day before. When a bird sneezes and looks lethargic on his perch, I don't take any chances. As it turned out, Big Bubba had merely been having a bad day. Dr. Layton had called the night before to tell me I could pick him up that morning, so I was there to take him home.

The crying girl and the man went in ahead of me. When I got to the reception desk, one of Dr. Layton's assistants was taking the bundle from the girl, and the receptionist was making sympathetic sounds and patting the girl on the shoulder. She was crying so hard that her words came out slurred and broken.

The only thing I could clearly understand was "He hit him!"

The receptionist and assistant looked up sharply at the man, who heaved a great sigh.

"It's a wild rabbit," he said. "It ran in front of my car. It was an accident."

The girl turned and screamed at him. "But it *matters*! It may just be a rabbit, but it *matters*!"

Now that I could see her face, she was older in the eyes than I'd expected, and they were a surprisingly pale aquamarine. With her tawny skin and wild black curls, the improbable eyes testified to ancestors from all over the world, a coming together of genes that can either be a societal blessing or a curse. From the set of her jaw that was both defiant and desperate, I guessed in her case it had not been a blessing.

Everything about her said, *I'm young, I'm pissed, and I'm miserable.*

The man said, "Okay, okay, okay," and looked around with jittery uneasiness.

Dr. Layton bustled out from the backstage labyrinth of examining rooms and boarding areas. A comfortably plump African-American woman roughly my age, which is thirty-three, Dr. Layton has the ability to soothe and command at the same time. With a quick glance at the injured rabbit lying suspiciously limp in its towel covering, she turned briskly to the man.

"It ran in front of your car?"

"It was an accident. I wasn't going more than ten miles an hour. It wasn't like I was speeding."

The girl seemed close to a complete meltdown. She buried her face in her hands, her whole body quivering with the intensity of her sobbing. The receptionist and the vet's assistant looked like they might cry at any minute, just in sympathy, and people and animals in the waiting area stretched their necks to look at her.

Dr. Layton said, "What's your name, dear?"

She said, "Jaz." At the same time, the man said, "Rosemary."

The girl shot him a hostile glare, and Dr. Layton studied him.

She said, "Are you this girl's father?"

Too firmly, he said, "Stepfather."

Dr. Layton put a calm hand on the girl's shoulder. "Jaz, go sit down while I check the bunny. I'll let you know if I can do anything for it."

To me, she said, "Dixie, do you mind waiting a few minutes? I want to have a word with you."

I nodded mutely and followed the man and girl to the waiting area. His hammy hand was wrapped around her upper arm in a tight vise, while she continued to heave with sobs. When she felt the edge of the chair against her legs, she shrank into it and drew her knees up to her face, sobbing as if she had lost her closest friend.

I took a seat across from her. Around the room, a handful of people and their pets were looking at her with sympathetic eyes. Two seats away from her, Hetty Soames was there with a new puppy. She gave me a quick smile and discreet wave, the way people do when they see somebody they know at a funeral, and then turned her attention back to the crying girl.

If Hetty weren't so busy raising future service dogs, she could be an Eileen Fisher model. An ageless take-charge woman, she has sleek silver hair and looks elegant in loose linen pants and tunics that would look like pajamas on any other woman. The new pup with her was the latest in a series of pups she raises for Southeastern Guide Dogs. Raising future service dogs isn't like raising other puppies. They need the same love and attention, but they have to be socialized differently. Those little guys will one day need to focus solely on doing their job and not get sidetracked by things other dogs might explore out of curiosity. Raising them takes thousands of hours of patient work, not to mention a heart big enough to pour out lots of love on a puppy and then hand it over to somebody else. Hetty has been doing it for years, and the only way you can tell she's sad when a young dog leaves is that the spark in her eyes dims for a few weeks, only to come back when a new pup comes to live with her.

The girl's distress obviously bothered Hetty. It bothered her new pup too. A three-month-old golden lab-shepherd mix, his little ears were up and he was watching the girl with concentrated attention. We all were.

Jaz was like the mutt you see at a shelter, the one that reason tells you is not a good choice to take home, but the one that tugs at your heart. Huddled as she was in the chair, we could see that the golden sparkles had mostly worn away from her green rubber flip-flops. Her toenails were painted black, and several of her toes were adorned with gold or silver rings. Her ankles were amateurishly tattooed with flower bracelets, but a well-done black tattoo in the shape of a dagger ran several inches up the outside of her right ankle.

If I'd got a tattoo when I was her age, my grandmother would have sanded it off with a Brillo pad.

The man kept making uneasy shushing sounds, as if the girl's despair embarrassed him. Teenage angst affects people the same way that a pet peeing on the furniture does—it brings out basic traits of either patience or meanness.

Hetty's pup must have decided that since no human was going to do anything constructive, it was up to him. He suddenly darted away from Hetty's feet, reared on his hind legs and pawed at one of the girl's toes. She took her hands away from her face, looked down at him, and laughed. Her laughter was a rusty, croaking sound, as if it had been jerked from her throat.

Hetty leaned forward in an anxious moment of hesitation, but the girl leaned down and scooped the pup into her arms. With no hesitation whatsoever, he proceeded to lick the tears from her cheeks and to wriggle as close to her as he could get. She giggled, and everybody watching gave a collective out-breath of relief at hearing that normal adolescent sound. Jaz wasn't so far gone that she couldn't laugh, then, not so damaged that she couldn't respond to love. I think we had all been unconsciously afraid she might have been.

Hetty said, "Looks like you've found a new friend. His name is Ben."

As if to make sure Jaz understood, Ben gave the tip of her nose a wet kiss, which made her giggle again.

Dr. Layton came from the treatment rooms and walked to stand in front of the girl. "I'm sorry, Jaz. There was nothing we could do for the rabbit. I think he died instantly. I don't believe he suffered."

That's what they always tell you. That's what they told me when Todd and Christy were killed. I never knew whether I could believe them, and I could tell the girl wasn't sure she could believe Dr. Layton, either.

She pulled Ben closer, took a deep shuddering breath, and nodded. "Okay."

The man came abruptly to his feet, digging in his hip pocket for a wallet. "How much do I owe you?"

Dr. Layton said, "There's no charge."

As she turned to walk away, a loud male voice yelled from the vet's inner sanctum.

"Get that man!"

The man swiveled toward the sound with his right hand diving under his suit jacket toward his left armpit.

Instinctively, all my former law-enforcement training made me leap to my feet with my arm stiffened and my palm out like a traffic cop. "Hey, whoa! No need for that!"

In the voice of one who hopes to defuse a tense situation, Dr. Layton said, "That was a bird. An African Grey."

As if on cue, Dr. Layton's assistant came out with Big Bubba inside one of my travel cages. Big Bubba hates little cages, which is probably why he swiveled his head toward me and hollered again, "Get that man!"

With an embarrassed twitch of his hand to the girl, the man said, "Come on, Rosemary."

Jaz and Ben exchanged a long sad look, which may have been the final impetus that caused Hetty to do something that made my mouth drop.

Getting to her feet and taking Ben from Jaz, she said, "I need somebody to help me with this puppy. Just a few hours a week. It doesn't pay much, but it's easy work and I think you'd like it."

Now that was probably the biggest lie Hetty Soames had ever told. Not the part about the work being easy, but the part about needing help taking care of Ben. She had simply taken a shine to the girl, knew she was in some sort of situation that wasn't good, and wanted to give her a helping hand.

Jaz and the man spoke over each other again. He said, "She can't do that."

She said, "Yeah, I can do that."

I tried not to grin. Anybody who knows Hetty knows she usually gets what she sets her mind on. I figured she would have the girl at her house within the hour, maybe sooner. Dr. Layton seemed to think so too. With a happier look on her face than she'd had before, she motioned me to the reception counter where Big Bubba waited in the travel cage.

At the counter, I looked over my shoulder at Jaz and her stepfather. He had jammed both hands in his trouser pockets and was gazing at the ceiling with the look of a man at the end of his rope. Jaz had moved to squat beside Ben and pet him while she talked to Hetty.

Dr. Layton said, "There was a touch of eosinophilia in Big Bubba's tracheal wash, but I suspect he's reacting to the red tide like everybody else. Keep him indoors until it's over. If it gets worse, I can give him some antihistamines, but I'd rather treat it by removing the allergen."

I wasn't surprised. A bloom of microscopic algae, red tide's technical name is *karenia brevis*, but by any name it's nasty stuff that causes respiratory irritations and watery eyes for people and pets. We get the bloom almost every September when Gulf breezes begin coming from the west, but this year it had started a month early. I promised Dr. Layton I would keep Big Bubba indoors for the duration of the bloom, and carried him out the door.

I don't imagine Hetty or Jaz or the man noticed me leave. They were all too caught up in their own intentions.

Afterwards, I would look back on that brief encounter in Dr. Layton's waiting room and wonder if there was any way I could have prevented all the coming danger. At the time, all I knew was that a girl who called herself Jaz but was really named Rosemary was desperately unhappy, that her stepfather's nerves were shot, and that he wore an underarm holster.